------- ★ -------

EDNA HOLZER HAD PROBABLY BEEN AN ATTRACTIVE WOMAN

The phone rang and Conway picked it up. "Say, where have you been? I've been trying to get you for an hour. This is Slattery down at the garage."

"We've been on a call. Did that car get brought in?"

"Well, that's what I'm calling about. I went up to Hollywood to get it, and you might have warned me, you gave me the hell of a shock. I mean, I've seen bodies before—I was two years in 'Nam—but I wasn't expecting it."

"A body?" said Conway.

"Yeah, in the back seat of this Chrysler. It's a woman."

------- ★ -------

SHANNON DELL

Exploit of Death

WORLDWIDE®

TORONTO • NEW YORK • LONDON • PARIS
AMSTERDAM • STOCKHOLM • HAMBURG
ATHENS • MILAN • TOKYO • SYDNEY

This one is for
Win Pendleton,
with thanks for
all past favors.

EXPLOIT OF DEATH

A Worldwide Mystery/December 1990

First published by William Morrow & Company, Inc.

ISBN 0-373-26061-X

"Know'st thou not any whom corrupting gold would tempt unto a close exploit of death?"

—William Shakespeare
Richard III

"Gold hath destroyed many and perverted the hearts of kings."

—Rabbi Jeshu Ben Sirah

ONE

THE MENDOZAS were on the way home. They had had an enjoyable, if tiring, five weeks' vacation, touring England and Scotland after a week in London. They had visited Bateman's, Rudyard Kipling's old home, and seen Pook's Hill. They had dutifully visited all the tourist attractions and they had called on Mairí MacTaggart's cousin Jennie in Inverness. They were both tired and it would be good to be home. Louis had needed a vacation, reflected Alison sleepily. But half the fun of going away somewhere was coming home. It seemed years since they had been home—since they had seen the twins, Johnny and Terry, and tomorrow was the twins' sixth birthday—and the baby Luisa would be a year old in a few weeks—and the cats and Cedric, the Old English sheepdog, and of course Mairí, the surrogate grandmother, and the Kearneys, and even the Five Graces, the sheep Ken Kearney had recommended for eating down the underbrush. It would be nice to get home to the big Spanish hacienda in the hills above Burbank, La Casa de la Gente Feliz, the house of happy people.

They had flown from New York this morning and had a two-hour wait at O'Hare Airport in Chicago for a flight to Los Angeles; when the flight was announced, there was quite a crowd of passengers flocking down the tunnel to board. The Mendozas were in the middle of the little crowd as the stewardess ushered them down the aisle of the big jet. The seats were in tiers of three across each side of the aisle, and there was a girl sitting in the window seat of the three the stewardess indicated.

Alison sat down in the middle seat next to her and Mendoza took the seat next to the aisle. The girl gave them a shy, tentative smile. She was a very pretty girl in the mid-twenties with a neat cap of smooth, dark hair, a pert triangular kitten face with a tip-tilted nose, and a wide, friendly mouth. Alison had noticed her before on the flight from New York, sitting several rows ahead of them. She was unobtrusively dressed in a smart navy-blue suit and a white tailored blouse.

When the jet began to roar and presently trundle down the runway and lifted off, the girl gave a little exclamation and said apologetically, "It is the first time I have flown, I am nervous," and laughed. "But it is exciting to see America for the first time."

"Oh, of course, it must be," said Alison politely.

"You see, my mother was American, but never have I been out of France."

"Oh," said Alison. She was feeling very sleepy and suppressed a yawn. "You are going to see relatives then, Miss—?"

"Martin," said the girl. "I am Juliette Martin." She gave it the French pronunciation. She spoke nearly unaccented English. "My grandfather, yes." She hesitated, considered Alison's friendly, encouraging expression and went on, "It is a funny little story perhaps. You see, my mother was studying to be a teacher of languages and she came to France with a scholarship for postgraduate work, and met my papa. And her father was quite furious that she wished to marry a foreigner, a Frenchman, and said he would have nothing more to do with her. My mother wrote to him when I was born, five years later, but never heard from him. But when my parents were both killed in the auto accident, that is six months ago, I thought he should know if he is still alive, and so I wrote, and he wrote back. We have corresponded, and he is most anxious to meet me. He is very remorseful now about how he treated my mother." She half smiled at Alison. "I think he is very old and lonely and sentimental as old people become. I am sorry for him."

"Of course," said Alison conventionally, suppressing another yawn. Mendoza had leaned back and shut his eyes. "That's very interesting. Are you going to stay long?"

"Not long. I have three weeks' holiday due to me because last spring I could not get away when we were busy in the office." She smiled slightly. "M. Trennard is not so easy an employer as his uncle, but he had to admit that I was owed a holiday."

"I hope you'll enjoy it," said Alison sleepily.

"Oh, yes. At first Paul did not want me to go. That is my fiancé, we are to be married in January. But he came to understand there is the family feeling. Grandfather is the only family I have, except for my two uncles. But you are having a holiday, also?" That was polite, conventional.

"No," said Alison through a large yawn. "We're on the way home," and how sweet it was to be going home. The vacation had been her idea, but she felt now that she didn't want to leave home again for a long, long time. She felt her eyelids drooping, but the girl had been friendly, perhaps was feeling lonely this far from home. Alison swallowed another yawn. "Do you live in Paris?" she asked at random. But the drowsiness was increasing. She thought the girl mentioned a rue de something and then her eyes closed and her red head fell back on the seat.

An unspecified time later she was jerked awake when the stewardess came round taking orders for a meal. When the trays were served, Miss Martin said, "You are tired. I should apologize for bothering you."

"Oh, not at all," said Alison. "It's just, I'll be so glad to get home." She had never been so tired in all her life.

Perhaps the girl was tired too. After that she slept a little and they exchanged only a little desultory conversation in the last half hour before the plane landed at International

Airport in Los Angeles. The last Alison saw of her, she gave Alison a shy, fleeting smile as she stood back for the Mendozas to precede her up the aisle.

AND IT WAS blessedly good to be home again, even in the midst of the twins' clamor, to find everything just as usual. The house was running like clockwork under Mairí's capable management. There was a boisterous birthday party for the twins. Everyone had to hear all about the vacation. And after Alison had slept the clock around, she felt a good deal better.

"And you don't have to go into the office right away," she said to Mendoza.

"Change of pace," he said. He'd been fidgeting around the living room most of the evening, unable to settle with a book. "It's time I got back to work, *mi vida.*" He hadn't been away from the thankless job so long in twenty-six years. These days, the thankless job at the Robbery-Homicide office at L.A.P.D. Headquarters.

HE HAD TALKED to Hackett on the phone briefly on Sunday night, the day after they got home. To the inquiry as to what was new on hand, Hackett had said merely, "Just the usual. You can look over the reports when you come in. Nothing very abstruse, Luis."

There wasn't, as a rule, anything very complicated or mysterious in the reports. Just more evidence of human nature. But when Mendoza showed up at the office on Monday morning, dapper as usual in silver-gray Dacron, only Hackett was in. Robbery-Homicide was a little busier than usual. At the beginning of September the worst of the summer heat was on them and the crime rate up in consequence. There had been, Hackett told him, a new bank heist on Friday, and these days the FBI left the bank jobs strictly to the locals. Landers, Galeano, and Grace were out talking again to the various witnesses but probably would turn up damn all. It had been a slick pro job. Two men on it, and nothing so far useful in the way of descriptions. They had the usual run of heists to do the legwork on. Higgins and Wanda Larsen were out on those. It was, of course, Palliser's day off. The perennial heisters were anonymous, coming and going. Only occasionally did they drop on one with sufficient evidence to pin down a court case.

"Of course," said Hackett, "we've got this and that on this Baby Face. I've got the latest witness coming in for a session with the Identikit for whatever it might be worth." He leaned back and the desk chair creaked under his wide bulk. "He's hit three times since you've been away. Two twenty-four-hour convenience stores and a liquor store. Everybody says he's big, blond, very polite, and sort of apologetic. Says please and thank you. No sort of description of the gun, what size or type, just a gun. He sounds like an amateur."

"No leads from Records," concluded Mendoza.

"Not a smell. Couple of descriptions could match but they both belong to tough pros. He's first time out," said Hackett with conviction. "Just luck if we ever drop on him. There's the usual run of corpses, O.D.'s and winos. No mysteries. You can look over the reports. And I'll bet you're glad to be back in this hellish climate again after the British Isles."

Mendoza lit a cigarette with a snap of his lighter and said, "No hot weather, and the people are fine, Art. But I was inviting high blood pressure driving on the wrong side of the road. So I'd better look over the reports."

They were shorthanded. Henry Glasser was off on vacation, wouldn't be back for another week. Hackett's witness arrived to be taken down to S.I.D. for the session with the Identikit. Hackett hadn't come back yet when Sergeant

Lake buzzed Mendoza and reported a new body. This time of year was always a busy one for Robbery-Homicide.

Nobody else being in, Mendoza went out on it. It was, to a veteran officer of Robbery-Homicide and a cynical cop, an uninteresting body. The body of a kid about sixteen sprawled alongside a bench at a bus stop on Alvarado.

The patrolman was waiting for him. There were a few curious bystanders hanging around. "A woman came up to catch a bus and noticed him," said the patrolman. "He could've been here for hours, everybody thinking he was passed out. Probably an overdose."

"Probably," agreed Mendoza, after a look. The kid was just an anonymous teenager. Long, greasy hair, jeans, dirty shirt; but there was ID on him, a detention slip from Manual Arts High School signed by one P. Siglione. The name on it was Anthony Delucca. After the morgue wagon came and went, Mendoza drove up to the high school and asked questions.

Siglione was an English teacher, fat and middle-aged and disgusted. "That one," he said. "What the hell are we supposed to do with these kids, I ask you? Stoned on drugs and/or the liquor half the time, passing out in class. I don't know if it's the right answer, but most of us just ignore them. Most of the parents don't care or can't do anything about it. Sure, Delucca's in one of my classes. He turned up drunk as a skunk yesterday. I gave him a detention and sent him to principal's office. I doubt if he went."

Mendoza asked the principal's office for an address and got one down on Seventeenth Street. There he broke the news to an indifferent neighbor, on one side of a dilapidated duplex, who said, "Mis' Delucca, she's at work. I don't know where. There's nobody home till about six."

Little job for the night watch, reflected Mendoza, breaking the news. He took himself out to lunch at Federico's and ran into Galeano and Landers. They had to hear all about the vacation, and told him this and that about the bank job. Not that there was much to tell. There weren't any leads on it at all.

Mendoza asked, "And how are the expectant ladies?" The joke around the office these days was that there was something catching going around. Phil Landers was expecting a baby in December, Galeano's new bride, Marta, in March. The Pallisers' second was due in February, as well as the Piggotts' first.

Landers said lugubriously, "She would rope me into that house in Azusa, for God's sake. It needs everything done to it, what else, when we got it for seventy thousand, and I just hope to God she'll use some sense and not start on the painting herself. Women."

When they got back to the office Higgins was there typing a report, and broke off to greet Mendoza and hear all about the vacation. "It's good to have you back, Luis. We could use a few hunches on some things that have gone down lately."

"I don't produce them to order, George."

"And sometimes we don't need the hunches," said Hackett behind him. "I just shoved that hooker into Pending. We'll never get anywhere on that."

"I said so the minute I looked at the damn thing," said Higgins.

"What hooker?" asked Mendoza.

"The reports are somewhere on your desk. No big deal," said Hackett. "Small-time hooker in business for herself, Mabel Carter. Typical two-room apartment on Portland Street. Girlfriend walked in and found her dead. Stabbed and cut up, it was a mess, but no weapon left. Well, for God's sake, it could've been any john off the street. The hookers lay themselves open to it and she was on the way down. A lush. She'd pick up any prospect who'd buy a bottle and pay her the ten bucks. The lab didn't come up with anything. All the girlfriend could say, she hadn't had any trouble with anybody she knew of.''

"So she picked up the wrong john," agreed Mendoza uninterestedly. But as he wandered back to his office, started to look over the recent reports, he felt vaguely that it was good to be back, to the shop talk. To all the many men he'd worked with so long, knew so well, to the never-ending monotonous crude jobs showing up to be worked. It might be a thankless and sordid job, but it was the job he knew. It was his job.

He left a note for the night watch about Delucca. That was probably an O.D. of one of the street drugs or a combination. On second thought, he sent a note up to Narco, to Goldberg's office, about it. Not that there was anything unusual about the O.D. The various drugs floating around, so easily obtainable, saw to that, and the damn fool kids getting hooked by the pushers. There wasn't much Narco could do about it any more than Robbery-Homicide.

He was still a little tired from the strenuous vacation, from the jet lag. He found himself yawning over the reports and left the office early. By all experience, he knew that the next couple of months would see a buildup in the cases on hand. The worst of the summer heat always brought the rise in violence.

THE NIGHT WATCH came on, and Rich Conway scanned Mendoza's note and uttered a rude word. "More dirty work," he said. "I hate breaking news to the citizens." But it was automatic complaint. Conway, that man for the girls, was resigned to a tour on night watch now. He was dating a nurse who was on night duty at Cedars-Sinai. Piggot was looking morose.

Bob Schenke said amiably, "I'll toss you for the job." Conway produced a quarter and flipped it. "Tails," said

Schenke. That was the way it landed, and Conway handed over Mendoza's note.

"So I suppose I'd better get it over," said Schenke, and collected his hat and went out.

Piggott said, "These interest rates." As a practicing fundamentalist Christian, Piggott was not a swearing man, but his pauses could be eloquent. "We should've started buying a house when we got married, but you always figure there's time. Now, an apartment's no place to bring up a family, but who can afford the payments, even on a little place? We've been looking, but it's just impossible."

Conway, the carefree bachelor, wasn't much interested, but offered token sympathy. They didn't have any calls until Schenke came back an hour later.

He said cheerfully, "She cried all over me. Fat Italian woman with seven other kids, and the husband's a drunk. Had to tell me seven times how hard she tried to get the kid to stop using this awful dope. But kids don't listen to sense. If us lazy cops would just stop these terrible people selling the stuff, the kids would be all right."

"Oh, tell us," said Conway. Sure enough, ten thousand street dealers out there, anonymous.

"The devil," said Piggott, "getting around and about."

At ten-forty they had a call to a new heist, and Schenke and Conway went out on it. It was a twenty-four-hour convenience market on Beverly Boulevard, and the manager had been there alone. His name was Bagby. He was a small man about forty, and he was still flustered.

"I don't like to ask the women clerks to take the night shift," he said, "just on account of this kind of thing. The terrible crime rate. But it's the first time we've ever been held up. I was just so surprised because he looked like a—like an average young fellow. Not anybody you'd suspect—well, I don't know exactly how much was in the register, but it must've been around a hundred bucks—"

"Could you describe the man, Mr. Bagby?" asked Conway.

"Well, yes, just an average-looking young fella, maybe about twenty-five. He was big, around six feet, and he had blond hair—he was wearing ordinary sports clothes, slacks and a short-sleeved shirt, and he was clean-shaved. In fact he looked pretty clean and neat altogether. Not the kind of lout you'd expect— Well, I don't know anything about guns—it was just a black sort of gun, not very big."

Schenke and Conway looked at each other resignedly. "Baby Face again. Did he touch anything in here, did you notice?'

Bagby shook his head. "I don't think so. He waited till another customer left and we were alone, and then he just came over to the counter and said, this is a stickup, give me all the money—and I saw the gun, so I did, and then he went out. No, I didn't follow him or look— I don't know if he got into a car."

The citizens. Well, faced with a gun in unknown hands, anybody would play safe. Schenke started to tell him they'd like a formal statement, if he'd come to headquarters sometime tomorrow. There'd be another report on Baby Face, and the way it looked, no more leads than the other reports had turned up.

They didn't have another call the rest of the shift. The beginning of the week was sometimes slow.

ON TUESDAY MORNING when Palliser came in, he wasted a little time hearing all about the vacation. "But it's good to have you back. With Henry off, we've been busy. And we'll be busier, with the worst of the summer still to come." He rubbed his handsome straight nose ruefully.

Hackett and Higgins had drifted into Mendoza's office after him. Hackett had the night report and said, "Baby Face again. And no leads. Well, how often do we pick up a heister? Go through the motions." He laid the report on Mendoza's desk.

It was Jason Grace's day off, and there was enough work on hand to keep the rest of them busy. They were still taking statements from the witnesses to the bank robbery, and two of the tellers were coming in again to look at more mug shots down in Records. The rest of them went out, and Hackett sat down in the chair beside the desk and lit a cigarette. "Have you had a chance to go through last week's reports?"

"Desultorily," said Mendoza. "Any one in particular?"

Hackett sighed. "These muggings. There's not a damn thing we can do about it, nowhere to go, but it looks like an organized effort to me. The first one was just after you left. So far there have been five. All of them in interesting places—the parking lots by the Ahmanson Theatre, that complex of shops around the Music Center, around those high-class restaurants in Little Tokyo. About the only places in downtown L.A. where you might reasonably expect to run into the well-heeled victims. And they've taken a little haul, all right. The jewelry, the cash."

"They," said Mendoza.

"Well, yes," said Hackett. "Only one of the victims was alone, an elderly widower. He's still in the hospital. The rest were couples having a night on the town. They all say it was three, four, five young louts. Moved in fast and didn't care how much damage they did. I know, Luis, but it smells to me like gang action. Fairly smart gang action. Picking those spots. It's funny when you come to think, these—um—fashionable places being right downtown in what used to be the real slums."

"Mmh," said Mendoza. He'd grown up in those slums before the fashionable places got built, or got to be fashionable.

"I talked to Slade over in Juvenile about it. He says there are four or five gangs who could be responsible, but no way to pin it down. Whichever, they know a fence. None of the jewelry showed up."

"And gangs down here," said Mendoza sardonically, "would know every fence operating."

"Well, it's just a thought," said Hackett. He sighed again and stood up. "And I would have a bet with you that it's a waste of time. That Bagby, Baby Face's latest victim, offered to come in and look at mug shots. Somehow I don't think Baby Face is anywhere in Records."

"You never know," said Mendoza. *"Buena suerte."* The phone buzzed at him as Hackett went out and he picked it up.

"Mendoza."

"I got your love note about your latest overdose," said Captain Goldberg. "What the hell do you suppose we can do about it? You haven't even had an autopsy report yet."

"I just thought you'd like the information for your statistics, Saul. No, I don't know what kind of an O.D. it was yet. But we all know the probabilities."

Goldberg sneezed and said, "Damn allergies. For a bet the Quaaludes—and/or liquor or PCP. Anybody can buy the stuff on any street corner, and when the kids are such goddamn fools to get hooked—well, let me see the autopsy report when you get it, just to pass the time. How was the vacation abroad?"

Mendoza told him and finished going over the reports he hadn't caught up on. He was just going down the hall to the coffee machine when Sergeant Lake on the switchboard beckoned to him urgently.

Mendoza halted. "What's gone down now?"

Lake proffered him the phone. He was smiling broadly. "It's Jase, Lieutenant, they've got one."

"¡No me diga!" Mendoza took the phone. "Congratulations, Jase."

Grace was in the middle of a sentence. "—and I've got to admit to you, we could've got one a year ago if we hadn't been particular. Us black folk get priority now, you know, and then too there are always plenty of black babies, but Virginia wasn't about to take just any baby and neither was I. Jimmy, you there?"

"It's me," said Mendoza.

"Oh, Lieutenant. That's good, you can tell everybody. We just got the confirmation an hour ago. Only heard about the possibility last night. We haven't even seen him yet, but he sounds just what we want. No, it wasn't the adoption agency, it was Virginia's doctor. He knows the family, very respectable family, good people, but the daughter got in trouble. He's only three days old, but the doctor's going to arrange everything—well, we don't know when we can see him, but we've already decided on Adam John and Virginia's crazy to go out shopping for baby clothes—"

Mendoza was laughing. "Good news, Jase, congratulations, just what you wanted." The Graces already had one adopted baby, little Celia Ann, and had been hunting another for a couple of years.

"You pass the word on, Lieutenant—tell you more tomorrow."

Mendoza grinned at Lake. "All of these pregnancies must've rubbed off on Jase."

Lake grinned back. "Just what he wanted. It's grand. I suppose he'll be raving about this one and taking all the pictures to show, the way he did with the first one. Well, kids, they can be a lot of trouble, but a lot of fun too."

Mendoza looked into the big communal detective office. Galeano and Landers were in and he passed on the news. They were pleased for Grace; he had felt a little resentful of all those pregnancies.

"At least," said Landers, "they already have a house. When I think of the payments on that old shack—"

Hackett and Higgins were apparently still down in Records with the witnesses. They hadn't shown up when the rest of them went out to lunch, leaving Wanda Larsen taking a belated statement from one of the witnesses to the bank robbery, and they had just landed back at the office at one-forty-five when a new heist went down, with a first report of a D.O.A. victim.

Mendoza went out on that with Galeano. It was a big chain pharmacy and on Olympic, and the D.O.A. was the head pharmacist, Dave Bryan. Everybody else around was in a state of shock. There were two other pharmacists, five women clerks, and seven or eight customers. Most of the heisters were shy birds, wary of operating in front of a crowd, but like everyone else they came all sorts. The two patrolmen had done their best to preserve the scene, but there had been some milling around. It probably wouldn't make any difference here.

"But it was so fast—" The older of the two pharmacists kept repeating that in a dazed voice. "So fast—in and out, and they both had guns— I don't know which of them killed Mr. Bryan—one of them asked for all the uppers and downers, and the other opened the register. I don't think anybody but us saw what was going on until they fired at Mr. Bryan—"

"And it was just a mistake," said the other one fiercely. "A damn stupid mistake! He didn't pay any attention because he didn't hear the bastards. He was getting deafer all the time and the hearing aid didn't help him much. He just turned away, he thought I was waiting on them, and I guess they thought he was going to call the cops and they—" The man lying face down at one end of the counter looked to be in his late seventies, with a scanty tonsure of gray hair and a spare figure in the white smock. He had been shot once in the head and there was no exit wound.

"There was just one shot?" They seemed to think so.

Stocky, dark Galeano stood looking at the corpse thoughtfully. "No powder burns," he pointed out. "The shot was fired from at least three feet off and got him square in the back of the head—either it was a fluke or the shooter's a pretty good marksman. Fairly small caliber, too. It looks like a very slick pro job."

Mendoza agreed, and talking to all of these people, getting all of the formal statements, was going to take up quite a lot of time. Go through the motions, he thought, with a vengeance—and likely come up with nothing useful. On the other hand, if this had been pulled by a pair of experienced pros, it was possible that one or both of them were in Records, and some of the witnesses might pick a picture. Even the experienced pros were quite often stupid, and it was also possible, given the stupidity of this caper—walking into a store full of people to pull a heist in the middle of the day— that they had both been high on something.

They started to ask for names, get the people sorted out. One of the patrolmen had called the lab; Scarne and Horder came out in a mobile truck and took some photographs, dusted the counter and cash register for any latent prints. Presently the morgue wagon came for the body. The other pharmacists said that Bryan had been a widower but had a married daughter in Pasadena. So they'd have to break more bad news.

ALTOGETHER, THERE WERE fifteen people to question, get the formal statements from, and it was going to go on a good part of tomorrow. Wednesday was Hackett's day off. By the end of shift on Tuesday afternoon, Mendoza and Galeano had taken four statements and set up appointments for the other witnesses to come in tomorrow.

On Wednesday morning Mendoza had just finished getting a statement from one of the clerks and had seen her out when Lake buzzed him from the switchboard. "You've got a new corpse," he said tersely. "Fourth Street."

"Oh, hell," said Mendoza. That was another thing about this job. It was like women's work, always more of it coming along. He looked into the big office. Grace, Galeano, Palliser, and Landers were all talking to witnesses, and Higgins had taken a couple more down to Records to look at pictures. Somebody had to tidy up the corpses as they came. He collected his gray Homburg and got the address from Lake.

It was a little way out on Fourth, in a very shabby block of old buildings. Most of the others along here were empty and boarded up and very probably the whole block was ready to be torn down to make way for the new high rises.

The address he wanted was a desiccated-looking old six-story apartment house. The squad was parked in a red zone in front. In the little lobby, Patrolman Hunter and three other people were waiting. Hunter stepped forward. "I kept him from going back into the room, sir. Not that I suppose it's important. Looks like a straight suicide." He added in a louder voice. "This is Lieutenant Mendoza. Mr. and Mrs. Daggett, they're the managers here, Mrs. Garvey," Daggett was a thin, medium-tall man in the fifties, with a lantern jaw and a prominent Adam's apple. He looked anxious and shaken. His wife was plump and maternal-looking, right now a little pale. The other woman was tall and thin with too much makeup and a lot of cheap costume jewelry. Daggett burst into speech rapidly.

"Like I was telling the officer here, I just found her. Never thought the poor girl would do such a thing. Take poison or whatever it was. She seemed like a nice girl. Her name's Ruth Hoffman, she rented the apartment last month, said she was from Chicago. See, I explained to her—

it says apartment hotel in front but the last ten years we just had permanent tenants— I explained to her I couldn't rent except on a weekly basis, the building's going to be torn down and we might get notice any day, but she said that was O.K. She seemed like a nice quiet girl. I don't think she had a job—she didn't go out regular—''

"Fred," said his wife, "don't get all upset now. It's nothing to do with us. I'm sorry for the poor girl, but it was her own doing."

"For love," said Mrs. Garvey unexpectedly in a dramatic tone. "All for love and the world well lost! I'm one of the few remaining tenants here, Lieutenant, and her apartment was just across from mine. I had met her when she asked to borrow some coffee once and the poor darling had confided in me." She sniffed into a handkerchief smelling violently of lavender. "How she had followed her true love here and he had spurned her. My heart went out to her, truly."

"Anyways," said Daggett rather desperately, "her rent was up yesterday and she hadn't come to pay me and I went up about maybe half an hour ago, forty minutes, to see if she was in, and the door was unlocked and, well, there she was, dead. Killed herself, with poison or something. And so I called the cops."

"All right," said Mendoza. "Which apartment?"

"It's number twelve—the right front. I don't have to go up again, do I?"

"Don't upset yourself," said his wife soothingly.

Hunter followed Mendoza up the uncarpeted stairs. "Dilapidated old place," he said. "Just what I could see, it looks like a straight suicide." The apartment door was open. Beyond it there was the expectable cramped living room, the tired old furniture, couch and one upholstered chair, a couple of small end tables. Visible through a doorway was a tiny narrow kitchen with just space for a minute table and two chairs. An old-fashioned wall bed which would fold up into the wall overnight was pulled down. The body lay on that, the face turned to the wall. On the bedside table was a half-full glass of water and a small plastic prescription bottle.

Mendoza bent to scrutinize that without touching it. Whatever label it had borne had been torn off. It was empty. On the cheap painted bureau were a worn billfold and two sheets of paper. Mendoza flicked through the billfold. Two hundred and twelve dollars in cash, a Social Security card with the name Ruth Hoffman. He took up the first sheet of paper. They were both letters. The first one was a half sheet of cheap stationery, evidently torn from a tablet. It was written in an overlarge, careless script, the writing of someone who did not often use a pen.

Dear Ruthie, I told you before you better just forget this guy. He is no good for you. You think he's serious, but believe me it isn't so what you tell me he said. You know the boss was kind of put out when you quit so sudden and he would take you back like a shot so you better come back home and forget this guy. You know we've been friends a long time and I'm just thinking of what's best for you.
Love, Jean.

The other letter was typewritten by somebody who wasn't a proficient typist, on a sheet of ordinary typing paper. It began abruptly without salutation.

Look Ruthie, I'm sorry if I hurt you. But I never was serious like you. I'm not ready to get married and settle down, and anyway, not with you. I'm sorry but you better stop pestering me about it. I like you all right, but nothing serious. You better go back to Chi where you got friends. Jim.

"*Así,*" said Mendoza to himself. The straightforward suicide. The silly girl in love. The lover spurning her, and a deliberate overdose. Where had she got it? And kaput.

Just more paperwork.

For the first time he looked at the old-fashioned pulled-down bed where the body lay. He went over to look at the body, and it was the body of the girl who had traveled with them on the flight from Chicago. Juliette Martin. She was unmistakable. The neat cap of dark hair, the tip-tilted nose, the wide mobile mouth. It was Juliette Martin, the girl from France.

And the identification said, Ruth Hoffman.

Why?

TWO

"WELL, OF COURSE it's the same girl, the girl on the plane," said Alison. The strip fluorescent lighting turned her fiery red hair nearly gold where she looked down unflinchingly at the white face in the cold tray in the morgue. "She was really lovely, a beautiful girl. But what a queer thing, Luis."

"You're sure. So was I." He steered her out to the corridor. They sat down on the bench along the wall and he lit cigarettes for both of them. "So tell me everything you remember about her. You're the one who talked to her. I was half asleep."

"We were both dead tired. She seemed like a very nice girl." Alison sounded troubled.

"Echoing Mr. Daggett," said Mendoza. "Yes, those Daggetts and the Garvey woman— And you know something *cariña,* it's fate—destiny or something. If I hadn't gone out on it to recognize her—well, I don't know that I caught all she said to you. Tell me what you remember."

Alison said dubiously, "Well, it wasn't much. All pretty casual. I was so sleepy, and I got the impression she was a little shy, not a chatty type—a nice girl, educated—well, a lady, I think"— Alison drew on the cigarette and looked at it thoughtfully—"well, that she said as much as she did because she was a little excited, a little nervous. She wasn't the type to come out with private affairs to a stranger—and she said that, that she was nervous. It was the first time she had ever flown. And she was going to visit her grandfather—"

"No name mentioned?"

"No. The grandfather had disowned her mother because she wanted to marry a foreigner. The mother had gone to

France for some postgraduate study—and she said her mother had written to him when she was born, Juliette, I mean, but never heard from him. But when her parents were killed in an accident of some sort she had written to tell him, and they'd corresponded, and now he was sorry about how he'd treated her mother, and wanted to meet her. And she worked in an office somewhere. She had three weeks' vacation coming that she hadn't taken because they'd been busy—"

"No mention of what kind of office?"

"No. And she was engaged to a man named Paul. At first he didn't want her to come here, but she said there was the family feeling. Her grandfather, the only family she had—except for two uncles."

"Who might," said Mendoza, "have been either her mother's or her father's brothers. *¡Mil rayos!*"

"Well, I suppose," said Alison. "And her boss was a Mr. Trenchard, Treuchard, Tenchard, something like that. I don't remember exactly."

"Helpful," said Mendoza. "It's a damn queer setup altogether. Somebody went to a little trouble."

"But why?" asked Alison. "She seemed an ordinary sort of girl. Prettier than average, but ordinary."

"Why indeed. Do you remember anything else?"

Alison considered. "I was so sleepy— I remember asking her if she lived in Paris and I think she mentioned a street name, a rue de something. But it was about then that I dozed off. I think you were already asleep."

"A handful of nothing," said Mendoza. "And the three helpful, innocent witnesses to back up the straightforward suicide—and those letters—*¡Dios!* Ordinary is the word, so very damned plausible. But I can't see exactly where to go on it except—mmh—yes, those Daggetts and Garvey, but—"

"Well, I hope you can find out what's behind it, but what a very funny thing, Luis."

"I could think of other words for it," said Mendoza in a dissatisfied voice. "Take care on the freeway home, *cariña*."

He had left the lab men going over the tired old furnished apartment. Now he drove back to headquarters, collected Higgins and Palliser into his office and told them about it. They were intrigued but doubtful.

"That's a damn queer setup if you're right," said Higgins. "But could you be absolutely certain it is the same girl?"

"Yes, yes," said Mendoza irritably, "and so was Alison."

"But that apartment manager, the other woman, telling the tale all straight-faced— She was supposed to have been here at least a month."

"That's right, and what's to say any different except that it's the same girl who was on the plane with us last Saturday. Juliette Martin. And they say that everybody's got a double, it's just my word and Alison's that it is the same girl, damn it."

"You're absolutely sure?" asked Higgins.

"Don't dither at me, George. Yes, I'm sure. Not going senile yet."

"Well, if we lean on those witnesses, they may come apart."

"And maybe not." Mendoza brushed his mustache back and forth in habitual irritated gesture. "Somehow I think they're—background. Just there for effect."

"I don't get you," said Palliser blankly.

"I'm not sure I know what I mean myself, John."

But there were a few obvious things to do. He went down to Communications and dispatched a cable to the Sûreté in Paris, requesting any information on Juliette Martin, French citizen, probably resident in Paris, probably on a

plane from Paris to New York last Thursday or Friday, and
appended a description. He sent a request to the U.S. Customs
in New York asking for any record of her arrival. Did
they take down the numbers of passports? He hadn't any
idea. He seemed to recall that when they landed in England
the Customs officers had simply glanced at the joint passport
and waved them on.

They drove back to the ancient apartment house in Higgins'
Pontiac. The lab men were just packing up to leave and
it was getting on for three o'clock.

"Why the full treatment on a suicide, Lieutenant?" asked
Duke. "And what a hell of a place to die. Damn pretty girl,
too."

Horder said with unaccustomed violence, "And so damn
silly, by those letters. Stupid. No real reason to kill herself,
over the silly love affair, but they will do it."

"I trust you got those close-up shots," said Mendoza.

"Yep," said Duke. "Doubt if we'll make any latents except
maybe hers. Place looks neat enough on the surface but
probably hasn't had a good cleaning in months. So it's all
yours."

They went out. Higgins picked up the old worn billfold
from the bureau top. "I thought you said a Social Security
card. Not exactly," he said, flipping it open.

"No, but a lot of people carry them," said Mendoza. He
looked at it again in the plastic slot of the billfold. The
original Social Security card was a rather flimsy small piece
of cardboard, easily misplaced or defaced. He had seen
these replicas advertised in a good many mail-order catalogs:
the numbers and name stamped onto a thin sheet of
metal. There was SOCIAL SECURITY at the top, an eagle with
wings spread, name and number below. The nine-digit
number was anonymous, the name Ruth Hoffman only
slightly less so.

Higgins, echoing the thought, said, "How many Ruth Hoffmans in the whole country?"

"No guesses," said Mendoza, "and I suppose the computers in Washington would trace down the number in time, if we're allowed to ask—which is debatable. The IRS can harass the citizens as much as they please, but nobody else is supposed to invade the citizens' rights."

They looked through the shabby old furnished apartment. The lab men had left a handbag on the bureau, the only handbag there, a big bone-colored plastic bag. There wasn't much in it. Two keys on a ring, one to the door here, one to the mailbox in the lobby. A couple of tissues, a soiled powder puff, a half-used lipstick. There was a shabby suitcase, unlocked and empty, and a meager wardrobe of clothes in the tiny closet, none new and no labels in any of them. There were four pairs of shoes, the labels of three of them indecipherable. The newest pair bore a logo from a local chain, Kinney's. All the clothes were size fourteen. In the kitchen cupboards was a modest stock of food—cereal, canned soups, canned vegetables, instant coffee. In the little refrigerator was a half-empty quart bottle of milk, an unopened package of hamburger, a quarter-pound of margarine, a loaf of bread. There were no dirty dishes.

"All very plausible," said Mendoza. "All very ordinary. Easy to read. Somebody went to a little trouble to set up the picture."

Palliser said doubtfully, "Well, it looks plausible all right. You *are* sure about the girl?"

"How often do I have to say it? Yes, it's a very pretty effort, and if I hadn't recognized the girl there'd be one stereotyped report getting filed away right now." Mendoza brushed at his mustache. He was looking exasperated. "Would you have thought twice about the missing envelopes, on those letters?"

Higgins massaged his craggy jaw. "Probably not," he admitted. "Nothing in the wastepaper basket, but the place is fairly neat. She could've emptied the trash last thing."

"We can guess those letters never went through the mail, and there'd be a chute to an incinerator in the basement, a place this old." Mendoza flipped through the billfold again and said, "*Así*, how nice." There was something else in the last plastic slot of the billfold. A library card made out to Ruth Hoffman, from the Los Angeles Public Library on Sixth Street. The date of issue was the sixth of August just past. "So that much we know."

"What?" asked Palliser.

"That this caper, whatever the hell it's all about, was set up that long ago, at least. I'll be damned, I will be damned," said Mendoza.

"But the witnesses—" Higgins still sounded doubtful.

"Oh, yes," said Mendoza gently. "Those witnesses."

HE HADN'T TAKEN formal statements from them yet. They brought them into the office that late afternoon and heard what they had to say again, Palliser taking notes. They told the plain, plausible story, and they looked like ordinary, honest people. The Hoffman girl had rented the apartment from Daggett just over four weeks ago, paying cash by the week, forty dollars. Daggett was less nervous now, and he showed the carbons of the receipts he'd given her, all correctly dated. That was the only time the Daggetts had seen her, when she paid the rent. "I don't think she'd got a job," said Daggett. "The only thing I remember her saying about herself, she came from Chicago." His wife nodded placid affirmation.

"That's right. She seemed like a nice, quiet girl."

The other woman, her garish makeup in the strip lighting revealing more wrinkles than it covered, was garrulous and confidential. Her name was Helen Garvey. She was a widow and worked part-time at a dress shop on Pico Boulevard. She had lived in the apartment house for nearly six years, and it would be hard to find another place at the same rent when the building was torn down. She'd met the Hoffman girl over the borrowed coffee. They'd got talking and the girl had told her how she'd followed her boyfriend out here and then found he didn't want to marry her after all, and she was all broken up about it.

Mendoza listened to them at length, leaning back in his desk chair, smoking quietly, giving them time. When Mrs. Garvey finally stopped talking, he sat up and said sharply, "Now that is all a damned pack of lies, isn't it? When did you first lay eyes on the girl? She hadn't been there that long, that we know."

Daggett's prominent Adam's apple jerked once, but his lantern jaw thrust forward and he said with just the right tone of indignation, "You've got no call to say I'm a liar. It was all just like we told you. Why'd we want to tell lies about it? None of us really knew the girl at all. It was just like I said, I went up to get the rent and found her like that. Poisoned herself, she had. Why'd we want to lie about it?"

"She'd been here a month," contributed his wife insistently. "I'm sure I don't know why you'd call us liars. We ought to know."

"She told me," said Mrs. Garvey emotionally, "how downright miserable she'd been about her boyfriend. His name was Jim. That was all she ever said. She thought he wanted to marry her—"

"Who primed you with the pretty story?" Mendoza's voice was sharp.

"I don't know what you mean. We just told you the plain truth." Daggett was defiant. They weren't showing any overt signs of nervousness, and when Higgins brought in the typed statements they signed them without a tremor.

Mendoza let them go. It was nearly five-thirty.

"You're absolutely sure—"

"For God's sake, don't say it again, George."

"Well," said Palliser, "it's just your word, but if we're working it by the book, there are obvious things to do."

"So go and do them," said Mendoza.

Palliser got waylaid in the hall by Jason Grace. Grace had been wasting everybody's time enthusing about the new addition to the family. They were planning a formal christening next week and Celia couldn't wait to meet her new baby brother. They would probably bring him home on Sunday. It had all been worth the long wait—

Palliser said yes and fine and just before the end of shift he got down to Communications. He sent off a teletype to the Chicago force asking for any information they could dig up about a Ruth Hoffman, description appended. Just on the very long chance he got hold of Duke in the lab and asked him to wire the girl's prints to Chicago. Mendoza sounded damn sure about the French girl, but on the face of it, it was an unlikely story. Mendoza had on occasion been known to be wrong. Palliser ruminated about it on the way home to Hollywood, but when he got there it slid to the back of his mind as he kissed Roberta.

"You feeling better?" She'd been having a bout of morning sickness.

She smiled up at him as two-year-old Davy came running. "I'm fine, the doctor said it's nothing to worry about. Don't fuss, John."

HIGGINS WAS WONDERING about Ruth Hoffman, too—a very offbeat thing, if Luis was right. But it was all up in the air and Luis wasn't infallible; and it was likely to stay up in the air because there was nothing to get hold of on it. Unless the French police came up with something definite. But a lot of queer things had shown up in Higgins' long years on this job, and he put it out of his mind as he pulled into the drive of the rambling old house in Eagle Rock.

Mary was just setting the table. The little Scottie, Brucie, was underfoot demanding his dinner. Laura Dwyer was busy over homework, Steve not yet home from basketball practice. Their own Margaret Emily was cuddling a stuffed toy on the living-room couch. Higgins built himself a drink and sat down to relax before dinner. Thank God tomorrow was his day off.

THE NIGHT WATCH didn't leave them anything new, and there were still a few statements to get on the pharmacy heist. Hackett was fascinated with the Hoffman-Martin thing. "But what the hell could be behind it, Luis?"

"I haven't the faintest idea," said Mendoza. "And don't ask me if I'm sure it's the same girl. Not a girl you'd forget. A good-looker in a distinctive way—"

"And you're just the boy to notice. I'll take your word for it."

"*Ya pasó aquello*— I'm a respectable married man."

"Well, we can try to pin it down. Wire photos and prints to Chicago and the French police."

"It's done," said Mendoza, "but damn it, Art, it's a long chance her prints would be in French records. The girl a perfectly respectable girl, what used to be called a lady, and they don't print all the citizens any more than we do."

"But eventually somebody will miss her," said Hackett reasonably, "and start asking questions. There was the fiancé, she must've had friends who knew where she was going here."

"*De veras.* Eventually. By God, I'd like to know what the hell is behind it, Art."

"These Daggetts. Do you think they were paid to tell the tale?"

"I'm damned sure of it, and they're probably regretting it now, but they're stuck with the story, and, *condenación*, I should've let them think we'd swallowed it until there's something concrete to throw at them."

"If there ever is," said Hackett.

Nothing had come in from Chicago. It was too early to expect it. The lab sent up the photos Mendoza had requested, full face and profile, close-ups of the lovely dead face, queerly more dignified in death.

Hackett looked at them and admitted it wasn't a face you'd forget. "But these Daggetts—what possible connection with a French girl?"

"How should I know? I don't think there is any. I think the Daggetts and the talkative widow are—mmh—just background. Put in for verisimilitude as it were."

"How?" asked Hackett.

"For the nice money. The setup cost a little something, if not much. The clothes, the stock of food, the cash on hand, enough to bury the poor silly suicide, so maybe we wouldn't try so hard to trace her back. And in a city the size of Chicago, how many Ruth Hoffmans? How many living in the bosom of families not listed anywhere? Those two letters, even minus the envelopes, a plausible substitute for a suicide note."

"Very neat," agreed Hackett. "If you hadn't just happened to have seen her before, it would've gone into a routine report and got filed away. Well, wait and see what may turn up."

"I want to ask some questions about that library card," said Mendoza.

JUST BEFORE NOON. Landers came in with one of the two pharmacists on that Bryan killing. He had unexpectedly picked out a photograph down in Records, identified it

positively as one of the heisters. The pedigree on file backed
him up.

Joseph Bauman, Caucasian, six one, black and brown,
one-seventy, twenty-four two years ago. He'd been charged
with one count of armed robbery and prior to that with assault and possession of controlled drugs. He'd got a one-to-
three on the robbery count. Landers got a statement from
the witness and called the Welfare and Rehab office to find
out what they knew about Bauman. The address in Records was two years old. A sergeant at that office looked up
their records and said Bauman was on parole since three
months ago. He was living at an address on Madera Avenue in Atwater and he had a job at a chain fast-food place
on Sixth Street.

Hackett went out with Landers to find him.

The manager at the fast-food store told him he hadn't laid
eyes on Bauman in a week. "And good riddance. That probation officer talked me into hiring him. I didn't like the
idea so good, and that Bauman, he just doesn't want to
work so hard—all the time goofing off."

So they tried the place on Madera in Atwater, which was
a modest frame house, neatly maintained, on the narrow
side street, and showed the badges to the fat, nondescript
middle-aged woman who answered the doorbell. She looked
at them, and first she looked alarmed and then resigned.
"He's in trouble again, is he? I just don't know why. I tried
to bring him up right. It was hard without my husband.
Joe's father got killed in an accident when Joe was only
four, but I tried. Lord knows I didn't spoil him. Tried to
teach him right from wrong."

"Is he here?" asked Hackett.

"Yes, he's not up yet. He got in pretty late last night. He
said he was out playing pool with some pals." She stepped
back, tacitly inviting them in.

Bauman was still in bed in the back bedroom, looking as if he had a hangover. He was dirty and unshaven. He snarled when he saw the badges, and he said exactly what they'd expected him to say. "I haven't done nothing. The fuzz got no call to come picking on me." It was automatic. Hackett told him to get dressed. The woman said she didn't mind their looking around, but they'd wait for a search warrant. He wasn't likely to get sent up for a long stretch within the courts in the state they were, but they'd take no chance on making the charge stick.

They took him in to the jail and applied for both warrants. Landers called the lab and talked to Scarne. "Oh, I was just about to make a report on it," said Scarne. "Yeah, the coroner's office sent the slug over and I was just having a look at it. It's out of an old beat-up S. and W. thirty-two. Probably hasn't been cleaned in years, it's a miracle the damn thing fired at all. Yeah, we can match them if you ever pick it up."

The search warrant came through after lunch. Hackett and Landers went back to Madera Street. At least Hackett's Monte Carlo was air-conditioned; it was up to ninety-four or so, humid and muggy. Madera Avenue was paved with blacktop and it looked as if it were ready to melt; it felt sticky to their feet. "Why anybody lives in this climate—" said Landers.

They hadn't questioned Bauman yet, just stashed him in jail. The witness had been very positive on the identification. The woman let them in silently, looked at the warrant. They started to hunt around Bauman's bedroom and within five minutes Landers came across a beat-up old S. & W. .32 under a pile of clean socks. It was unloaded. There was a box of ammunition for it in the next drawer down.

Landers said sadly, "And some people think it's a glamorous job, or that you've got to be big brains to do it."

"And in all the brainy arch-villains," rejoined Hackett. "All I can say, Tom, is that I hope to God some soft-headed judge doesn't give him a slap on the wrist and six months in the joint."

"I won't hold my breath," said Landers.

They poked around some more but didn't come up with anything interesting. So they started back to the jail to talk to Bauman. When he knew they had the nice evidence, he might be inclined to tell them who the other heister had been on that job, and they were both aware, as certain as death and taxes, that Bauman would claim it was the other fellow who fired the gun and the other fellow—if they picked him up—would claim it was Bauman.

The job wasn't glamorous, but it was often discouraging.

"OH, DEAR ME, I couldn't say at all," said Mrs. Marsh blankly. She stared at the glossy eight by ten enlargement. "She looks sort of dead."

"She is," said Mendoza. "You've never seen her?"

"I just don't know." Mrs. Marsh was thin and sharp-nosed, about forty, with pale blue eyes and over-large round glasses. She was one of the assistant librarians at the big main library on Sixth Street. She looked back at the library card and shook her head.

"Who would be the one to issue cards?" asked Mendoza.

"Any of us. Anyone on duty at the check-out desk." She had laid the photograph down hastily, pushing it toward him. "It would depend who was on duty when—when the person requested a card. I don't think anybody would remember. I mean I don't think anybody would recognize that—any photograph."

"Why not?" asked Mendoza.

She wet her lips. "Well, we have a lot of people in. It's a big library, and we issue a lot of new cards. Unless the person was a regular, who came in a lot—they're just faces. If you see what I mean. And at least I can tell you that the girl wasn't a regular. I don't think I ever saw her in my life."

It was what he had expected, a slight gratification. "But whoever took out the card, it's not so long ago. If we can locate the librarian who issued it—"

She was still shaking her head. "You mean, maybe to tell you what she looked like. Oh, I shouldn't think so. You just don't realize, we're always pretty busy. We get a lot of students in, you know, and we're always issuing new cards. It's—it gets to be automatic. Like filing or checking books in and out. And it doesn't take five minutes—you know. You get the name and type it on the card and put in the date and that's that."

Mendoza was aware that they didn't ask for identification. It was like a driver's license—anybody could apply for one under any name. In this big, busy place, very likely whichever librarian had issued the card had hardly glanced at the female who announced herself as Ruth Hoffman. In fact, the library card told them only one thing, that it had been a female who took it out. Young, old, fat or thin, whatever color. Mrs. Daggett? Mrs. Garvey? Or Anonyma?

It said, of course, something else. It said, for about ninety percent sure, that the pseudo suicide of Ruth Hoffman had been planned at least since the date on that card and probably before.

And he was no stranger to homicide of any kind. But at the thought a small cold finger touched his spine. He picked up the photograph and glanced at it before he slid it back into the manila envelope. The lovely face with its pert nose, wide mouth, tender skin, looked so very young. And death didn't reckon by age. But suddenly he saw again, as he had seen it only once, the rather shy, friendly smile of the pretty girl on the plane. Whatever was the reason, it was a sad thing that she was dead and cold down there in the morgue.

Being thorough, he talked to every one of the librarians on duty. They all shook their heads at the card, except one, a Doreen Minor, who said brightly, "Oh, I know the name. Ruth Hoffman. But now I see it can't be the same one. The same Hoffman. This is a new card—August sixth—and Ruth Hoffman's been coming in for years. She's a student at L.A.C.C., I know her pretty well. But she only got her card renewed last year. So it must be a different Hoffman. Of course, it's a common name."

So it was, and that had been part of the plan, too. There wasn't anything to be got from the library card. Mendoza hadn't really expected there would be.

He had talked to the coroner's office and asked for the autopsy to get priority. The lab report on that apartment would be along sometime. It was never any use to prod the lab boys. They took their own time.

PATROLMAN DAVE TURNER was on swing shift, and at this time of year he was just as glad. The darkness after the sun finally went down gave a sort of illusion of coolness, and by the time he came on shift at four o'clock it must have gone up into the high nineties. Turner was only twenty-four, but he'd heard a lot of old folks claim that it never used to get this hot in Southern California, that it was the rise in population and all the watering of gardens that had changed the climate. He would just as soon live in a cooler climate, but he'd also like to make rank on this top force.

He took over the newly gassed-up squad after the briefing in the Traffic squad room, at one minute past four. He was on a beat right in the heart of the oldest part of the city, and parts of it were quiet as the grave and parts of it could get pretty hairy. But they didn't have the manpower to run two-men cars anymore. He had covered the beat once by five o'clock and had just turned back onto Alameda when he caught the light a half a block down. As he sat waiting for it to change, somebody honked at him urgently and he looked around. There was a big truck looming up at the left of the squad and its driver was leaning across the seat of the cab beckoning at him. Turner pointed up toward the side street, and the driver nodded and put up a thumb. The light changed, Turner pulled into the side street and parked and in the rearview mirror saw the truck ease cautiously across traffic into the right lane to follow him. It pulled into the curb ahead of the squad. It was a Goodwill truck, the familiar logo across each side of the body. Turner got out, automatically putting on his cap, and the driver slid down from the cab. He was a thick-shouldered, stocky man in the forties with thinning red hair and freckles.

He said to Turner, "Say, I don't want to give you a bum steer, you know? God, it's hot. What a climate. Seems to get worse every year." He brought out a handkerchief and mopped his forehead. "I was just figuring maybe I oughta tell somebody about it, just in case it is anything."

"About what?" asked Turner.

"Well, I figure I got sent to the wrong address, see. Nobody down here in this neck o' the woods would have much good salvage to give away. It's an address back there on Banning Street," and he gestured. "I nearly didn't get out of the truck. Old shack of a place. But it was the address the dispatcher gave me so I went up and rang the bell. This was about ten minutes ago. Had to wait awhile, nobody ever did answer the door, but I could swear I heard somebody callin' for help from inside. Kind of a weak voice— Help me, somebody."

"I'll be damned," said Turner.

"I come away, but I was still thinking about it when I spot your squad car, and I just figured I'd feel better if I told somebody about it."

"Yes, sir," said Turner. He got the man's name for the record, Bill Cotter. "Thanks very much, Mr. Cotter. We'll check into it."

"I suppose it could've been kids, but you never know. Helluva thing. Kind of scared me."

"Yes, sir, I'll have a look."

Cotter went back to the truck and pulled out. Turner went around the block and headed back to find Banning Street. He knew generally where it was, a short and very narrow old street on the wrong side of Alameda, not far from the railroad yards. A street of ramshackle old houses dating from the turn of the century and never very fancy to start with, houses unpainted, with narrow front yards bare of grass or flowers. Peering against the too-bright late afternoon sun, he spotted the address. It was an ancient frame house ready to fall down. One of the front windows to the right of the tiny porch was broken—a whole pane missing. He parked the squad in front, went up to the porch and pushed the bell. He listened and in thirty seconds he heard it—a thin, faint voice moaning, and then "Somebody—please help me—somebody." He pushed the bell hard again. There was a shuffling step inside and the door was pulled half open to reveal a tall thin old man in stained cotton pants and a ragged shirt. There was about a week's growth of gray stubble on his chin. He looked at Turner and he said, "I got no time for niggers. What do you want?"

Turner showed him the badge. "There seems to be somebody in trouble here, sir. May I come in?"

"Ain't no trouble here," said the old man brusquely. And the faint voice came again, "Please, help me—help me—"

"Let me in, sir," said Turner gently. For one moment he thought the old man would slam the door in his face, and then he stepped back reluctantly.

Turner went in past him to a little living room nearly bare of furniture, only a sagging armchair and an old console T.V. He turned right into a short hall and faced a closed door which must lead to the room where that broken window was. He opened it, took one look and said sickly, "Oh, my God!"

It was a bedroom containing only an old twin bed, a small table, a rickety unpainted chest. It was a shambles of squalor and filth. There was long-dried excrement on the floor and bed, a thousand flies zooming around, and on the bed, in a tangle of dirty bedclothes, was an old woman, emaciated to skin and bones, gray hair wild about her witless face. She was moaning weakly.

Turner swung back to the old man. "What's your name, sir?"

After a dragging moment he said, "Leach. Ben Leach."

"Is this your wife?"

"Ain't got no wife. No use for females. She's my sister."

"What's her name?"

"Mary. Mary Leach. I don't purpose to have no dirty niggers asking no questions nor coming in my house—"

"Please leave the door open, Mr. Leach," said Turner sharply. He went back to the squad and put in a call for an ambulance. While he waited for it, he went back into the house.

The old woman's eyes were dazed, unfocused, and she twisted her thin body feebly. "Please—help me—so hungry—"

The old man had the television on.

"My good God," said Turner to himself. "People." On this job you saw everything.

THE NIGHT WATCH came on. "At least," said Bob Schenke cheerfully, "we get to stay in air conditioning part of the shift."

Piggott was studying the real estate section of the Times. "There's nothing within reason," he said dismally.

"Take it to the Lord in prayer," said Conway flippantly.

"Oh, don't think we haven't. If it's intended—" Piggott sighed.

"You're just the born pessimist, Matt," said Schenke kindly. "Hold the positive thoughts."

"You're not looking for a home with reasonable payments," said Piggott peaceably.

"Well, no. Maybe I was born to be a bachelor."

At least the day watch hadn't left them anything to do.

They didn't get a call until nine-forty, from a squad out on Alvarado—a mugging. Piggott and Conway went out on it. The victim was D.O.A. and there were witnesses: people up the block, one elderly man, who had also been waiting for a bus at the corner like the victim.

"They just came up and—and attacked him. Slugged him and knocked him down—and I guess got his wallet and just ran off. It all happened pretty fast, and I got a pacemaker— I couldn't do much even if it hadn't been so fast—" The couple of people farther up the block hadn't seen the assault so clearly. There were, of course, no descriptions. Only that there were two muggers, both men and probably young.

About twenty feet up the street they found a worn old billfold. It was empty of cash, but there was identification in the plastic slots. At a guess, of course, homicide hadn't been intended. He'd been knocked down hard against the bus-stop bench and probably died of a fractured skull. His name was Vincent Carmody and he'd lived on Coronado Street in the Silver Lake area, by the driver's licence. He was twenty-five and he had been good-looking. Piggott and

Conway went up to break the news and tell the family about the mandatory autopsy, when they could claim the body.

"He was just going to see Judy," wept Mrs. Carmody, "the girl he was engaged to—such a nice girl—just waiting for a bus to come home, his car was on the fritz in the garage. Just coming home from seeing Judy—it doesn't seem fair— It isn't fair—"

Carmody had been a clerk at a Sears warehouse, with a blameless record. It didn't seem fair, but that was the way things went.

THREE

HACKETT WAS THE FIRST MAN in on Friday morning. The heat was getting to him. It had been consistently in the high eighties for weeks, but lately it had been a lot worse. He'd be ready for his vacation six weeks from now—they weren't going anywhere, they couldn't afford it and they couldn't take Mark out of school—and that monster of a dog Angel had saddled them with ate as much as a horse—but it would be nice just to relax and not have to get up so early.

They hadn't got much from Joe Bauman yesterday, just profane denials. They'd tackle him again today. But before Landers came in Sergeant Lake buzzed him and said somebody at the hospital wanted to talk to police, a Dr. Richter at Cedars-Sinai. Hackett picked up the phone and said, "Robbery-Homicide, Sergeant Hackett."

"Rob— Well, I just wanted to report the death," said a doubtful masculine voice. "We understood the police were concerned. This Mrs. Leach."

"Leach. I'm afraid I don't know—"

"Well, she died last night. I don't know the details, but the ambulance man said it was a police officer had called him."

"I don't know anything about it. What did she die of?"

"My God, she was in a terrible state— I was at the end of my shift in Emergency when she was brought in— I never saw anything like it," said Richter. "Gross malnutrition, and she was filthy. Hadn't bathed or eaten in God knows how long. We took it that she lived alone and hadn't been able to look after herself, and she was probably in the late seventies. She was dying when she was brought in, there wasn't much we could do. She went into a coma about seven P.M. and died a couple of hours later. The heart just gave out. All we have is the name. I understood the police had the background—it was an officer called the ambulance.''

Hackett was a little annoyed at new business. He called down to Traffic—they would have the records of what went on in all the beats in Central Division, if it had been Central business—the fact that the hospital was Cedars-Sinai said nothing, that was the emergency hospital. Traffic eventually found the record for him. The patrolman was a Dave Turner, the address Banning Street. It didn't sound like any business for Robbery-Homicide, a natural death; but he got Turner's phone number and woke him up.

What Turner had to say put a little different look on it. They'd better talk to this Leach anyway. "I mean, Sergeant, he acted a little bit senile as far as I could see, but he looks O.K. physically. He could've helped the old lady if he wanted.''

"Yes,'' said Hackett. The other men were drifting in. It was Galeano's day off. It still didn't sound like much and it would take some time, but he started out to talk to Leach.

Palliser and Grace were talking to a couple of witnesses—probably on that mugging last night. The paperwork went on forever.

It was already at least ninety outside. He had to look up Banning Street in the Country Guide. At the ramshackle little house he waited awhile before the door was opened.

"Mr. Leach?'' He proffered the badge. "I'm sorry to have to tell you that your sister died last night. I'd like to ask you a few questions if you don't mind.''

The old man peered at him blearily. "I got no money to pay for a funeral,'' he said.

"How long had she been ill?''

Leach said indifferently, "Awhile. It was a damn nuisance. Leave me to do the cookin'. She allus did. But it sure

saved on grocery money. Yes, sir. Time she took sick"— He
worked his slack mouth as if savoring something—"said all
she wanted—tea and toast. I brung it to her a time or two,
but it was a damn nuisance. But it sure cut down on expenses." Suddenly he cackled gleefully. "I come to see that,
first week or so—reckon I got by for no more than six, seven
bucks a week."

"Why didn't you call a doctor for her?" asked Hackett.

Leach said, "Doctors, they cost a lot of money."

"You hadn't been giving her anything to eat?"

"She wanted, let her get up and get it. Leavin' me do all
the cookin'. She allus been a pretty good worker up till
then." Leach gave Hackett a furtive, silly smile. His mouth
was slack and he dribbled a little.

Hackett swore to himself. The old man going senile, that
poor damned old woman left helpless. They'd have to find
out if there were any responsible relatives, get Leach safely
tucked away. It was a little mess and not really police business. It wouldn't add up to any charge but contributory
negligence, and Leach obviously wasn't in possession of all
his faculties.

He started to ask another question, but Leach suddenly
turned and went over to the T.V. and switched it on, blar-
ing.

Hackett looked through the house. There wasn't much in
it and it was filthy. The kitchen was piled with dirty dishes,
alive with flies, and the whole place stank like a sewer. He
didn't find an address book or any letters. There wasn't a
phone.

The house to the left side was boarded up and empty. The
house on the other side was occupied by a fat, mustached
Mrs. Sanchez who said in thick English that she didn't know
none of the neighbors—she just moved in.

Hackett went back to headquarters and talked to the
Health Department. Then he called the appropriate Social

Services office and talked to a Mrs. Peabody. They would get the old man committed, sort out who owned the old house, get the old lady buried. And by that time he'd wasted half the morning on it.

Nobody was in the office but Higgins, sitting at his desk, smoking and staring into space.

"Goofing off," said Hackett. "Where is everybody?"

"Tom went to talk to that heister, and Baby Face's latest victim came in to make a statement and Jase took him down to look at mug shoots—not that he'll make one."

"No," agreed Hackett. "I don't think Baby Face is in anybody's records. What's the boss up to?"

MENDOZA WAS TALKING to a Sergeant Donovan in Chicago. "Listen," said Donovan plaintively, "what do you expect, bricks without straw? All you give us is a name—Ruth Hoffman—you know how many pages of Hoffmans there are in the phone book?"

"I can guess," said Mendoza. "We're just going through the motions, Donovan. But we'd like you to prove there never was a Ruth Hoffman who came out here last month from Chicago."

Donovan groaned. "Not a hope in hell, either way. There could be a dozen Ruth Hoffmans, anywhere in greater Chicago—you want us to check through the whole damn phone book?"

Mendoza said brusquely, "Just the usual cooperation. If you can't find a trace of a Ruth Hoffman who left Chicago recently, that'd be very gratifying."

Donovan groaned again. "I'll set a couple of boys to phoning. Just hope we can get you to return the favor sometime."

Mendoza put the phone down and wandered out to the big detective office. Hackett and Higgins were there and he passed on what Chicago had to say, which was expectable, and heard about Leach.

"And damn it, no lab report on that apartment yet. We should get an autopsy report today or tomorrow or something from the French police, or the airlines, or Customs. Where the hell is everybody, on what? Anything new down?"

Higgins said, "A squad called in about an hour ago. Body in an alley on Skid Row. John went out to look at it. Probably nothing to work. I'd just as soon nothing new went down to take us out of the air-conditioning."

Palliser came in and said, "My God, it must be nearly a hundred out there." He looked tired and yanked his tie loose, sitting down at his desk and pulling the cover off his typewriter, rummaging for report forms in the top drawer.

"What was the body?" asked Hackett.

"Nothing much. Looked like an old wino. Either natural causes or the alcohol. Man about sixty, little I.D. on him— Manuel Garcia. Lived at one of those dollar-a-night flophouses on the Row—the city will have to bury him." Palliser started to type the triplicate report.

It was getting on for noon. Landers came in looking hot and tired and said, "There's going to be a riot over at the jail—the air-conditioning's broken down and it's like a damned oven. My God. But Bauman had been thinking things over and decided to tell us who his pal was—one Albert Gerber."

"And Gerber was the one who fired the gun and killed the pharmacist," said Hackett.

"Naturally." Landers picked up his phone, told Sergeant Lake to get him R. and I., and asked if they had a package on Gerber. "Bauman gives us an address—Houston Street in Boyle Heights. We'd better go and see if Gerber's home."

"After lunch," said Hackett.

Five minutes later R. and I. called back to say that Gerber had a package with them of two counts of armed robbery.

It was a quarter past twelve. Palliser finished the report and they all started out for lunch. But as they passed the switchboard, a uniformed man came in and handed Lake a manila envelope.

"Cable from Paris. You've been asking about it."

Mendoza seized it eagerly and slit it open with his thumbnail. Twenty seconds later he said exasperatedly, *"¡Diez millones de demonios!"* He thrust the cable at Hackett. That prestigious police force, the Sûreté Nationale, had nothing to say. PRINTS WILL CHECK. INSUFFICIENT DATA YOUR REQUEST INFO MARTIN NO AVAILABLE INFO UNLESS SUPPLY FURTHER DETAILS.

"¡Condenación!" said Mendoza. "If we had any further details, don't they suppose we'd have said so?"

"I said you'd never get anything more on it. It's all up in the air," said Higgins. "You don't know anything about the girl—what to ask for—or where. Where she was bound for here. Anything—it's a dead end. If there's anything to it all." And Mendoza gave him a bitter look.

"In other words, I'm just woolgathering."

"Don't rile the man, George," said Hackett. "Maybe the lab report will have something useful."

THE LAB REPORT wasn't in when everybody came back from lunch. Hackett and Landers took off to look for Albert Gerber, and ten minutes later a new call went down to a bar on Temple. Palliser and Grace went out on that. Five minutes after that information started to come in all at once.

American Airlines called Mendoza from New York to confirm as requested that a Juliette Martin had been booked on that flight from New York to Los Angeles with a stopover at Chicago and a change of planes, last Saturday. Air

France called from its New York office to confirm that Juliette Martin had been on its flight from Paris to New York—leaving Orly Airport at eight P.M. a week ago today. "Something to tell the Sûreté anyway," grunted Mendoza. Then the Customs office in New York called to confirm that French citizen Juliette Martin had passed through Kennedy Airport with a French passport at approximately five P.M. a week ago today. They gave him the passport number.

"Something concrete," said Mendoza pleasedly.

"For what it's worth," said Higgins.

"You're just a little ray of sunshine, aren't you?"

"And that's impossible. If she left Paris at eight that evening she couldn't get here at—"

"Time differences," said Mendoza tersely. "Europe's eight hours ahead of us."

"But it's nothing you didn't know already," said Higgins.

Then a uniformed man came in with a manila envelope. The lab report on the apartment. Mendoza scanned it hastily and said, "Hell, *nada absolutamente*—or nothing useful."

The only latent prints the lab had picked up in the apartment were the girl's. There had been a clear print of her right thumb on the top of the handle of the refrigerator—just where it might be expected—and others on the kitchen counter, a table in the living room. Nothing else but smudges anywhere, except for one clear print of her right forefinger on the plastic medicine bottle. There hadn't been enough residue of anything in that for analysis. And that was all the lab had to tell them. Mendoza passed the report over.

"And I'm wondering now—how did she get there?" he said dreamily. "Already drugged, already unconscious—" He stabbed out his cigarette and immediately lit another, his gaze abstracted on the view over the Hollywood Hills in the distance through the big window behind his desk. "Going to visit her grandfather! No possible way to find out the name this side of France—anywhere in greater Los Angeles—and where the hell was she between Saturday and Tuesday? We haven't got an estimated time of death yet but it looked as if it could've been Tuesday night. No address book there. Well, they'd have got rid of anything informative, of course."

"The Daggetts?"

"I don't know," said Mendoza in a dissatisfied voice. He had asked Records about the Daggetts and Helen Garvey. They looked simply like ordinary little people—unimportant. "They know something but it might not be much. But Grandfather comes into it somewhere, George."

"And how the hell do you make that out?"

"Grandfather would've been expecting her. Knew she was coming. Was he going to meet her at the airport? We didn't see anything of her after we got off the plane. Grandfather is probably an elderly man—maybe he doesn't drive. Was she expecting to be met? —And—Hell and damnation!" He sat up with a jerk.

"I just saw that too—not operating on all cylinders," said Higgins. "Better ask the cab companies if she picked up a cab at the airport."

Mendoza already had the phone off the hook. "And damn it—no way to be sure but show the photos to any cabby who had a fare there. A little legwork. But George, the reason I say Grandfather's in it somehow—he'd be expecting her. If she was intercepted somehow, by whoever, for whatever reason only God knows—and didn't show up, Grandfather would be concerned. The natural thing to do would be to check with the airline, and he'd find out she landed here. If he isn't in on the caper—whatever the hell it is—why hasn't he reported her missing?"

Higgins passed one hand over his prognathous jaw. "Maybe he has."

Mendoza shut his eyes. "*Muy bien*. Not operating on all cylinders you can say. Grandfather may not be a villain. He could live anywhere from Malibu to Monrovia, Tujunga to Lakewood—and he may have reported her to one of a hundred police forces. Thank you, George."

"Well, it was just a thought."

"So we get on the phone and start asking. The logical force would be Inglewood where the airport is. But what in God's name it's all about—*Por Dios,* I swear that was a cold-blooded killing, and it was planned out right here, whatever the hell was behind it—and there have got to be some leads if we dig deep enough." He picked up the phone again. "Jimmy, I want to talk to some cab companies."

Higgins yawned. "There must be people who knew where she was heading. She'd have had friends—there's the boyfriend."

"Don't suggest that I cable to the Sûreté again," said Mendoza bitterly.

HACKETT AND LANDERS were trailing Albert Gerber in ninety-eight-degree heat. Gerber wasn't at the Houston Street address, which was an old four-story apartment building, and the only tenant at home didn't know him, but the manager lived on the premises and said helpfully that he knew Gerber had a pal who worked at the Shell Station up on the corner of Soto. He didn't think Gerber had a job since awhile back but he was up to date on the rent all right. They had queried the DMV about a car and knew Gerber was driving a ten-year-old Chevy, plate number so-and-so.

They tried the Shell Station. An indolent-looking fellow with a big paunch, shirt opened to his belt, looked at them lackadaisically over a canned Coke and said, "Oh, him. Yeah, he hangs around here some—working on his car. He's a friend of Mike's—Mike Sullivan, he spells me part-time and nights, he's supposed to show up at four if you want to talk to him.''

"Do you know where he lives?" asked Landers.

The man said reluctantly, "Oh, hell, I got it wrote down somewhere." He moved slowly into the grubby little office, rummaged and found an address scrawled in a ragged ledger. It was Cornwell Street, only a couple of blocks away, a shabby old duplex. The girl who answered the door had a luscious model's figure, clearly visible in a pair of shorts and a halter, and she didn't know where Mike was but she knew where Gerber might be. He'd been dating Marlene Foster pretty heavy lately, she said, she and Marlene had been to school together, and Marlene had just got laid off her job so she might be out somewhere with Al. That address was Pennsylvania Avenue. The air-conditioning in the Monte Carlo barely had time to get going when they found the place, a single frame house with peeling paint. A shapeless woman in a wrinkled tent dress opened the door.

"Oh," she said to the question. "No, Al's not here. Him and Marlene went to the movies. Mostly for the air-conditioning. They went to the first show when it opened at one o'clock.''

"Do you know which one?" asked Landers.

"Sure, the Bijou over on Whittier. Unless they changed their minds. You're cops, aren't you?" She looked doubtfully at Landers. "Even if you don't look old enough to be.''

Landers with his perennially boyish face would be hearing that one until he was a grandfather.

It was a little past three-thirty then and the first show was probably about over. They looked up the address at the nearest public phone and got to the theater fifteen minutes later. There was a public parking lot half a block away. They looked and spotted Gerber's old Chevy, so they waited.

There wasn't any shade and the sun beat fiercely on the sticky blacktop. They waited another fifteen minutes and a couple walked up to the car laughing and talking.

"Albert Gerber?" asked Hackett.

"Yeah, that's me." He recognized them for what they were instantly and said, "What the hell you want anyways?" He was tall and dark with a heavy tan and bulging muscles. The girl was small and blond. She looked scared.

"You," said Landers and brought out the badge. They had already applied for the warrant.

Gerber came out with a string of obscenities and the girl began to cry. "You promised you wouldn't get into any more trouble," she wailed.

"I haven't done a thing, the dirty fuzz just pick on anybody got a little pedigree—"

"Well, Joe Bauman says you were with him on that heist the other day, and it's a charge of murder two this time, Gerber. That pharmacist is dead."

Gerber said this and that about Bauman. "I don't know what the hell you're talking about."

"Come on," said Landers. "We're taking you in."

Gerber fished out his car keys and gave them to the girl. He said, "You get hold of Mike and tell him I'll need some bail money. The goddamn fuzz."

They ferried him down to the jail and booked him in. Hackett said, "We can talk to him some more later on, Tom—after they've got the air-conditioning fixed."

The air-conditioning was still off at the jail and it felt hotter than it had outside, stuffy and stagnant.

MENDOZA LEFT EARLY and got home by six o'clock. It was a little cooler up in the hills above Burbank, but the sun was still fairly high and unrelentingly bright. Beyond the tall iron gates which opened politely as he shoved the gadget on the dashboard, the green pasture on either side of the drive looked pleasantly pastoral. The Five Graces, the woolly white sheep to keep down the weeds, were peacefully huddled in a little cluster grazing industriously. Ken Kearney had the sprinklers going on the pasture. The Kearneys would be relaxing over dinner in their apartment attached to the stables for the ponies, Star and Diamond.

At the top of the hill, where the big old Spanish ranch house sprawled behind its concrete block wall, Mendoza slid the Ferrari into the garage beside Alison's Facel-Vega and Mairí's old Chevy and went in the back way. In the rear patio, Cedric, the Old English sheepdog, greeted him amiably. His long pink tongue was out; in this weather his heavy coat must be a burden. He followed Mendoza in through the service porch.

Mairí MacTaggart was at the stove, Alison busy making a salad. She glanced up. "You're early, *mi vida*. The rat race just as usual?"

He bent to kiss her. "*Estoy rendido*— I'm exhausted, for no good reason."

"Is there anything new on the Martin girl?"

"*Nada*—and maybe nothing ever will show," he said moodily.

"Now that," said Mairí, shaking her silver curls at him, "is a verra strange business indeed. I wonder what happened to that poor thing? Now, you go and sit down with the man, *achara*, I'll finish that."

"I need a drink," said Mendoza.

El Señor, the half-Siamese, could hear that particular cupboard opened the length of the house away, and came floating up to the counter top demanding his share in a raucous voice. Mendoza poured him half an ounce of rye in a saucer. "Shortening your life," he said.

"I'll have a glass of sherry, *cariño*."

In the living room the twins scrambled up from coloring books to greet him. Baby Luisa was staggering around with

a stuffed dog in her arms. The other three cats, Bast, Ne-
fertiti, and Sheba, were dozing in a tangle on the couch.
Cedric sprawled at Alison's feet and Mendoza gratefully
sank into his big armchair and sipped rye. It cost a fortune
to run the air-conditioning in the big house, but it was worth
it.

"Have you heard from the French police?" asked Alison.

"That's a dirty word," said Mendoza.

"I wish to goodness I could remember anything else she
said. I've got the definite feeling there was something more,
but it just won't come."

"And it could turn out to be a dead end." Mendoza
sipped rye and tried to turn his mind off. No use worrying
at the thing; it was futile. He sighed and leaned back.
Someday maybe he would retire and be rid of the thankless
job.

LANDERS' SPORTABOUT wasn't air-conditioned and he was
perspiring and exhausted when he got home to the Hollywood apartment. The apartment, thank God, was air-
conditioned, and Phil—whose parents had christened her
Phillipa Rosemary before she decided to be a police-
woman—looked cool and comfortable. She had got home
just ahead of him, but she had spent the day in air-
conditioning down in the R. and I. office. She was bulging
a good deal in the midsection these days; the baby was due
at the end of December, and at the end of this month she'd
be taking maternity leave and then she could stay home until the end of March. And by that time, he reflected without much enthusiasm, they'd be moved into that claptrap
house in Azusa—Azusa, my God, forty miles farther to
drive—and her car was eight years old and sooner or later
she'd have to have another one, and he wasn't due for a raise
until next year—and there'd be the house payments—and a
baby-sitter—

"You look as if you had quite a day," said Phil in a concerned voice.

"Well, you look fine," said Landers. He kissed her, his cute little blond Phil with the freckles on her nose. "The rat race. I need a drink before dinner."

"It's just cold cuts and potato salad and odds and ends, unless you'd like a hamburger."

"That's fine. I'll fix us some drinks and we can take our time."

THE BRAWL in the Temple Street bar had been time-consuming and took a little sorting out. There was only the one patrolman there and he said apologetically that a couple of witnesses had been long gone before he could get their names. There had been quite a little crowd in the place and most of them excited, but he'd done his best. Both Palliser and Grace had served apprenticeships riding squads and knew how awkward that kind of situation could be. "But I've got the one who did the knifing. His name's Tony Aguilar." He had the man in cuffs, sitting at one of the battered wooden tables. "I got here just about as it happened. The owner had called in—"

"Because I don't want no trouble." The man leaning on the bar was thickset rather than fat, with a flourishing full black mustache and bushy black eyebrows. He looked nervous. "Tony, he's got a temper on him. He starts to cuss out this guy, I don't know the dude—he just come in off the street—and Tony's started fights before, I don't want no busted furniture and bottles, I says to him, Cool it, Tony, but I see he's about to blow up, and I'm sorry, I don't want to get him in trouble, Tony's a right guy mostly—it's just he's got a temper on him. He's not drunk. You can see he's not drunk. I don't let guys get stoned in here. I run a quiet place."

"All right, Mr.—"

"Perez, I'm Bob Perez."

"Mr. Perez. What were they fighting about, do you know?" asked Grace.

Perez licked his lips. "I'm an honest man," he said irrelevantly. "I don't run no clip joint, boys. It was just a little game of draw—nothing important."

That, of course, spelled out the situation. Unrealistic as it might seem, it was against the law to gamble in public, except inside the racetrack—the only place it was legal around here was down in Gardena where all the cardrooms were located.

Aguilar raised his eyes from the handcuffs and said morosely, "He was cheating. He had cards up his sleeve or something. He took every pot and Diego called him a cheat and quit the game. I was fool enough to stay in, but I'm not fool enough to let him get by with a royal flush when one of the high cards already got played, and I said—"

The dead man still had the knife in his chest, a big horn-handled jackknife.

"You shoulda listened to me, Tony," said Perez mournfully. "Now what's your wife gonna say? So he was a cheat, you didn't have to go and kill him, Tony."

"I didn't mean to kill him, for God's sake."

There were eight or ten other men there standing around watching. The squad-car man had a list of names. "Does anyone know who this is?" asked Grace.

Perez shrugged. "Who knows? He just come in off the street. Had three or four beers and got into the game."

Palliser squatted over the corpse and felt in the pockets, came up with a billfold. There were eighty-four dollars in it and in the first plastic slot a driver's license for Alfredo Delgado. He'd been a moderately handsome man in the mid-thirties, and the address was Brooklyn Avenue in Boyle Heights.

They talked to the other three men who had been in the game, who told the same story. "Diego who?" asked Grace.

"Diego Allesandro. He's a regular here. He left before it happened. He wasn't here," said Perez. "You going to lay a fine on me?"

Grace surveyed him amusedly, brushing his narrow mustache in unconscious imitation of Mendoza. "I don't know, Mr. Perez. It would be up to the district attorney's office, but I don't suppose they'll bother." The token fine, the unrealistic rules weren't going to stop the card games in bars or anywhere else.

"It was just a friendly little game," said Perez uneasily. "I mean it started out like that, see. The guys don't get to playing cards in here—I mean all the time, I mean it's not a regular thing. Just once in a while. You can tell them, can't you?"

Grace exchanged a cynical look with Palliser, who shrugged. But it took the rest of the afternoon to clear it away. The morgue wagon came for the body and they took Aguilar down to the jail and booked him, went back to the office. Palliser set the machinery going on the warrant. It would get called murder two and might easily be reduced to plain manslaughter under the circumstances.

Grace typed the report and then they went over to Boyle Heights and talked to Delgado's landlady. He'd been renting a room in an old single-family house. The landlady's name was Bream and she didn't seem very much upset to hear about her roomer. "Well, he wasn't here much. I never had much talk with him. Couldn't say if he had any relatives." She agreed indifferently to let them see his room and they looked through drawers and pockets, but found no address book or letters. Delgado had probably been a drifter and somewhere there might be people concerned about him, but there was nothing to say so here. They let it go. And that

took them nearly till the end of shift, and thankfully they
both left early.

As Palliser drove home, he was thinking vaguely about
the way the crime rate was up in Hollywood. But they had
an equity in the house, and Trina was a good watchdog.
Maybe when he got his next raise they could look somewhere farther out.

And Grace, easily shelving the routine job, was thinking
fondly and fatuously about the new baby. The plump brown
little boy who would be christened Adam John at the Epis-
copal Church next Sunday. He'd been worth waiting for.

IT WAS Piggott's night off. Schenke and Conway drifted in
together at eight o'clock to the big communal detective office that always seemed so much bigger and emptier at night
than when it was full of busy men on day watch.

"What do you bet we'll have a busy night?" said
Schenke. "The heat building and the weekend coming up."

The switchboard was shut down. Any calls would be relayed up from the desk downstairs.

Conway assented cheerfully. He had a date set up with his
new girl, Marilyn, tomorrow afternoon. They were going to
one of the few new movies worth seeing and out to an early
dinner at that Italian place on the Strip. She was on the
eleven-to-seven shift at Cedars-Sinai. He thought about
Marilyn happily. A nice girl, no nonsense to her, perfectly
happy to have the date without going all serious. He'd just
met her last month when they had that rape case. After his
latest couple of girls starting to talk suggestively about real-
estate prices and what good cooks they were, Marilyn was a
joy—pretty, too, with her glossy brown hair and blue eyes.
Conway was a good-looking man himself with his regular
features and cool gray eyes, which he appreciated without
undue vanity.

He was sitting at Higgins' desk and there were a couple of glossy eight by tens on the desk blotter. Conway looked at them appreciatively. He could see that the poor girl was dead, but she'd been a hell of a good-looker. "I wonder what this is about," he said.

Schenke, also a born bachelor, but not particularly a man for the girls, said indifferently, "No idea."

They got their first call at eight-fifteen, a heist at a liquor store on Third Street. The address rang a faint bell in Conway's mind. They both went out on it, and when they got there, the owner was mad as hell. "It's the third time I've been held up in five months, goddamn it. I have had it. I have had it up to here, I've goddamned well had my fill of this goddamned business. My wife's been after me to retire and move up to Santa Barbara— Hell, who can afford to retire with the goddamned Social Security about to go down the drain, and I'm only fifty-five but these goddamned punks roaming around—"

He looked vaguely familiar to both Schenke and Conway. His name was Bernard Wolf and he was a short, stocky, dark fellow with an unexpected bass voice.

Schenke said, "Yeah, the latest one was back in July, wasn't it? We were both out on that then."

"I remember you," said Wolf. "You goddamned well were, and goddamn it, you never picked up that bastard, he got away with a hundred and seventy bucks—it was a Saturday night. You had me down there looking at pictures of all the punks and I couldn't make any, all of these goddamned louts look alike—"

"Well, can you give us any description of this one tonight, Mr. Wolf?" asked Schenke patiently.

Wolf let out a long exasperated sigh of resignation. "I don't know that I can, goddamn it. There'd be ten thousand punks look like him—all over this goddamned town. I was alone in the place—my wife's nervous about me being here at night, but the young guy I hired to come in, he's in the hospital with a leg in traction. Do I shut at six and miss all the busines—the weekend coming up? There'd been a customer just left, the punk came in and showed me the gun and I gave him all the paper in the register and he went out—call it three minutes. All I can tell you, goddamn it, he was a spick.''

"Latin," said Conway.

"Sure, maybe five ten, thin, black hair, little mustache, and he couldn't talk English so good, had a thick accent. He got maybe a hundred and fifty bucks. Goddamn it. Goddamn it, I have had it. I can't afford to retire, but the hell with it. I'll get something for the business and maybe I can find a part-time job up in Santa Barbara. I have had it with this goddamned business and this goddamned town—''

"Did he touch anything in here?" asked Schenke.

"Nothing but the goddamned money," said Wolf.

They went back to the office and Conway typed the report on it. It was probably the only report there'd be. There would be a hundred possible heisters conforming to that description in Records, and they'd never pin the charge on any one of them. He stopped typing to light a cigarette. "At least it would be cooler up in Santa Barbara," he said. He had just finished the report when another call came in, and another a minute later.

The first was a heist at an all-night pharmacy on Beverly Boulevard, and the other was a body on Rosemont Avenue in the Echo Park area. Schenke went out on the heist and Conway looked up Rosemont Avenue in the County Guide.

When he got there, it was a narrow, shabby old eight-unit apartment building. Four apartments down, four up. The man waiting for him at the entrance was about forty-five, a heavily built man with a bald head and rimless glasses. His name was Robert Peterson. He was the manager of the apartments, lived in the right front one downstairs. The door was open and an anxious-looking gray-haired woman was visible in there listening.

"I don't know what happened, Officer, but it's Mrs. Eberhart. Maybe a stroke or something, only she's not that old. Why, she could've laid there hours before anybody found her—a terrible thing—the Kohlers are off on vacation, they've got the apartment across the hall, they've gone to visit their daughter—you see Mrs. Eberhart's apartment is on the rear right. Why, she could've laid there all night, except that I took the trash out and naturally went out the back door and passed her apartment."

"So, let's have a look," said Conway.

Down the dim hall the door of the rear apartment on the right was open. With Peterson dithering in the background, Conway took a quick experienced look. The woman was dead. A big, buxom blond woman, the blond courtesy of peroxide, wearing a flowered cotton house robe. She was sprawled just inside the door and there was dried blood on one temple—just a trace. There was a table beside the door, standing sideways out from the wall. You could read it. She'd been knocked down, hit the table. The autopsy report would probably say, fractured skull. He thought resignedly, better get out the lab. It could, of course, have been accidental: Maybe she'd been drunk and fallen down, but also it could be something else.

He asked questions. Peterson said, "Well, her name's Rose Eberhart. I don't know about any relations. She's lived here about six years. Well, yes, I do know where she worked. It was McClintock's Restaurant on Sunset. She was a nice quiet tenant, Officer, never any trouble and always on time with the rent. I suppose it could've been a heart attack. That can happen to anybody, age doesn't seem to matter. Oh, for goodness' sake, no, I'd never seen her under the influence of alcohol."

A couple of men from the night watch at the lab showed up in a mobile truck. Conway said, ''You better give it the full treatment, boys.''

Just in case. And leave it to the day watch to look at further.

FOUR

SATURDAY WAS Sergeant Lake's day off and Rory Farrell was sitting on the switchboard. Mendoza glanced over the night report and passed it on to Hackett. "So we'd better find out something about this Eberhart woman, in case it is a homicide. Wolf's coming in sometime today to make a statement, but there's damn all on that, we can file it and forget it."

Hackett said, "I wonder if they've got the air-conditioning back on at the jail. We've still got to talk to Gerber. Of course, Bauman had the gun, it's likelier he did the shooting. Which reminds me—" He called the lab and talked to Horder. He had dropped the gun off at the lab on Thursday. Horder said, "Oh, yeah, that's the equalizer, O.K. Matched the slug out of the body." So they could write a report after they got the statement from Gerber, if he'd say anything, and send in the evidence to the D.A.'s office and forget it. This time, Bauman might go up for a sizable stretch.

It was Landers' day off.

On the other heist last night, the pharmacist had given a fairly good description, volunteered to look at mug shots. He'd be in this morning. Hackett went over to the jail to talk to Gerber. Palliser said, looking over the night report, "I suppose this restaurant won't be open until ten or so. Has the warrant come through on Aguilar?" It hadn't, but would be showing up sometime today.

Bernard Wolf came in about nine and made a brief statement, and Wanda Larsen took him down to look at mug shots. But there could be a thousand walking around who conformed to that description.

And finally the coroner's office sent up the autopsy report on the supposed Ruth Hoffman. Mendoza read it over rapidly, one hip perched on a corner of Higgins' desk, and passed it over. "So, a few possibly suggestive things," he said.

The report said that the girl had died of a massive overdose of a common prescriptive sedative, a phenobarbitol base. Interestingly, there were indications that it had been accumulative over a brief period of time. There had been the equivalent of a couple of strong drinks in the stomach contents. The percentage rate was .010, and .014 was the rate for legal intoxication. The estimated time of death was between eight and midnight last Tuesday night. There were no bruises or other marks on the body. She had been a virgin. She had had a meal about six hours prior to death, consisting of some sort of fish, potatoes, green vegetables.

"This is your offbeat one," said Palliser.

"The wild blue yonder," said Higgins.

"Well, it says a little something." Mendoza lit a cigarette with a snap of his lighter. "But there's a gap between Saturday and Tuesday. Where was she? That library card—this was set up awhile ago. If they, whoever, had arranged the killing, why not do it right away? Grandfather! Could she have been with Grandfather? I can't see any pattern to it at all, damn it."

"Have you heard anything about the possible missing reports?" asked Higgins. Mendoza had sent out queries to every force in the country about that.

"Nothing's come in yet. Where the hell was she and why? We should be hearing something from the cab companies, if there's anything to get."

"Those Daggetts could tell us something," said Higgins.

"I wonder," said Mendoza. "They know something but maybe not that much. I haven't leaned on them because we haven't a damn thing to go on, for God's sake. There's no smell of legal proof that the girl was the Martin girl. And whoever primed the Daggetts with the Hoffman story, all they have to do is stick by it, we can't prove it's a lie. What the hell use would it be to lean on them, George? They're not big brains, but they understand that much. Grandfather, Grandfather! If only there was some way to find out where she was going, or thought she was going—" He brushed his mustache back and forth angrily.

"There's just no handle to any part of it," said Higgins. Mendoza picked up the phone, asked Farrell to get Communications, asked if there was anything in, from any force, on a possible missing report on the girl. So far most of the police forces in the country had responded and none had any record of such a report.

"So what does that say?" Mendoza emitted a long angry stream of smoke. "Grandfather!" The phone buzzed at him and he picked it up.

"You've got a new body," said Farrell. "Hoover Street."

"Hell," said Mendoza and took down the address and passed it on to Higgins.

Palliser and Higgins went out on that and Mendoza wandered back to his office and sat staring out the window at the view of the Hollywood Hills, chain-smoking, until Farrell rang him and said he had somebody from the Yellow Cab Company on the line. "Put him through," said Mendoza.

The man on the line was a Mr. Meyers, sounding efficient. "You wanted to know about any passengers picked up at International Airport a week ago today. I've got a list for you from the dispatcher. There were only nine."

"Fine," said Mendoza. "We can cut corners here and save some time. I'd like all those drivers to come in to headquarters to look at a photograph."

"Oh, my God," said Meyers. "What a hell of a nuisance, but we do have to cooperate with the police. All right, where are they supposed to come?"

THE ADDRESS on Hoover Street, a secondary main drag, was in the middle of half a dozen little shops, all in an old building stretching for half a block. There was a shoe-repair place, a women's dress shop, a little variety store, a photographer. Three of the shops were empty, with for-rent signs, and there was a dingy independent drugstore on the corner.

The squad and the uniformed patrolman were in front of the little variety store. Higgins slid the Pontiac into the curb behind the squad and they got out.

There was a woman with the patrolman, a stout middle-aged black woman. She looked neat and respectable in a dowdy blue cotton housedress, but her round face still wore a shocked expression.

"There are the detectives, ma'am. This is Mrs. Sadler, she found the body."

"That's right," she said. "It's just awful, the poor soul lying there dead, it's terrible the things happen nowadays, all these criminals running around. Mrs. Coffey was such a nice woman, she wouldn't have hurt a fly. To think of a thing like that happening to her—"

The faded sign over the front door said VERNA'S VARIETY. "Mrs. Verna Coffey?" asked Palliser. She nodded. "Just tell us what happened, Mrs. Sadler."

"Well, I'd run out of green thread. I'm making a dress for myself for my daughter's wedding next week, and I just stepped over here to get some thread. Mrs. Coffey's store is real handy for lots of little things. I just live up the block on Twenty-fourth, it's only a step, and she's always open by eight. The door was open and I went in, but she wasn't there and I waited a few minutes but I didn't hear her in the back. She lives in the back of the store, has a little apartment there, you see. And I called her name and then I went back and just looked in the door and—Oh!'' She put her hands to her mouth. "Oh, just terrible! The poor soul, her head all bloody and the place in a mess, I could see she was dead and I called the police on the phone there—''

So they'd have to get her prints for comparison with any others the lab might pick up. But the honest citizens didn't know much about scientific investigation.

There were a few curious bystanders out now, from the shoe-repair shop, the drugstore. Palliser and Higgins went into the little store, dim without lights on, past double counters stocked with the cheap cosmetics, shoelaces, sewing materials, plastic dishes, all the odds and ends of variety goods, to the door at the rear. It led into a small living room, crowded with old furniture—couch, two upholstered chairs, end tables, a T.V. on a metal stand. One of the tables had been knocked over, the drawer from the other one dumped on the floor, three pictures pulled off the wall and thrown facedown. The body was sprawled between the T.V. and the couch, the body of a fat black woman. There was a faded pink nylon housecoat rucked up around her legs. Under it she'd been wearing a pink nylon nightgown. There was dried blood on one temple and the white of the skull showed where one blow had landed on vulnerable thin bone. On the floor beside her was an ordinary hammer with black tape on the handle. On the other side of the body, in front of a side window, a big potted plant on a metal stand had been knocked over and spilled wet earth and leaves over the thin carpet.

"No sign of a break-in in front," said Palliser.

"No. She was undressed for bed, she could've done that early in the evening, but it was after she'd closed the store," said Higgins. "Somebody knocked at the door—somebody she knew?''

They looked through the rest of the small shabby apartment. There was a tiny bedroom with a single bed neatly turned down for the night but showing no signs of having been occupied. The bedroom had been ransacked too. There was a tiny kitchen with a clean sink and counter tops. There was a back door giving on an alley that ran behind this block of shops, and that door was locked and bolted.

"Somebody she knew," said Palliser. "Which could be anybody around here. But she probably wouldn't have opened the door to a stranger. Living alone, she'd keep the doors locked after dark." The dumped drawers, the pictures pulled off the wall, were the earmarks of the pro burglar.

They went back out to the street and Palliser used the radio in the squad to call the lab. Higgins asked Mrs. Sadler, "Do you know anything about Mrs. Coffey's family?"

"Well, I know she had a married daughter in Pasadena. She had another daughter who died. Her husband, I guess he died quite awhile back."

There had been an address book beside the phone. They would find out.

"Do you know if she kept much money here?"

"I don't know at all. I don't suppose she got an awful lot from the store—enough to get by on—but I don't know."

Higgins started to explain to her why they'd have to take her prints. She just nodded dumbly. This looked like the crude attack, and there might be prints. It might get unraveled rather easily, or never.

"She was such a nice woman," said Mrs. Sadler. "It's just awful, a thing like that happening."

The mobile lab truck came and later the morgue wagon. Higgins and Palliser waited while Horder dusted the address book, and took it to look at. There was a phone number listed simply under JULIA at a Pasadena exchange and they tried it, but there wasn't any answer.

NICK GALEANO got to McClintock's Restaurant on Sunset at eleven o'clock. It was an old place, but good middle-class, middle-priced. He talked to the manager, Don Whitney, who was shocked to hear about Rose Eberhart.

He said, "What a hell of a thing. I tried to call her when she didn't show up. Thought maybe she was sick. What the hell was it?— I don't think that she was more than in the forties. She was a good waitress—reliable. She'd worked here for nearly ten years. What the hell happened to her?"

"We're not sure yet, Mr. Whitney. She was here yesterday?"

"Sure, just as usual. She was on from ten to six. She'd been on the evening shift up to last month. All the girls would rather work that because you get better tips through the dinner hour, but we change around—give all of them a chance at it."

"She left about six?" By the night report, Eberhart's car had been at its usual slot at the apartment, an old two-door Ford.

"That's right. My God, this shakes me. Like it says—in the midst of life."

"Had she had any trouble with anybody lately, would you know?"

"My God, not that I know of. Rose was an easygoing girl, got along with everybody fine. I can't get over her being dead."

"Well, I'd like to talk to some of the other waitresses, if you don't mind," said Galeano.

"Sure, sure, anything we can do to help you find out about it. There's not much trade in until noon. You can use this booth, let me get you a cup of coffee. I'll send the girls over."

There were four waitresses, only one of them under forty. They were all upset to hear about Rose. Apparently they'd all been friendly with her but not close, they were just surprised and sorry. The one who seemed to have known her best—the two of them had worked here longer than the others—was Marie Boyce. She was a plain-faced thin dark woman about forty.

"Was she a widow, divorced, or what?" asked Galeno. "Did she have any family?"

"She was divorced. Second time about three years back. Yes, she had a daughter from her first husband, she lives back East somewhere— I think it's Cleveland."

"Could you say if she was much of a drinker, I don't mean on the job, but just to relax at home?"

She looked indignant. "She sure wasn't. Not that I do much of it, either, but I don't feel as strong as she did about it. Rose was just death on liquor. She wouldn't take a drink on a bet. She'd seen too much of that with her first husband, he was a lush."

"Well," said Galeano. "Do you know any of her other friends? Did you see much of her aside from on the job?"

She shook her head. "I only saw her at work, but Rose wasn't one to socialize much. She always said she was just glad to get home at the end of the day and put her feet up. This job can be tough on a person's feet, you know."

So Eberhart hadn't been drunk and fallen down. Galeano came out and got into the car, automatically switching on the air-conditioning, and drove down to Rosemont Avenue.

The manager, Peterson, wasn't home. His wife said the police had asked him to go down to headquarters to make a statement. Galeano went down the hall and looked at the door to Rose Eberhart's apartment. The lab men had put a seal on it when they finished work. She'd been right in the open doorway—the door was open—that's how the manager had spotted her when he came past with the trash. The door just opposite bore the name KOHLER in the name slot beside the bell. He pushed the bell and faced an elderly little woman with gray hair and glasses. She looked at the badge and started to talk without any questioning.

"Oh, about Mrs. Eberhart, it's an awful thing. The police were here when we got home and Mr. Peterson told us. Was it a heart attack? She wasn't all that old."

"We don't know yet, Mrs. Kohler. You were out last night?"

"Yes, at our daughter's place in Glendale. It was my birthday, we had an early dinner about five-thirty and played bridge all evening, we didn't get home until eleven."

Galeano reflected, so there had been nobody close enough to overhear any argument in the hall, with that apartment door open. He talked to her another few moments, but she hadn't any more to tell him. They hadn't known Rose Eberhart except casually, exchanged the occasional hellos and that was all.

Galeano came back to the car and decided it was time for lunch. He stopped at a café on Silver Lake Boulevard and after debate ordered the chef's salad. Marta was too good a cook, he'd put on a few pounds lately and he'd better watch it. And this Ebérhart thing now looked definitely like a homicide. See what the lab turned up, but before that, have a look through the apartment for addresses and phone numbers, talk to everybody she'd known. In fact, the usual legwork.

THE CAB DRIVERS had been trooping in most of Saturday afternoon, from two cab companies—Yellow and Checker. Among them, fourteen drivers had picked up fares at International Airport between noon and one o'clock last Saturday. They all had a look at the close-up photos. One of them said, "In the usual way I wouldn't be sure. You're only looking at the fare for just a minute, but I think for damn sure I'd have remembered this girl. She's a real beaut." And several of the other cabbies echoed that in different words.

Only one of them, who came in at about four o'clock, shook his head at the enlargement. "I'm not sure. It could be, it couldn't be. The fare I picked up at International, as far as I recall, was a girl about this age, I guess."

Cab drivers got around and saw a lot of people and he didn't remember where he'd taken her, but the dispatcher had the record. It was an address in West Hollywood, Norma Place. Mendoza could guess what the fare had been from Inglewood. Most people flying in here, to any airport in a big city, would be met by friends or relatives, or rent a car at the airport. Nobody took a cab here unless it was necessary.

When the last driver went out, he looked into the detective office and beckoned to Hackett. Higgins was on the phone, Palliser typing a report. Nobody else was there.

"A possible lead on Grandfather," said Mendoza. By now all the various police forces had reported in, and nobody had received any missing report on Juliette Martin.

They drove out to West Hollywood in the Ferrari. The address was a dignified old Spanish house with a red-tiled roof and neat green lawn, a well-tended rose bed in front. In a quiet way it said Money. Mendoza shoved the doorbell and after a moment the door opened and they faced a nice-looking middle-aged woman with dark brown hair, intelligent eyes; she was very smartly dressed in a beige sheath and high-heeled sandals, She looked at the badges in surprise. "Police—what's it about? Not an accident! My husband?"

"Nothing like that, no, ma'am," said Hackett hastily.

"But then, what is it?"

"Someone took a cab to this address from International Airport last Saturday, Mrs.—" Mendoza waited, watching her.

"Lucas, I'm Mrs. Lucas, Mrs. Timothy Lucas. Do you want to see Linda? What on earth **about**?"

"Linda who?" asked Hackett.

"Well, for heaven's sake, Linda Barlow, my niece, she's not here right now, she's at the college, and what the police want with her I can't imagine. Yes, she got in from Chicago last Saturday, and my car was in the garage and Tim had to drive up to San Francisco on business, so I told her to take a cab at the airport and I'd pay the fare."

Mendoza asked, "She's visiting you, or does she live here?"

"Well, you could say she lives here now. She's starting out at U.S.C, the semester begins on Monday. Her home is in Bloomington, Illinois, but she'll be staying with us during the college year."

"She's at the college now?"

"Yes, she had to finish up registering for classes. My husband got her a good used car for transportation. But what on earth is this all about? Police asking about Linda?" She was indignant now.

"Sorry to have bothered you, Mrs. Lucas. It was just a little mistake in the name."

She was still looking bewildered as they turned back down the front walk. In the Ferrari, Mendoza automatically switched on the air-conditioning, but made no move to pull out into the street. The powerful engine purred in a low voice. He lit a cigarette.

"Dead end, Arturo. But, Grandfather, where the hell and who the hell is Grandfather? Damn it, Grandfather's got to be mixed in somehow."

"I don't exactly see how you make that out," said Hackett dubiously. "The little she said, it sounds as if it was a, well, a friendly relationship, if she hadn't ever met the man before. She was coming to stay with him, presumably, and now we can assume that he or somebody met her at the airport with a car."

"And took her where? To Grandfather's? And subsequently to the apartment. When? Monday? Tuesday? That place all stocked and set up to be the plausible background for the nonexistent Ruth Hoffman. I don't think Juliette ever saw it until she was drugged far enough that she wouldn't care where she was. By the autopsy, it's a distinct possibility that she'd been kept under sedatives for several days, since Saturday."

"Yes," said Hackett. "But it's so damn shapeless, Luis. No rhyme or reason."

"And," said Mendoza savagely, "Grandfather knew all about it."

"You're picking him for the arch-villain again?"

"Read it, for God's sake. He was expecting her. He knew which plane she'd be on. She was met at the airport by somebody. If she didn't reach Grandfather's and he doesn't know anything about all this, why hasn't he been making waves? Reported her unaccountably missing? Two plus two. But I'll tell you something else. There's more than one X. Somebody besides Grandfather. Because a woman applied for that library card in the Hoffman name."

"Yes," said Hackett. "Yes, it seems to add up that way. But there's nowhere else to go on it, now. There's only one more thing I can see. The answers are in France and we'll have to wait for them. She told Alison she'd be here about three weeks. Well, somebody in France, the boyfriend, any girlfriends, her employer, knows when she'd be coming home. They wouldn't expect to hear from her while she's here and I think airmail takes about a week to get to Europe anyway. They'll be assuming she's all right for another couple of weeks, but when she doesn't turn up and they don't hear anything, somebody will report it to the French police and they'll ask us some questions, and they'll be able to tell us who Grandfather is."

"That's a bunch of ifs, Arturo," said Mendoza. "Or am I being pessimistic? Yes, surely to God, her fiancé, her best girlfriends knew where she'd be staying here. You're probably right, we'll have to wait for it. But whoever took her off, for whatever reason, they'd know that too. That it was only a question of time before we found out that Juliette was missing and could trace her to Grandfather and ferret out the substitution."

"Well, I wonder," said Hackett. He hunched his wide shoulders in the low bucket seat. "Is there a Grandfather?"

Mendoza turned to stare at him. "That's a new harebrained notion. You're saying she told a tale, as an excuse to fly to Los Angeles, maybe? *Por la gracia de Dios,* that was a perfectly respectable honest girl. But more to the point, if the story was a lie, why should she come out with it voluntarily to a stranger in a plane?"

"True," admitted Hackett. "But so, somebody tells us about Grandfather and we go to ask and he says I thought she changed her mind about coming. What's to prove different? And as far as Hoffman goes, you said it yourself, if you hadn't been the one to look at the corpse, it's on the cards we'd have bought that suicide at face value and written it off. Asked Chicago to do a little checking for a family, but with such a common name we wouldn't have been surprised when they couldn't find any. There was enough money left on her to pay for a funeral—and, *adiós.* A month, two months later, what's to connect her with a Juliette Martin reported missing from France? Even if they wired photos, how many bodies per week do we see?"

"More than most divisions," said Mendoza.

"I still think we ought to bring the Daggetts in and grill them, hot and heavy."

Mendoza laughed sharply. "And on two counts I don't think it'd be any use, Art. In the first place, unless we could

show them proof that we know they're lying, they'll stick to
their story. But more important, I don't think they know
much to tell. That was such a—what's the word I want—a
very crafty little operation."

"How do you mean?"

"So simple, so plausible, but showing the ultimate cunning. I think all X wanted of the Daggetts was that convenient apartment, the key to it, the nice rent receipts, and the
story. Somehow I don't think this particular X would lay
himself open to possible blackmail from the Daggetts."

"There is that. All I say is we'll have to wait for any answers. Eventually, somebody will miss her and ask questions."

Mendoza stabbed out his cigarette and at last released the
parking brake and pulled the Ferrari out to the street.

GALEANO HAD ROPED Jason Grace into helping on the legwork. They had broken the seal on the door and gone
through the Eberhart apartment. There was an address book
with not many names in it, but among them was an Alice
Bickerstaff, an address and phone number in Cleveland,
Ohio. Galeano let Grace do the calling. Grace's soft voice
was always reassuring to witnesses.

It was the daughter. And of course she reacted expecta-
bly. When Grace got her talking coherently, she couldn't tell
him anything useful. She hadn't heard from her mother
since last week, and the letter hadn't said anything about any
trouble, any worry, just how hot it was and how tired the job
made her. Her mother hadn't had any really close friends.
She didn't go out much. About her best friend was a Mrs.
Cora Delaney. "But, of course, it must have been a burglar. The crime rate is so high and that wasn't a very nice
part of town, only it's anywhere these days—and it's awful
to say, but we couldn't afford anything for a funeral, my
husband's been out of work—"

Grace assured her that there seemed to be nearly a thousand dollars in her mother's checking account. They had found the bankbook. He told her about the mandatory autopsy. "Would you like an undertaker here to arrange a funeral, Mrs. Bickerstaff? We can give you a couple of names."

"Oh, it's just awful to say—" But she sounded relieved. "Oh would you? I guess that'd be the easiest thing to do, thank you."

There were still a couple of hours till the end of shift. They drove up to Hollywood to locate the only man who figured in the address book—a Pete Openshaw, at an address on Kingsley. It was an apartment house very much like the one Rose Eberhart had lived in, and Openshaw was sitting in a shabby living room with the door and all the windows open and an electric fan going three feet away. He'd been reading a paperback western. He was a nondescript fellow, about fifty, partly bald, with a snub nose and friendly blue eyes. He was astonished and grieved to hear the news.

"Say, that's a hell of a terrible thing, Rose dead. An attack of some kind? My God, I'm sorry to hear it."

They asked questions and he answered quite openly. "Well, she always brought her car into the station where I work down on Alvarado. That's how we got to know each other. And since I lost my wife, I didn't fancy getting hooked up again and neither did Rose, she'd had two marriages go sour on her—but sometimes it's nice to have somebody to go out with, know what I mean? Neither of us had the money to go to fancy restaurants or shows, but we went to a movie now and then or to some place for Sunday breakfast. You know, like that." The last time he had seen her was last Sunday. They had gone to a movie in Hollywood.

"Did she mention anything about any trouble with anybody? Any argument?"

Openshaw said, "Nothing like that, Rose was easygoing. She wasn't one for árguments or to go faultfinding. She never said nothing about any trouble."

"Would you know who her closest woman friend was?"

"I guess I'd say Cora Delaney. They'd known each other a long time."

That address had been in the book too, Beachwood Drive. They found it, a modest frame house, but the open garage was empty and nobody answered the bell.

"Anyway," said Grace, "we'd better see what the autopsy report says so we know what we're talking about."

They drove back to Parker Center and called it a day.

HACKETT WAS LATE getting home. The traffic on the freeway was murder at this hour. It was farther to drive, to the rambling old house on a dead-end street high in Altadena, but it was just slightly cooler up there. He came out of the garage to head for the back door, and Mark and Sheila came shrieking a greeting with the monstrous mongrel, Laddie, bounding after them. Hackett hugged the children and was nearly knocked down by Laddie, who seemed to be getting bigger by the day. Fifty-seven varieties all right, and the new higher fence had cost a bundle, but he was good with the children. The only member of the household who didn't appreciate Laddie was the dignified great Persian, Silver Boy, who was a middle-aged cat and resistant to change. After a few indignant claws had connected, Laddie had learned to keep his distance, wistfully. There was nothing Laddie loved more than new friends.

Hackett went in the back door to blessed air-conditioning. Angel was setting the table. "I was just starting to worry about you," she said.

"Traffic," said Hackett, bending to kiss her.

"Murder, I know. Good day, darling?"

"Unproductive," said Hackett. "It got up to a hundred, by the radio."

"I know. Thank God I didn't have to go out anywhere, and I've kept the kids in until it started to cool off about an hour ago. Do you want a drink before dinner?"

SATURDAY NIGHT on the Central beat could be busy. But if the heat stirred up the violent emotions, it also kept people ready to stay inside. The night watch got called out only twice the whole shift. The first call was a hit-run on Beverly with a young woman D.O.A, and there had been plenty of witnesses to say the car had run a light and was going about forty, but no one had got the plate number and there was confusion about a description of the car. The consensus was that it had been a medium-sized sedan, not very old, not very new.

Traffic was probably busy writing tickets and dealing with drunks, but the night watch sat and waited until the second call came in at just on midnight. Piggott had finished the report on the hit-run. Schenke was reading a paperback historical novel. Conway was just sitting. When the desk called, it didn't sound like much. A body in the street. Conway went out to look, expecting the drunken derelict, and that was almost what it was. On a quiet, run-down side street, just up from Venice Boulevard, the man dead in the gutter wasn't more than twenty-five. He hadn't been dead long and the minute Conway laid eyes on him in the glare of the squad-car headlights he knew what the autopsy report would say.

"Christ," he said disgustedly to the uniformed man. "These stupid damn punks. Rotting what brains they have on the dope."

The uniformed man said succinctly, "They've got no brains to start with or they wouldn't."

Conway went over him. There wasn't any I.D., but in one of his pants pockets was a cardboard box with about fifty Quaaludes in it. "My God," said Conway, "if the dope hadn't got him, he might've got taken off for this. Let's have that light closer." The patrolman shifted the flashlight. "I thought so. More of the fake stuff. It's coming in by the ton, by what Narco says. Mostly from South America."

"It isn't the real stuff?" The patrolman was interested.

"Oh, it's the real stuff. It'll kill you as quick as the bona fide American-made, but look at the little stamp mark." The pills were slightly smaller than a dime and in the beam of the flashlight they could make out the tiny legend stamped on each. LEMMON 74. "The real pharmaceutical company doesn't use that mark, but it looks like a guarantee that these are American-made. Real Quaaludes."

"I'll be damned," said the patrolman. "I suppose we want the morgue wagon?"

"What else?" said Conway. "I'll see these get handed over to Narco, as if they needed any more."

AT ELEVEN-THIRTY, one of the sergeants sitting on the central switchboard at Hollywood Division got a call from a frightened citizen. At first she was rather incoherent, but he calmed her down and got her talking straight. "Now, have I got your name right, Frances Holzer? Yes, Mrs. Holzer. Start out again, it's about your mother?"

"Miss," she said. "Miss Holzer. Yes, I'm just worried to death because she should've been home hours ago, she's a good driver, but an accident—but she's carrying identification, I would've heard about it, somebody would've called. And she was only going to stay a little while, Mrs. Lincoln's been pretty sick and visitors aren't supposed to stay long—"

"Just let me have your address, Miss. O.K, Del Mar Avenue. What's your mother's name?"

"Mrs. Edna Holzer. She was going to the French Hospital to see Mrs. Lincoln. She left about seven and she should've been home by at least eight-thirty, I've been worried to death. She was coming straight home, she said so, and—"

The sergeant thought rapidly. That was a pretty classy address, up above Los Feliz, and the girl sounded straight. "What's she driving?"

"A Chrysler Newport—two years old—navy-blue." She was more businesslike now, reassured by the solid masculine voice. "Wait a minute, I've got the license number. It's one-E-D-seven-four hundred."

It passed fleetingly across the sergeant's mind that these seven-digit plate numbers, issued since the state ran out of different six-digit ones, made life a little complicated. He wrote it down. "I'd like a description of her, please."

"Of M-mother?— She's f-forty nine, five six, a hundred and t-t-twenty," and the girl burst out crying.

"Now, Miss Holzer, try to get hold of yourself. Miss Holzer?"

She hiccupped and sobbed once more and said, "I'm sorry. I don't want to sound stupid, but it's just, she was so p-p-proud of herself, she'd been on a diet and lost twenty pounds—she's got brown hair and blue eyes and she's wearing a sleeveless blue nylon dress and bone sandals."

"All right, Miss Holzer. That's fine. We'll have a look around. Check the hospitals, and so on. I'll get back to you."

He did the obvious things on it. Called the emergency rooms, the Highway Patrol. If the woman had been heading for Hollywood from downtown she'd likely have been on the freeway and the Highway Patrol handled freeway accidents. He drew a blank. So then he called Central Traffic, explained and asked them to look around that area for the car. The woman could have had a heart attack, a lot of things could have happened.

At twelve-fifty, Central Traffic called back. A squad had checked the parking lot at the French Hospital. The Chrysler wasn't there. The squad had looked all around side streets there and it wasn't anywhere. Funny, thought the sergeant. What could have happened to the woman? Of course, without knowing anything but what the girl said—she could have stopped for a drink, she could have gone to see a friend and lost track of time, she could have—

He called the girl back. "No, she hasn't come home. What have you found out?"

"I'm sorry, I haven't a thing to tell you. But we'll keep looking. Miss Holzer, have you checked with any of her friends? She could have stopped in to see someone. She could have—"

"At nearly one A.M.?" she said. "She told Mr. Shepherd she'd be in the office at nine, she's his secretary. Mr. Lynn Shepherd, he's the head of the firm—Shepherd, Lynch, and Morse. Mother's been his secretary for twenty years, and there was this important tax case, there has to be a deposition and the witness could only come in on Sunday. She said she'd be home by eight-thirty."

They both sounded like responsible citizens, but of course even that kind came all sorts. The sergeant said, passing the buck, "Well, we've done all we can do, Miss Holzer. I tell you, if your mother hasn't come home by morning, you can file a missing report with Central Headquarters."

"And what would they do?" she asked wildly.

The sergeant wasn't too sure. He said stolidly, "Well, that's what you'd better do. All I can tell you, your mother hasn't been involved in an accident in the last six hours."

"That's all you know?"

"I'm sorry, Miss Holzer. That's al ."

"Well, thank you," she said.

THE MISSING REPORT on Edna Holzer got filed at nine A.M. on Sunday morning, but that was not a busy office, Missing Persons. Their business was quiet and slow, and Lieutenant Carey was off on Sunday. The sergeant in that office filed the report without thinking much about it. Carey didn't see it until Monday morning.

On Sunday morning there was another cable from the Sûreté. They had turned up Juliette Martin's passport number. She had applied for it on the first of August. It had been issued on the nineteenth. No information was required for a passport except evidence of citizenship. There was no address available. No further information.

"*¡Diez milliones de demonios desde infierno!*" said Mendoza.

FIVE

ON SUNDAY Wanda Larsen was off. Higgins and Palliser might have taken her along to help break the news to Verna Coffey's daughter; a woman officer was helpful at that sort of thing. The address corresponding to the Pasadena listing was one side of a duplex, on a quiet middle-class street, but nobody had been home. Now this morning they tried there again and found the family just starting off for church, Robert and Julia Elmore and an eighteen-year-old daughter, Lila. There was the usual reaction to news of violent death. Palliser and Higgins gave them time. These were more honest solid citizens, as Verna Coffey had been. The husband worked at a Sears store here, the girl was a senior in high school. But Julia Elmore was a sensible woman and when her first grief subsided, she answered questions readily.

"I couldn't say exactly how much money might've been there. Mother only went to the bank once a week, on Wednesdays." She was a thin sharp-faced woman, not very black. "She didn't drive and her arthritis bothered her. She had to take the bus, she used to close the store for a couple of hours—same as when she went up to the market once a week."

"I don't suppose," said Elmore, "she made an awful lot out of the store, but more than you might think. It was a steady trade." He was a heavy-shouldered man, medium black. "I suppose she might've had a hundred bucks or so, in cash, maybe more."

"Where did she keep the money, do you know?" asked Palliser.

"She kept it all in an old handbag in the closet," said Julia Elmore. "But she was careful about keeping the doors locked, Sergeant, living alone like she did—and that's an old building and it was lonely at night there—you know, she was the only one lived there, all the rest of those stores were closed and empty at night." She was crying a little again. "Oh, we worried about it—"

Elmore said, "But there were good deadbolt locks on both doors, I'd seen to that, I don't see how anybody could break in, but you say it looked as if she'd opened the door to somebody." He shook his head. "She wouldn't have let anybody in after dark."

"Unless it was someone she knew," said Palliser.

"But nobody like that would've hurt her." They were incredulous.

"She knew a lot of people around that neighborhood," said Julia. "She'd lived there for more than forty years, but I don't think she'd have opened the door to anybody after the store was closed."

He said, "She'd had some trouble with kids. Some of the kids there—coming in and stealing candy bars. She was always having to chase them off. But no kid—"

"Oh, we did worry," she said. "I wanted her to close the store and come to live with us. She was sixty-nine and her arthritis was getting worse all the time, and she had Daddy's Social Security, but she'd had the store so long she didn't want to change. That isn't too good a neighborhood now, not like it used to be. Oh, I can't stand thinking how scared she must've been—the last time we saw her was a week ago today, she had a little birthday party for Toby—"

"Who's that?" asked Higgins.

"My sister Eva's boy, Toby Wells. Eva died last year. We were all there, she had a cake and ice cream and she gave Toby ten dollars for a birthday present. It was his twenty-fourth birthday. He's a nice boy, Toby. Got a good job at a Thrifty drugstore up in Hollywood.'' She wiped her eyes.

Higgins asked, ''Was she hard of hearing at all, Mrs. Elmore? How was her sight?''

She was shrewd enough to catch his thought. ''You mean she might've thought somebody she knew was at the door when it wasn't? Oh, no, I don't think so. She wasn't deaf and her eyes were good. It was just the arthritis bothered her. I just can't imagine her opening the door to anybody after dark.''

''Do you know anyone in that area? Does anyone there know your name?'' asked Palliser.

What had occurred to him, someone like that might have got her to open the door with a tale that the family had tried to call her—that the phone was out of order.

''Not for twenty-four years—since Bob and I were married,'' she said. ''Of course, we didn't live in the store, then. We had a house on Twentieth. It was just since Dad died that she lived in the back of the store. And the neighborhood had changed, not the same kind of people around.''

Higgins explained about the mandatory autopsy. That they'd be told when they could have the body. They just nodded quietly.

''Did she have any close friends around there?''

''Well, there's Mrs. Wiley. She lived next door on Twentieth Street and she's still there, she's a widow now. She came to see Mother now and then—and Mrs. Buford, but she's in a rest home on Vermont. Sometimes Mother went to see her.''

Back in the car, Palliser rubbed a finger along his handsome straight nose and said, ''Ways it could've happened—so she was a careful old lady. If somebody banged at the door and said the building was on fire—''

"She wasn't attacked in the store," said Higgins. "Not until they'd gone into the living room at the back." He hunched his bulky shoulders.

"Well, the women friends. Nothing likely there."

"I suppose they had families and she'd know them. But damn it!—that was a crude spur-of-the-minute attack. I don't see any rudimentary planning to it. She was an old lady, John. She'd been familiar with that neighborhood for years—before the crime rate started to climb. Maybe she wasn't just as cautious as the family thinks. She might've opened the door for any reason. Wait and see what the lab report has to say. There just could be some prints on that hammer."

"Wait and see," agreed Palliser.

WHEN IT COULD BE EXPECTED that people would be up and dressed on Sunday morning, Galeano drove up to Beachwood Drive and at the little frame house found Cora Delaney at home. She looked at stocky dark Galeano—according to regulations in a whole business suit, white shirt and tie, when most men wore casual and sports clothes, and at the badge in his hand—with surprise and curiosity. She was somewhere around Rose Eberhart's age, short and plump and defiantly blond. She let him into a neat living room with a collection of old but good furniture, and Galeano told her about Rose Eberhart. She broke down and cried for five minutes and then sat up and blew her nose.

"We knew each other for forty-five years, since we were in kindergarten together. She was only forty-nine. But how could it have happened? You said it looked like she was attacked by somebody. I don't understand—a burglar—"

It hadn't been a burglar. The apartment had been intact, not ransacked, and there'd been thirty dollars in her wallet, a modest amount of good jewelry undisturbed.

"That's what it looks like, Mrs. Delaney. When did you see her last?"

"I talked to her on the phone Wednesday night. She sounded just her usual self, but of course she wouldn't know she was going to be attacked. She'd been feeling run-down lately, said she was taking extra vitamins." She blew her nose again. "Oh, and she was annoyed at some woman who'd been pestering her. Some woman named Arvin."

"What about?" asked Galeano.

"Oh, she was claiming Rose owed her some money and she didn't. It was some woman she used to work with. She hadn't seen her in a long time and ran into her at the corner market. She wasn't really worried about it, just annoyed. Have you talked to Alice—her daughter? Does she know?"

He told her about that, gave her the name of the funeral parlor. The body would probably be released tomorrow.

"Oh, I'd better call Alice, I'll be glad to make the arrangements. This is all the poor girl needed, a sick baby and her husband laid off. Yes, I've got her number, thanks." She began to cry again. "We were going out to lunch together today. It's her day off. I said I'd meet her at the Tick-Tock at twelve-thirty. It just doesn't seem possible she's dead."

Galeano drove up to McClintock's Restaurant. It was just open, no customers in yet. He ordered a cup of coffee from Marie Boyce, who said blankly, "I don't think I ever heard the name. Arvin? I can't recall anybody named that ever worked here. Since I've been here anyway."

Whitney came over and sat on the opposite side of the booth. "Arvin," he mused. "It seems to ring a faint bell. I've heard the name somewhere." He accepted a cigarette and brooded over it. "Somebody she used to work with. Well, she'd been here ten years. About as long as I've managed the place. I tell you, in that time there's been a little turnover in the staff. Most of our girls are pretty steady, but now and then we get one who isn't satisfactory and I let her go, or one doesn't stay for some reason. It could've been one like that—here for just a short while—sometime back. I just don't remember, Mr. Galeano.''

Galeano went back to the office. Jason Grace had just come in, having taken the morning off. He had just bought himself a Polaroid camera, and he was passing around shots of the christening, a broad smile on his face. Galeano grinned at him over the snapshots. Grace's wife, Virginia, was a nice-looking woman, and the baby was a cute one, round and brown with solemn eyes and a little fuzz of hair. The little three-year-old girl was a honey, in a starched white dress and a red hair ribbon. "Nice family, Jase." Galeano had been a bachelor for a long time and he was looking forward to a family of his own.

He told Grace what meager information he had turned up and Grace said, "It doesn't sound like much, Nick, but we don't know one hell of a lot about this anyway."

MENDOZA WASN'T supposed to come in on Sunday, but he usually did for a while, to keep track of what was going on. He drifted in about two o'clock and Lake said that Sergeant Donovan from Chicago had been asking for him. "So get him on the phone." Mendoza swept off the Homburg and went into his office.

"We've got damn all for you," said Donovan. "There are about a thousand and one Hoffmans in the greater Chicago area, but none of them seems to be missing a Ruth."

"I didn't expect so," said Mendoza. "That must've been a hell of a job. Thanks very much, Donovan."

"At least we could check by phone, didn't have to do the legwork in this damn heat. But thank God, it's beginning to cool off now, getting into fall."

"I wish I could say the same." He was just off the phone when an autopsy report came in from the coroner's office on Anthony Delucca. He had to think before he remembered—the teenager on the bus-stop bench. It had been an overdose of Quaaludes. He filed it and forgot it.

The office was humming along quietly, Higgins typing a report, Palliser on the phone, nobody else in. Hackett and Landers had gone over to the jail to talk to Gerber. Mendoza swiveled his desk chair around to the window and sat smoking, staring at the view over the Hollywood Hills, and tried to think if there was anything else to do on Juliette Martin. There wasn't. Wait for the French police. Hell, he thought. There must be a catch to that somewhere. X would know about that possibility, too. Wait and maybe never hear anything from France on Juliette. Why not? He didn't have any ideas about it at all.

Lake brought him a cable. It was from the Sûreté and said simply, PRINTS UNKNOWN OUR RECORDS. Mendoza snarled at it.

Of course, strictly speaking, it wasn't the Sûreté's fault. Passports didn't carry a typed address, only one filled in by the holder. But the French passport bureau might, for God's sake, have noted down something about the girl. What the proof of citizenship had been, something.

And he reflected moodily, they'd have to bury the poor girl eventually. They couldn't leave her down in the cold tray at the morgue indefinitely.

Hackett looked in the door and said, "Gerber gave us a statement. He admitted he was on the heist with Bauman, but it was Bauman had the gun and fired it."

"*Naturalmente.*"

"So it's up to the D.A.'s office what to call it. Want to bet it'll start murder two and get reduced? Tom's doing the final report on it. Anything new gone down?"

"I don't know. Everybody seems to be out somewhere on something." Sunday was just another day to the men at Robbery-Homicide.

HACKETT WENT DOWN the hall for a cup of coffee, but he hadn't taken more than three sips before Lake buzzed him.

"Attempted heist, it's a liquor store on Wilshire and the squad's got him."

"No rest for the wicked," said Hackett, annoyed. He abandoned the coffee and went back downstairs to the parking lot. The liquor store was a little way out on Wilshire.

The heister had picked a wrong target on this one. The store owner was a hefty ex-Marine by the name of Nolan who worked out at a gym regularly, and the gun hadn't scared him worth a damn. He said to Hackett disgustedly, "For Christ's sake, the damn punk didn't even have his finger in the trigger guard! Does he think I'm a goddamn idiot? I just took one swing at him and put him out cold, and called for cops, and I bet some goddamn fool judge sends him up for sixty days, poor guy not responsible because his mama spanked him too much."

The heister was sitting on the floor propped against the counter. The patrolman had put the cuffs on him, and he was feeling his bruised jaw with both cuffed hands. He raised his head to look at Hackett, and Hackett said pleasedly, "Well, I will be damned if it isn't Baby Face."

The various descriptions had been faithful. The man looked about twenty-five and he was fairly tall and husky but he had a round, boyish face, a shock of white-blond hair. He was very neatly dressed in brown slacks and a clean white sports shirt. He looked as if he was ready to cry.

The patrolman handed the gun to Hackett. It was an old .32 Colt automatic and it wasn't loaded.

"All right, let's have your name," said Hackett.

The heister said in a thin voice, "Ricky Davies. I'm sorry. He didn't need to hit me that hard, I wouldn't have done anything to him. The gun's not loaded. I don't even know how to load a gun."

Nolan said, "Oh, for Christ's sake."

Hackett reached down and helped Davies onto his feet. "Come on, I think we want a little talk with you." The uniformed man went out to go back on tour and Nolan said to nobody in particular, "These goddamn punks."

At least the air-conditioning was back on at the jail. While Davies was getting booked in, Hackett called the office and told Lake to start the machinery on the warrant.

Davies had I.D. on him, a driver's license, a couple of credit cards and nineteen-sixty-four in cash. He sat hunched in the cramped little interrogation room, and asked in a subdued voice, "Can I call my wife? She's going to be upset as hell about this and I don't know how to tell her. She thinks I'm out with a buddy of mine. She's going to be mad as hell at me and I don't blame her."

Hackett offered him a cigarette and he said he didn't smoke. "You can call your wife whenever you like, and a lawyer. How did you get into this?" Davies was hardly the seasoned criminal by his looks and manner.

Davies said miserably, "It was on account of all the bills. I never did anything wrong before in my life—never wanted to. But it's just, everything costs so much. I've got a good job— I work at Desmond's men's store up on Western—and I thought Stella and I could get by O.K. on what we both make, we just got married six months ago—but we had to get an apartment, I'd been living at home with Mom and she'd been with her folks too, and the rent's three-fifty—you can't find anything much cheaper and it's not a high-class place at that, and Stella's used to nice things— I wanted her to have nice things—and we had to get furniture and a lot of things. She works too, she's a cocktail waitress at the Tail o' Cock, but even between us there's the payments on her car, and my car, and the rent, and all the groceries, I never realized how much groceries cost. And then she said she'd always wanted a diamond watch and I got her one for her birthday—and you got to dress pretty sharp in my job and even when I get a discount it adds up.'' He took a breath. ''And Stella likes nice clothes—all pretty girls do. And the Visa account got up to the limit, a thousand bucks, and I missed one payment on the car, and then Stella got the flu and was off work a week, and she'd used up her vacation and sick leave when we went on the honeymoon. We went up to Tahoe and that was part of the Visa account. And I got so I just didn't know which way to turn,'' said Davies helplessly. ''And Stella wanted to get me a nice birthday present, it's this gold ring with my initials, she put it on our account at Bullocks', it was ninety-four bucks—and I was feeling kind of desperate, if you get me. I got that gun at a pawn shop for thirty dollars. I don't know anything about guns, I never had any bullets for it—and people just handed over the money. I thought if I came right downtown here there wouldn't be the chance of anybody recognizing me from up in Hollywood. I felt pretty bad about it, it was all wrong, but I got the Visa account nearly cleared up. Stella never looks at the statement— I knew she wouldn't notice.'' He looked at Hackett, his face haggard. ''She's going to be mad as hell at me, get into all this.''

''Have you ever been in any trouble before?''

He shook his blond head. ''I never even had a parking ticket.''

Hackett stood up. ''Well, you can get bail and your wife can get you a lawyer.'' It was funny in a way, and he felt sorry for this stupid kid. It would probably end up as a reduced charge. Call it a year in and probation. ''You'd better call your wife and break the news.''

''Thanks,'' said Davies meaninglessly. Hackett turned him over to the jailer and started back to the office to write the final report on this.

MENDOZA HAD GONE HOME and nobody else was left in the office at five-fifty, except Higgins and Palliser. They were on their way out past the switchboard when Lake beckoned, put down the earphone and said, "Something funny, boys. It's the California Community Hospital and they say they've got a murder. The desk downstairs relayed the call. It's a Dr. Rasmussen. Says one of the patients has been murdered."

"For God's sake," said Higgins. "And hell, the night watch won't be on for a couple of hours. We'd better have a quick look and see what it is anyway. O.K. John? Jimmy, call our wives and say we'll be late."

"Murder at a hospital," said Palliser as they waited for the elevator. "Funny isn't the word. I didn't think anybody was ever alone long in a hospital, and you usually need privacy to commit a murder." They took Higgins' Pontiac and drove down to that fairly old hospital on Hope Street. In the main lobby, Higgins asked one of the receptionists for Dr. Rasmussen.

"That's me," said a voice behind him. "The other one doesn't look much like a cop, but I spotted you when you walked in." Big craggy-faced Higgins might as well have COP tattooed on his forehead. Rasmussen was a young man with crisp light brown hair, a nearly handsome face with a long nose and bright eyes. "This is the damndest thing I ever heard of, but when I saw what it was I thought we'd better rope you in. Your business. The damndest thing." He yawned. "Look, can we sit down to talk? I'm bushed. Had a hell of a day, and now this—and I'm not off till seven and I suppose you'll keep me hanging around. You'll want to talk to all the nurses—"

"Let's take one thing at a time," said Higgins. They sat down in one corner of the lobby and he offered Rasmussen a cigarette. "What's this all about?" Rasmussen was probably one of the interns here, about the right age.

"This patient, Carlo Alisio, cancer patient—man seventy-four and pretty far gone. He was riddled with it. He was in for radiation and therapy, and oddly enough—but it's unpredictable—he'd suddenly gone into remission. We thought he was going any time, about ten days ago, warned the family. But he'd perked up and was doing pretty well. Just a question of time, of course. He was due to be transferred to the V.A. hospital tomorrow. His Medicare had run out and he was eligible." Rasmussen drew strongly on his cigarette. "I saw him for just a minute this morning—no occasion to again, until the nurse called me. That was about five o'clock. She'd gone in for a routine check and found him dead."

"Was he in a private room?" asked Palliser.

"You know what year it is? Hell, no, who can afford it, and we don't have any left. He was in a three-bed room, but the other two patients are fairly comatose—not up to noticing anything—and the curtain was up around Alisio's bed. I thought, of course, he'd just passed out naturally, and I was a little surprised, I must say. Then when I took a look at him—well, the nurse had seen it too— I was even more damned surprised. He was smothered with the pillow. All you have to do is look, it was still over his face. But I looked at it— I don't suppose even your smart lab men could get fingerprints off a pillowcase—"

"You'd be surprised at that, too," said Higgins.

"— And there is the plain evidence. He'd struggled and bitten a piece out of the pillowcase. There's saliva and mucous stains, and a piece of cloth and thread still in his mouth. The damndest thing."

"Do you know if he had any visitors today?"

Rasmussen said, "The nurse can tell you, but I'd have a bet on it. There was a big family—Italians after all—and all evidently pretty close. Somebody always coming to see him and calling in. Sisters, brothers, nieces and nephews. He was a widower. But we chase the visitors away about four-thirty. The nurses like to get dinner over with early.''

"How long do you think he'd been dead?" asked Palliser.

Rasmussen shrugged. "He was still warm. I'd say not over an hour—possibly less. What do we do about the body? I thought you'd want to see it, told the nurses to stay out."

Higgins looked at his watch and swore. "We'd better have some pictures, at least. And unless somebody's working overtime in the lab—" He got up, went to call in. Then Rasmussen took them up to the third floor and pointed out the room halfway along the hall. There was a little huddle of nurses gathered at the station at that end, whispering excitedly together. They eyed Higgins and Palliser with avid curiosity. "He's in the bed by the window," said Rasmussen, following them in.

The patients in the first two beds, two old men, seemed to be asleep or in comas; neither stirred. The white curtain was pulled across the side of the bed by the window. They stepped around it and looked at the dead man. Alisio had been a small old man, thin and bald with a big nose. The gray-stubbled face was contorted, his mouth and eyes open, the body twisted to one side, right arm up over his head—he had struggled for his ebbing life. The pillow was on one side of the body and they could see the little piece bitten out of the casing, the stains on the rest.

"I will be damned," said Higgins. "I left word at the lab. Somebody will be out as soon as the night watch comes in. I don't suppose it'd disturb the other patients in here, if you just leave him a couple of hours."

Rasmussen said, "Unlikely."

"Well, after our men have got some photographs, we'd like you to send the body down to the coroner's office for autopsy. The nurses on now don't go off shift until eleven, is that right?''

"Right."

"What I'd like you to do," said Higgins, massaging his jaw and thinking, "is to notify the family that he's dead. Just that. They'd been expecting him to go—they won't be surprised."

"They'll want the body," said Rasmussen. "What do we tell them?"

"Oh, we'll be around asking questions," said Higgins. "I guess we can leave it for the night watch, John. And I think I'll call Luis. He always likes the offbeat ones. He's going to love this one, in spades."

MENDOZA HAD EXCHANGED the orderly peace at the office for the bedlam of an obstreperous family at home. "They've been wild as hawks all day," said Alison crossly.

The twins flung themselves at him and pummeled him. "Daddy, Daddy! I galloped real fast on Star and Uncle Ken says I'm a tomboy, what's a tomboy?" "Daddy, Mama says we can't take the ponies to school, why couldn't we ride the ponies to school?"

"It wouldn't be good for them to walk on the street," said Mendoza at random.

"Mairí's been fixing my uniform. Girls get to wear a uniform because they're more important than boys," said Terry loudly.

"Are not! Girls aren't important to anybody! And I galloped faster on Diamond! Why wouldn't it be good for them, Daddy?"

"Nobody's more important than anybody else," said Alison. "For heaven's sake, go to your rooms and play quietly at something and give your father some peace. It's the school, of course. They'll settle down in a couple of days, I hope."

Tomorrow was the opening day of the semester for both public and parochial schools. Having completed kindergarten, Johnny and Terry would be starting first grade at the Immaculate Heart Parochial School down the hill in Burbank. And as Alison said, her good Scots Presbyterian father was probably turning in his grave, but it couldn't be helped. At least they'd get a sounder education than most public schools offered these days.

"Why wouldn't it be good for them, Daddy?"

"It would hurt their feet," said Alison. The cats, affronted at all the noise, had departed huffily. Cedric began to bark.

"But we want to ride the ponies to school! It'd be lots more fun than riding an old school bus. Why can't we—"

"We've told you why," said Alison.

"And besides, if girls aren't more important than boys, how come I get to wear a uniform and Johnny doesn't? A uniform is special."

"Because that's the way the school rules are," said Alison. "And we'll hear no more about it. You two go and see what Mairí's doing."

"I know what she's doing, she's fixing my uniform because the skirt was too long."

"And I don't see a uniform is so special, she's got to wear it, it's a rule, and I can wear anything I want. So—"

"No, you can't. You have to wear dark pants and a white shirt, so that's like a uniform too. And now we'll drop the subject. Why don't you go out and see the ponies again?"

"We want Daddy to play with us," shouted Terry promptly. "Play bears and lions!"

"Oh, Terry, you haven't played that since you were a baby. Daddy's too tired to play."

"*¡Demonios, qué relajo!*" said Mendoza. "*Basta,* you two. Daddy's got too much to think about to play. You chase off and visit the ponies."

"We already did. We just came back, and Uncle Ken said we was little devils."

"So you are," said Alison. She finally persuaded them to begin practicing their reading for school, and they made as much noise on the stairs as both the ponies. Alison sank down on the couch. "What a day, and what a relief to have them in school all day! I'll bet you in a week's time it'll be, why do we have to go to school?"

Mendoza laughed. "I wouldn't doubt. They'll grow out of it sometime, *cariña.*" He went out to the kitchen for a drink. El Señor heard the cupboard open and was on the counter before he had the top off the bottle. Mendoza said, *"Borracho,"* and poured him half an ounce. Back in the living room he said, "The Sûreté hasn't a damn thing to tell us. And you know we can't leave her in the morgue. There ought to be some sort of funeral."

"Oh, dear," said Alison. She sat up and lit a cigarette. "I know there was something else she said that just escapes me—and you know it sounds silly, Luis, we didn't know the girl at all, but I feel somehow that we ought to send flowers or attend the funeral or something."

"Yes, I know." Mendoza had the same queer feeling.

He was still thinking about Juliette, which was futile, because there wasn't anything else he could do about it, when they settled down after dinner. For once Kipling couldn't hold his interest. But at eight-thirty Higgins called to tell him about the new offbeat one and that gave him something else to think about.

"WELL, OF ALL THE RIGMAROLES," said Conway, scanning Higgins' note. "The day men have left us a little work. On the other hand, we may meet some pretty nurses." He shoved the note over to Piggott.

"Somebody's got to mind the store," said Schenke. "I'll toss you for it."

"No, I want to go talk to the nurses. What a hell of a funny thing," said Conway. "Why bother to murder a man who's as good as dead already?"

"Could've been what they call a mercy killing," suggested Piggott. "Some people don't think so straight about things like that."

"Or a homicidal maniac among the orderlies," said Conway. "O.K, Bob. You sit on the store and if you get swamped, you know where we are. Come on, Matt. Let's see what we can find out about the maniac."

Schenke sat and finished his historical novel in the unnatural gloom and quiet of the big office, before the desk relayed a call. It wasn't a heist this time, but a mugging, and it looked like another in that series that was probably organized gang activity. It was the parking lot at Madame Wu's in Little Tokyo, and the couple were fighting mad. They looked like money, a couple in the thirties, Mr. and Mrs. James Ferguson, dressed to the nines. Her expensive evening gown had one sleeve ripped nearly out. He had the start of a fine shiner and his sport shirt was slashed. "Goddamn it," he was saying to the patrolman, probably for the tenth time, "I tried to put up a fight, but there must've been six or eight of the damn bastards—"

"We never saw them, they came out from behind some cars—just *grabbed* us and held us while the rest of them tore off my necklace and earrings—"

"And got my billfold— I tried to get loose and put up a fight but they were all damn big bastards—"

Schenke got them calmed down a little and sorted things out. "Well, I don't know to a dime how much I had on me, but it must've been close to a hundred bucks, and damn it, that diamond necklace set me back seven thousand—"

"Could you give a description of any of them?"

"It was too damned dark and it happened too fast. But they were Latin," said Ferguson. "Just a couple of things the one said—just take it easy and you won't get the knife in your throat—he had a heavy Spanish accent. Hell, no, neither of us could recognize any pictures. I don't suppose there's much the police can do about it.''

"Well, we'd like a description of the jewelry, sir, to put it on the hot list to pawnbrokers." That was just a gesture. None of the loot this bunch had got away with had shown up, which said they knew a tame fence. "Are you all right to drive home, Mr. Ferguson?" Their address was Pacific Palisades.

"Yes, yes, We'll be okay. They just roughed us up. Come on, Myrna."

Schenke went back to the office and typed a report on it. That was about all there was to do.

PALLISER WAS OFF on Monday, but they got Henry Glasser back. When Mendoza came in, Grace had already corralled him and was showing all the pictures, and sandy middle-sized Glasser was grinning amiably at them. "Welcome home, Henry," said Mendoza. "Good vacation?"

"I went up to Big Bear," said Glasser. "But even up there it was too damned hot." He was looking over at Wanda Larsen at her desk in the corner and she was smiling back at him. There'd been a little speculation about those two, nobody knew if they were dating or not.

"I want to see the night report, and you'd all better hear what we've got on this so far." They were all in by then, Hackett and Higgins, Galeano, Grace, Landers. They dragged chairs into his office and heard about the new one from Higgins while Mendoza read Conway's report.

"So, there's legwork to do," said Mendoza, passing it on to Hackett. "This Alisio had a big family and he'd been in the hospital nearly a month. The nurses knew them casually. He had eight or nine visitors yesterday, between about one and four-thirty or a little before four-thirty. They didn't all stay in his room all the time, there wouldn't be room for them, they went in and out. Sat in a little lounge down the hall. The hospital just had one brother's name as the responsible relative—Joseph Alisio—an address in Hollywood. He'll give us the names of the rest of the family.''

"You don't think it was one of the family?" asked Galeano.

"Who knows? No, I don't. From what the nurses say it's a big loving family, concerned and attentive. But on a Sunday there were a lot of visitors coming and going, and they can probably give us a better idea than the nurses who was there, the nurses were busy. They'd all been visiting the hospital quite a bit and may have got acquainted with some other visitors."

"Reaching," said Higgins. "And one of them suddenly had the urge to smother a patient—any patient?"

"You know, Luis," said Hackett, "just off the top of my mind, there are always a lot of people wandering around a big hospital, and nurse's aides, orderlies, even nurses—they're just people—come all sorts. You know what I'm thinking about?—that case in Santa Monica last year, where that male nurse was giving the senile old patients the overdoses of morphine. Just out of kindness, they were better dead.''

"Yes," said Mendoza. "It's possible it could be something like that, and we want to question these nurses again in depth, and damnation, none of them is on until three P.M. Though the ones there now can tell us something about the visitors starting at one o'clock. However you slice it, we've got a lot of people to talk to so—*¡Sigan adelante!*" He stabbed out his cigarette and stood up.

But as he followed the twin looming bulks of Hackett and Higgins down the hall, Lieutenant Carey of Missing Persons came past the switchboard and said, "I'll take twenty minutes of your time, Mendoza."

"What the hell do you want? Don't tell me you've turned up a body for us."

"No, but we just might," said Carey seriously.

Slightly annoyed, Mendoza took him back to his office, gave him a cigarette and asked, "What have you got?"

"It's what we haven't got," said Carey. His snub-nosed bulldog face looked rather solemn. "It just shapes up as a probable abduction. Possible rape, possible homicide, after this long a time. I just thought I'd brief you about it in case the body shows up, because it's got to be the Central beat. The woman's been missing for thirty-six hours, and a rapist doesn't usually hold them that long. It's possible she's dead."

"Why, how, and who?"

"Well, this Edna Holzer. I didn't see the report until an hour ago. I've just been talking to the girl—Frances Holzer. Edna Holzer's the mother. We've got a description I won't bother you with, but she sounds like an attractive woman. She left home, which is Del Mar Avenue in Hollywood, at about seven on Saturday night to visit a friend in the French Hospital. She didn't intend to stay long—should've been home by eight-thirty, but she wasn't. The daughter called Hollywood about eleven-thirty. They called Traffic and a squad looked around, but no show. She was driving a two-year-old Chrysler Newport, we've got the plate number and there's an A.P.B. out." Carey emitted a stream of blue smoke, put out his cigarette, and asked, "You know the French Hospital?"

Mendoza was sitting back with eyes shut. "West College Street." Mendoza knew his town, from twenty-six years on the job.

"That's right. And look, Mendoza. She wasn't five minutes from the Stack where all the freeways come in. In five minutes she'd have been on the Hollywood Freeway heading for home. The girl called the hospital on Sunday—well, so did my office after she filed a missing report—and Mrs. Holzer had been there, left about a quarter of eight. Well, you can see how it shapes up. She must've run into trouble between the hospital and the Stack, within about five blocks.''

"Less," said Mendoza, lighting another cigarette. "Her nearest route was the Pasadena Freeway down to the Stack and that's three blocks from the hospital."

"Well, there's no sign of her or the car," said Carey. "She's a responsible woman. Legal secretary to a big firm. You can see it smells of abduction, robbery, possible rape, and possible homicide."

"Es cierto," said Mendoza. He was sitting back smoking lazily. "So you think she's going to turn up as a corpse for us."

"It's a possibility. I thought I'd tell you. Wherever she does turn up—whenever—it's got to be a hundred percent sure whatever happened to her, it happened on the Central beat."

SIX

By the middle of Monday morning, Hackett and Higgins were talking to Joseph Alisio and his wife in their home. It was an old house in a once very fashionable area of Hollywood and still a good residential area, Outpost Drive. Some of the furniture looked like valuable antiques. Alisio was in the main executive office of a big chain of markets. He looked like his brother, a small man with a big nose and a bald head. His wife was a fat motherly-looking woman. They had both reacted to the news about Carlo with more incredulity than grief. "There's just no sense to it at all," said Alisio, rubbing his naked bald head. "Of course we were upset when the hospital called last night. Carl had seemed to be a lot better the last week or so, but the doctor had told us it was just a temporary state of remission. But this—it doesn't seem possible. Anything that could happen in a hospital."

His wife said, "With so many there—"

"Just who had been to see him?" asked Higgins. "When did everybody leave?"

Alisio said promptly, "We got there about two o'clock and I think it was just after four we left, wasn't it, Amy?"

She nodded. "We were having some friends in for dinner. I'd left the roast on but there were still things to do. Ruby and Arthur came just after we got there. That's my nephew and his wife, and their daughter and her husband came just a while later. Then Randy and Rosa and Bill came—"

"That's my sister Rosa, Randy's mother—the Nicollettis—and then I think about three o'clock my brother Dan and his wife, Selma, and their two girls dropped by. It's a little drive for them from Long Beach, but we're a pretty close family—we thought a lot of Carl.'' Alisio took off his glasses to polish them with a handkerchief. ''My God. A thing like this. Some lunatic—and in the hospital—it's just senseless. Dan and Selma hadn't got up the Sunday before, Carl was so glad to see them—and Randy. Randy was his favorite nephew. That's our sister Rosa's son. She's our youngest sister—baby of the family—and later on some old friends of Carl's came by, Jeanette and Paul De Angelo.''

''You were all in and out of his room most of the afternoon?'' asked Hackett.

''Yes, that's right. Just as usual. There wasn't space for more than three of four visitors at once. We'd go down to sit in the little lounge and then take turns going in to Carl.''

''Did either of the other two patients ever have any visitors?''

''No, they never seem to. I guess they're so far gone they wouldn't realize if anyone was there or not. I don't know if they've got any families.''

''But the other patients in the wing had visitors,'' said Higgins.

''Oh, yes. There were people coming and going most of the time, but of course we didn't know any of them. There were people we'd seen there before, I suppose seeing patients who'd been there as long as Carl had, but we wouldn't know their names. But who in God's name would want to do a thing like that? I can't take it in. It's just insane. Just insane.''

There had been nurses going around, naturally, and a couple of doctors, all the nurses and aides at the station in the hall. But Alisio was firm that the family were the only ones who had been in Carlo Alisio's room until they left.

''Who was the last to leave? Do you remember?'' asked Hackett.

He said at once, "I think it would be either Randy or Rosa and Bill. They were still there when Amy and I left. Everybody else had gone. But, my God—how such a thing could've happened—it must've been some lunatic, doing a thing like that, but in a hospital with so many people around like Amy says—" He supplied names readily. Randy Nicolletti and his parents. His niece Ruby and her husband, Arthur Overman. The De Angelos—his brother Dan and his daughter, Kathy Penner.

"And we'll have to look at all the employees," said Higgins back in the car. "What a hell of a job, Art. We'll have to talk to all the family."

When they got back to the office to parcel out the names and addresses, Grace and Galeano had gone over to the hospital to start talking to the staff. This was going to pose some legwork with a vengeance. They would have to get the names of all the patients on that floor, try to find out who their visitors had been, when they'd been there, and talk to everybody on the hospital staff with any reason to be in that wing. And this looked like the irrational thing, but a good many people with some mental quirk were walking around looking as sane as anybody else. That kind of thing wasn't always plain to see.

Landers looked at the list of names and addresses and sighed. "Have to talk to all the family. Somebody may have noticed something. The last ones to leave." He ran a hand through his dark hair. "The time seems a little tight. That doctor thought he'd probably been killed between four and four-thirty—"

"And just about then," said Higgins, "all the visitors were leaving and the nurses getting the patients ready to have dinner in an hour or so. Hell, anybody could've wandered into that room without being noticed, and it wouldn't have taken two minutes to kill the old man—"

"Well, you know, George," said Glasser ruminatively, "hospitals these days—there aren't the same standards there used to be. They hire a lot of their lower-echelon people from the immigrants coming in, people who don't know English—willing to take menial jobs at lower pay. Besides all the nurses and aides and orderlies, there'll be the clean-up people and kitchen staff—all sorts of people. I know the immigrants are supposed to be screened, but who knows what could slip through?"

"Lunatics," said Hackett. "Well, we'll sort out who saw him last, if they noticed anything. Anybody coming into the room or just outside when they left."

They divided up the names and started out. Hackett drew the Nicollettis and went down the hall to the men's room before he headed for the elevator. When he passed the door to Robbery-Homicide again, Sergeant Lake called his name and he turned in. "Lady asking to see you," said Lake.

Alongside the switchboard was a girl about twenty-two, a very pretty blond girl with a beautiful figure. She was smartly dressed in a blue sundress and high-heeled white sandals, with a big white handbag. She said, "I wanted to talk to the officer who arrested my husband. Is that you? I'm Stella Davies."

"That's right, Mrs. Davies. I'm Sergeant Hackett." He took her into the office and gave her the chair beside his desk.

She said drearily, "I wanted to ask you, you'd know about it, I guess. What Ricky might get."

"Well, it's a first count on him and he's got a good record. I don't know, but it's probable the D.A. would accept a plea bargain. He might get sent up for a year and get probation."

"I see," she said. "Thanks for telling me. Of course he was an awful fool for doing that, but I've got a sort of feeling it was partly my fault, too. I should've been a lot more careful about expenses. Neither of us had ever had to budget very tight, if you see what I mean. I'd been giving Mother forty a week to help pay for groceries, but she owns the house and I wasn't used to paying rent, and neither was Ricky. And I guess we just thought we could go out and get whatever we wanted. I didn't have any idea those credit cards had gone so high, but it's just too easy to say charge it and give the account number." She accepted a cigarette and a light apathetically. "I really didn't have to pay forty dollars for this dress."

"He told you how worried he'd been," said Hackett.

"I let him keep track of everything. I just hadn't any idea."

"Well, maybe it's been a lesson for both of you."

She said, emphatically, "It sure has been, Sergeant. And I guess I'll feel guilty the rest of my life. It's partly my fault Ricky'll be getting a prison record—but maybe it won't-be so bad at that. I talked to his boss this morning, Mr. Willard, and he's always liked Ricky and he said he'll let him have the job back afterward. We'll both just try to use more sense and do better." She stood up. "Thanks, Sergeant. I'll be moving back in with Mother and try to save up all I can so we'll have a little backlog when he gets out, and we'll both watch it. And I'm going to get rid of those credit cards," she added vigorously. "They just make it too easy."

Hackett grinned to himself, following her out. Maybe it had been the necessary lesson for both of them. Sometimes the stupid kids grew up a little and got some sense.

MENDOZA AND LANDERS had talked to the Overmans in Pasadena and Dan Alisio and his family in Long Beach, stopped for lunch on the way back and found Mrs. Rosa Nicolletti at home in West Hollywood. They had some idea now who had been at the hospital at what time. Mrs. Nicolletti said her husband was at work, he owned a sporting goods store in Santa Monica. Joe had called to tell her what the police said about Carl and she just couldn't believe it, it must have been a crazy person. She was better-looking then her brothers, with graying black hair and a figure slightly too plump.

"What time did you leave the hospital?" asked Mendoza. "Was anyone else with your brother then?"

"Well, as I recall we left together. Bill and I and Randy. Mary's expecting a baby and she hasn't been feeling too good, the doctor says she has to take it easy, that's Randy's wife—so she didn't come. It was about a quarter past four, and they like all the visitors to be out by around four-thirty, they bring the dinners around a little after five. I think we left together. No, I'm wrong, but it came to the same thing— Randy left his cigarettes in Carl's room and went back to get them, and we all went down to the elevator together. Randy's all broken up about Carl. He was Carl's favorite nephew. They thought a lot of each other."

"Your brother didn't have any family of his own?"

"No, he and Annie never had any children. They were sorry about it. It was a shame because Carl did a little better than the rest of us, in a money way I mean. Not that he was awfully rich, but he built that drugstore into a good business, he was a pharmacist, you know, and I guess he had a nice savings account. He was always a great one to save and watch the pennies. Oh, dear God," she said suddenly. "We knew he was dying—he was the oldest of the family— the first to go. But to have it happen such a way—"

She told them where to find her son Randy. He worked at a big tax-accountant's office in Glendale. There they talked to him at his desk in a big communal office on the third floor of a new high-rise building. He was a good-looking dark young man about thirty, and he said wretchedly, "I feel terrible about Uncle Carl. I nearly didn't come to work. And when Dad called about noon— Oh, hell, I couldn't

believe it—to think of— Well, that's right, I guess Mother
and Dad and I were the last ones to leave. I went back after
my cigarettes and came back out and—no, I didn't notice
anybody in particular near the door. There were quite a few
people in the hall, the elevator was crowded. Yes, Uncle Carl
was alone in the room then, except for the other two patients."

What with all the driving, they'd spent the whole day
finding out that much and it still looked shapeless. Anybody could have gone into that hospital room between four-
fifteen and five o'clock when Alisio was found dead. They
drove back downtown to Parker Center nearly in silence.
When they came into the office, only Hackett was there, and
he was on the phone. He was looking amused, and when he
put the phone down minutes later he said, "The things that
happen. That was that Peabody woman from the Social
Services Department. You'll be interested to hear that when
the Health Department went to look at Ben Leach's house
they found a hundred and four thousand dollars in cash
hidden away at the back of a closet."

"*Maravilloso,*" said Mendoza. "So the county won't be
paying for his board at a nursing home."

"The court will appoint a conservator and it'll probably
take care of him the rest of his life. It's funny," said Hackett, starting to laugh again. "People—those young Davies.
There doesn't seem to be any happy medium between the
ones who throw it away and the misers. What have you
picked up?"

"We've sorted out who saw him last," said Mendoza.
"And damn it, it's still all up in the air. My next thought, we
take a good look at the hospital staff—at backgrounds—
something suggestive may show. Hell, there must be a couple of hundred people on that staff—more—and anybody
in a uniform could saunter down that hall without anybody
paying any attention—and we haven't talked to those nurses

on this shift again. Damnation. We'll be doing some overtime tonight.''

THE OFFBEAT ONE at the hospital took up time. There were
a lot of people to talk to, to question. Palliser was off on
Monday, Grace on Tuesday. Even with Glasser back they
were shorthanded. And with all the answers they got, it was
still a shapeless thing. All the comings and goings—anybody at all could have gone in and smothered the old man.
Nobody had seen anything, anybody out of the ordinary. It
was just a lot of tiresome legwork for nothing.

Galeano and Higgins landed back at the office about
three o'clock on Tuesday afternoon and found that the autopsy report on Rose Eberhart had just come in, and also a
report from the lab. Galeano looked them over. She had, of
course, died of a fractured skull, between six and midnight
Friday night. They kicked it around a little and looked at the
photographs.

''That table by the door,'' said Galeano. ''There was just
a smidgen of blood on it. She wouldn't have bled much
when she fell.''

''Got knocked down,'' amended Higgins. ''By these
shots, she was a good-sized woman and she must've hit with
some force to do herself that much damage, Nick. What it
adds up to is, with the open door, she was talking to somebody in the hall, somebody she wasn't going to let in, and
the somebody knocked her over backwards. A sudden violent argument over something? And the only thing you've
turned up about any little trouble she'd had lately was—''

''This Arvin woman. Not sounding like much of anything,'' said Galeano. ''Some woman she'd worked with.
Hadn't seen in a while, and ran into at the corner market.''

''And no lead on locating her,'' said Higgins.

''Well, I had a thought or two,'' said Galeano. ''Jase always saying he's got a simple mind. I've got a fairly simple

mind, too, and I thought of the phone book first. But if Eberhart hadn't seen her in a while and then met her again just recently, it could say that the woman had just moved into that area recently, too. A *corner* market, not a big supermart. It sounds like a place they'd both walk to. A local independent store—handy to where they both lived. And if she'd just moved, she wouldn't be in the phone book. She could also have an unlisted number. A lot of women living alone do.''

"True," said Higgins. He massaged his jaw thoughtfully. "We can give it a try."

"That's what I thought," said Galeano. He looked in the phone book for Central L.A. and there were only five Arvins—four more who spelled it with a y. None lived any closer to the Echo Park area than Alhambra, City Terrace, Monterey Park, Lincoln Heights. He dialed the information operator, introduced himself, invited her to call back to verify that she was really talking to police.

"I'm looking for an Arvin— I'm not sure just how it's spelled. Somewhere in the downtown area. The number may have just been changed to that name or it may be unlisted. No, I don't have any first name."

"You don't want the ones listed in the Central book, sir?" She sounded like an intelligent girl.

"Anything else you've got, please."

"Just a moment sir. There's an unlisted number, Linda Arvin, on Cadillac Avenue."

"I don't think that's it."

"A J. Arvin, Durango Avenue. Oliver Arvin, Langford Street—that's just been listed."

"Keep going," said Galeano.

"Myra Arvin, Santa Ynez Street—that's a new listing too. There's a D. Arvin on—"

"O.K., thanks. If I want that I'll get back to you." Galeano put the phone down. "Bingo, maybe," he said to

Higgins. "Santa Ynez. That's right in the middle of that area. Let's go take a look."

They took his Ford and after a little hunt found the address. Santa Ynez was an old narrow street in that old residential area, and the address was a small apartment house dating back to the twenties. In the little uncarpeted lobby, they found Myra Arvin listed, by the mailbox, in apartment 4-B, upstairs. They climbed worn old wooden stairs and found the door. It was the right front apartment. Galeano pushed the bell. In a moment the door was opened by a short stout woman with suspiciously black hair and snapping black eyes, a sallow complexion, innocent of any makeup. She was wearing a flowered cotton houserobe and ancient bedroom slippers. Galeano showed her the badge and she stared at it.

"And what would the police want with me?" she asked sharply.

"Do you know Mrs. Rose Eberhart, Mrs. Arvin?" asked Higgins.

Her mouth went tight and she looked very angry. "For the Lord's sake, has that damned woman sicked the police on me? That's just like her nerve! I don't know what the police would have to do with it, if anybody's got reason to call the police it was me, and I'm not sorry I knocked her down either. Her trying to tell me that lie about Bert! She had it coming. I'll never see that fifty bucks again, might as well forget it."

Galeano said gently, "I think you'd better let us in, ma'am." She marched across the room and plumped herself down on the couch, and Galeano and Higgins took the couple of chairs opposite. This was a typical furnished apartment, nondescript furniture, a T.V. in one corner, glimpse into a kitchen at one side, a bedroom at the other. Galeano said, "Suppose you tell us your side of the story, Mrs. Arvin."

She lit a cigarette with an angry snap of the lighter. "I suppose she's claiming that I tried to rob her or swindle her or something. And I thought she was a nice woman when I first knew her. You bet I'll tell you my side of the story, and if I can't prove it, she can't prove that damn lie about Bert."

"When did you first know her, Mrs. Arvin?"

"When I had that job at McClintock's. I was only there six months, it was three years back. She worked there, too, I don't know if she still does." She was smoking rapidly. "Damn it, I was sorry for her then—the reason I loaned her the fifty. She was married to a drunk, she wanted shut of him, can't blame her for that—and she needed the money to hire a lawyer. She said it was just temporary till payday, and I let her have it. And she never paid it back. Well, I had reason enough for it going out of my mind for a while. Bert died of a heart attack about a month later—my husband— and it was a big shock to me. After the funeral I quit my job and moved up to Fresno to live with my son and his wife— them saying it was the sensible thing to do—all over me that snippy little girl was, and didn't I find out why, all they wanted was an unpaid housekeeper and baby-sitter!" She snorted. "I never did get on with that girl, anyway, don't understand what Roy sees in her." It was possible that there were quite a few people Myra Arvin would not get on with. "When I remembered the money, I wrote Rose at the restaurant, I didn't know her address, but I never got an answer, and I know she must've got the letter. I was mad about it but there wasn't anything I could do up there, and I don't know why I stuck it out as long as I did, but I finally had it with that girl and her two spoiled brats, and I came back down here a couple of weeks ago—found this apartment and got a job at Denny's—the one on Santa Monica, I'm on the night shift—and when I got settled I was going up to McClintock's, see if Rose was still there, only I ran right into her at that little market on the corner. I didn't know she lived around here. So I asked her about the fifty and she tried to put over this damn lie. She said she paid it back, she gave it to Bert when he came to pick me up one night at the restaurant. She said I was back getting my coat, and Bert thanked her and put it in his pocket. I ask you!''

"You didn't believe her?'' asked Galeano.

"Listen,'' she said, "I was married to Bert Arvin for thirty-two years. You think I didn't have him trained to hand over all the money to me? He wasn't just so smart about handling money and I'm a good manager, I always handled all the money. He wouldn't have held it out on me. And anyway, she knew he was dead and couldn't speak up for himself—just a plain lie to get out of paying me back.''

"You went to see her about it again last Friday night?'' asked Higgins.

"I sure did. I'd already had a couple of arguments with her. I'd looked up her address and found she lived just a couple of blocks away. I could use that money—just moving back here like I said—and I wasn't going to let her get away with it. I don't know what she told you, but I went there and she wouldn't let me in. She stood in the door and argued with me—said she wasn't going to pay the money twice—and I just got mad. I saw there wasn't one damn thing I could do about it, I couldn't prove she never paid Bert, but I know she hadn't. And finally I just gave her a shove, I was damn mad, and I guess I caught her off balance and she fell down—and I can't say I'm sorry. I haven't been near her since. I don't care what she told you.''

"She didn't tell us anything, Mrs. Arvin,'' said Higgins. "She's dead. She hit her head when she fell down and fractured her skull.''

She stared at him with mouth open, and her complexion went muddy gray. "You mean when I pushed her—you mean—Oh, my God—my God— I never meant to hurt her any way—Oh, my God.''

Galeano said, "I'm afraid you'll have to come downtown with us."

"You're arresting me for murder—for killing her? I never meant—"

"Well, it won't amount to that," said Higgins. The charge would probably be involuntary manslaughter and she wouldn't serve much time.

"Oh, my God," she said dully. "Can I go get dressed? I can't go anywhere like this." They didn't think she'd try to cut her throat, alone in the bathroom; she wasn't the type, so they let her go.

Galeano lit a cigarette. "The poor henpecked husband," he said. "Seeing a chance to keep a little cash for himself."

"I wonder what he did with it," said Higgins.

"Maybe blew it on a more congenial female," said Galeano.

They were never to know that two and a half years ago Mrs. Amelia Brown, moving into a cheaper apartment on West Adams Street, had with surprise and gratification discovered two twenties and a ten in an envelope at the back of the closet shelf in the bedroom. She had decided not to mention it to the manager. It was her business. It had meant a few little extra luxuries that month, and a really nice birthday present for her oldest granddaughter.

GALEANO GOT HOME to the little house in Studio City at six-thirty. It had been murderously hot again today. He looked at the house as he turned into the drive and thought again that it could stand a coat of paint, but with the baby coming—maybe next year they could afford it. Marta hadn't heard him drive in. She was in the backyard, sitting on the grass playing with the little gray tabby kitten she'd got from the people down the street. He stood for a moment looking at her fondly, his darling Marta, with the tawny blond hair and dark eyes. She wasn't showing the baby much; it was due in March. She had on a green sundress and she was laughing down at the kitten. It would be funny if the baby should arrive on their first wedding anniversary. It was going to be Anthony for his father or Christine for her mother.

"Nick, I did not hear you come in." She scrambled up and came running to him and he kissed her soundly.

"I was just thinking, I wish I could afford a better house for us."

She laughed. "But you do not know how rich it makes me feel to own a whole house, with a nice yard to make a garden?" She'd never lose her little German accent. She'd had a rough time for a while—her first husband killing himself, and losing the baby. He hoped he could make it all up to her from now on. "You look tired, *liebchen*. Come in and sit down, I have dinner nearly ready."

That night about eight-thirty, Patrolman Manuel Gonzales was peacefully cruising on his regular tour in Hollywood. He'd turned on to Vermont for the second time and presently came to the L.A.C.C. campus. Several of the buildings were lit up—for evening classes probably, he thought—and there were cars in the parking lot. Just doing the routine, he turned in and drove around there. He had nine A.P.B.'s posted on the squad's dashboard, plate numbers to look for. He didn't know why the front-office boys were after them, it could be anything from a stolen car to a heist suspect to murder. But that wasn't his business. He drove slowly around the lot, looking casually at plate numbers, and suddenly, down at the end of the lot, he spotted one. He braked and checked the number with the posted A.P.B. They matched. A two-year-old Chrysler Newport, navy-blue, and it was the right number. He got on the radio to report it.

IT WAS SCHENKE'S night off. Piggott and Conway got sent out once, early, to a heist at a pharmacy on Sixth. There wasn't a decent description of the heister to be had, the owner was the only witness and he was too shook to say what color the man had been. They came back to the office and Piggott started to type the report. And then Hollywood Division called to say that the A.P.B. had turned up a car they wanted. Neither of them knew much about Edna Holzer, but enough to know that it probably wouldn't be any use to stake out the car and wait for somebody to come back, the car belonged to a missing woman. Conway called the police garage and asked for somebody to go up there and tow it in for lab examination. He supposed there wasn't any hurry about that and didn't bother to call the skeleton night crew at the lab.

Piggott hadn't finished the report when they got another call to another heist. There were five witnesses to this one and all good witnesses. It was a liquor store and both owners had been there with three old friends, just about to start a friendly game of draw in the back office after the store was closed. They were all older men who had seen military service and didn't scare easily. They hadn't wanted anybody to get hurt so they hadn't put up a fight, and the owners had only left enough cash in the register to start with change tomorrow; he'd only got about twenty bucks. But they all described him graphically. A Negro about twenty-five, six feet, small mustache, dark pants and yellow shirt, no discernible accent. They all agreed on the gun—a revolver, either a .38 or .45, probably a Colt.

"This will give the day watch some legwork," said Piggott. On a lot of the recent heists, there wasn't much to do. When there was a good description, there was. They looked in Records for men who matched the description, went and looked for them, brought them in for questioning. It could be tedious and largely futile, but once in a while they hit a jackpot.

The phone rang and Conway picked it up. "Say, where have you been? I've been trying to get you for an hour. This is Slattery down at the garage."

"We've been on a call. Did that car get brought in?"

"Well, that's what I'm calling about. I went up to Hollywood to get it, and you might have warned me, for God's sake, you gave me the hell of a shock. I mean, for God's sake, I've seen bodies before— I was two years in 'Nam— but I wasn't expecting it."

"A body?" said Conway.

"Yeah, in the back seat of this Chrysler. It's a woman."

"Well, surprise, surprise," said Conway. "I suppose the Hollywood man just checked the plate. Just leave it alone, I'll see if I can get the lab out." He called and somebody named Steiner said through a yawn that they'd get on it.

"You want the works—pictures and all? O.K. You boys do pick the goddamndest time to find corpses."

"I TOLD YOU SO," said Carey. He and Mendoza stood in the cold room down at the morgue looking at the body in its tray. Edna Holzer had probably been an attractive woman, but you wouldn't know it now. She'd been stripped and her clothes sent up to the lab, and nothing had been done to the body pending the autopsy. There were ugly cyanosed stains on her throat and shoulders and her face was twisted into a grimace.

"And I don't need an autopsy to know she was strangled," added Carey. "Knocked around a little first. The doctors will say if she's been raped."

"And not very long after she left the hospital on Saturday night," said Mendoza. "There wouldn't have been much traffic at that hour along the couple of blocks before she'd hit the freeway, but—"

"But," said Carey, "woman driving alone at night, it would've been dark for about half an hour, she'd automatically keep the car doors locked. Even if she caught a light, how could anybody have jumped her? I suppose he could've been waiting in the parking lot—grabbed her when she came back to the car. It's about the only way it could've happened. She wasn't planning to stop anywhere between there and home."

"*¡Condenación!*" said Mendoza, brushing violently at his mustache. "We've got a hell of a lot too much on hand already, with that damned hospital staff to delve into, and another homicide, and that new heist. All we need is something like this. Of course, the lab might pick up something on the car. Well, no rest for the wicked, as Art says. We'll have to work it."

They drove up to Del Mar Avenue in Hollywood in the Ferrari. The Holzer house was a comfortable old Spanish place with a manicured lawn in front. Frances Holzer was home and Carey broke the news to her.

She was a pretty girl about twenty-five with brown hair, a fair complexion, and hazel eyes. She had looked a little haggard already, and she broke down and wept for quite a while. They gave her time. Finally, she sat up and blew her nose and said in a shaking voice, "I knew she was dead— I just knew it. I knew she had to be when she didn't come home. I said to her when she left that night, I wished she wouldn't go, I said she could go on Sunday—in daylight. That's right downtown—that hospital. Not a good part of town. But she said there was that deposition to do in the morning, and she wanted to wash her hair in the afternoon. Maybe I had a premonition. I just couldn't go to work all week, I called in sick. I knew she'd never come home again."

"Would she have had much money with her, Miss Holzer?" asked Mendoza.

"No, just a few dollars. But all her credit cards— I did have enough sense to call and put a stop on those. Just in case—in case—"

Mendoza made a mental note to find out which cards they were, ask the central clearing office to notify them on the outside chance that somebody might try to use those accounts.

"Oh, my God, I've got to call Mona—my sister. They've been just frantic too, but they live in Bakersfield and couldn't come—they'll have to now."

"Was she careful about keeping the car doors locked?" asked Carey.

She gave them a wild look and began to cry again. "But that's why I'd been so worried about her going out alone— at night— I begged her not to go—she said, the freeway nearly all the way—"

They gave her another minute while she sobbed. "What do you mean, Miss Holzer?" asked Mendoza.

"The l-l-lock on the right front door was b-b-broken. They had to send for a part. It wasn't going to be fixed until next week. Oh, my God, I'd better call Mona right away—"

Mendoza and Carey looked at each other. Such a simple explanation when you knew.

ON WEDNESDAY, just before noon, the autopsy and lab report on Verna Coffey arrived at about the same time. Palliser was alone in the Robbery-Homicide office. He'd been delegated to write the latest report on the Alisio case. It was Hackett's day off and everybody else was over at the hospital.

There wasn't much in the autopsy report. She'd been beaten to death and, from the lab report, apparently by the hammer left beside her. There was blood, hair, and brain tissue on that. There hadn't been any readable prints on the hammer, but they had picked up quite a few around the little apartment. Most of them were hers. There were nine others belonging to three different people, probably, unknown to Records—very likely the rest of the Coffey family. And somebody ought to get their prints for comparison. There had also been two good prints identified as those of Toby Wells—record appended. Palliser sat up in surprise, but when he had read the attached Xerox copy, his interest faded a little. It wasn't much of a pedigree—an arrest for theft from an expensive men's clothing store a couple of years back. Disposition, goods paid for and the court ordered a year's probation. The only reason he'd been printed and got into Records was that it was a technical felony, theft of goods valued at more than a hundred dollars. It was natural enough that his prints should be there. He was Verna Coffey's grandson. They had been picked up from the side of the washbowl in the bathroom, and the family had all been there the Sunday before the murder. They could easily have stayed there for six days without getting smudged. But they'd talk to him and find out where he'd been that Friday night.

The phone rang and he picked it up, still looking at the report. "Robbery-Homicide, Sergeant Palliser."

"Say," said Duke at the lab. "Did you get that report yet? Good. I meant to put a note in with it. We've been kind of busy and it slipped my mind. I'll tell you what, Palliser, if you ever pick up a good solid suspect on this Coffey homicide, you bring all his shoes along to us. We'll maybe give you some beautiful scientific evidence."

"Shoes," said Palliser blankly. "Why?"

Duke laughed. "Just don't forget it. We all have our professional secrets, Palliser."

On Thursday afternoon, the tedious checking into backgrounds of all the employees at the hospital turned up something interesting, and Grace and Galeano brought it to

Mendoza rather with the air of two well-trained retrievers fetching in a bird that had been lost in the underbrush. *"¡Vaya por Dios!"* said Mendoza, looking at the record.

One Alfredo Diaz, employed as a chef in the hospital kitchen, had turned out to be a former mental patient at the Norwalk State Hospital. He had been released after a couple of years there, three years ago. One of the doctors on the hospital board had got him the job. "We just talked to that one," said Grace, "and he nearly bit our heads off."

"Time is money, Jase. We interrupted his schedule," said Galeano. "All these people are growing a prejudice for the damn suspicious fuzz, Lieutenant. They were excited over the murder, but when we came nosing around suspecting that somebody at the hospital did it—"

"Medical people," said Grace, "are all temperamental. Supposed to be all efficient and scientific but they're so used to being in charge of everything they're apt to have a tantrum when they're not—if you take me." Grace might know. His father was the chief of the Gynecology Department at the General Hospital.

"Well, mental patients come all kinds like other people," said Mendoza. "One of the chefs—"

"I know," said Galeano. "That's the little stumbling block. He says he was in the basement kitchen fixing the dinners with everybody else. He never goes up to the wards—wasn't interested in the patients, and there seems to have been about forty other people there, but that cancels itself out in a way. If he was gone for fifteen minutes—said he was back in the john—would anybody have noticed?"

"What in hell is one like that doing on a hospital staff?"

"The doctor we riled—a Dr. Ackerwood—told us he'd got him the job as a favor for a friend of his, one of the psychiatrists at Norwalk—a Dr. Silverman."

"I'm not," said Mendoza, "constitutionally disposed to believe automatically anything a psychiatrist says, boys. I think at least half of them are a little bit touched themselves. But I suppose it wouldn't do any harm to hear what Silverman has to say about Diaz."

He saw Silverman on Friday morning at his private office out on Chapman Avenue in Fullerton, and was, grudgingly, favorably impressed. Silverman was fat, bald, friendly and not given to the six-dollar words.

"Well, the man has a low-normal I.Q., Lieutenant. He's a mildly schizoid personality, but I never detected any tendency to violence in the three years I was treating him. He had a great lack of self-confidence—understandable with his mentality, but it took the effect of suicidal impulses rather than outward aggression. As I had rather expected, when we found him a job he could perform satisfactorily, a mechanical job he could do by routine, he responded quite well. He's made a good adjustment." Silverman was academically interested in the homicide. "I don't know anything about it, Lieutenant, except what you've just told me, but from my experience with aberrations, I might hazard a guess that you should look for someone with a fixation about death—perhaps," he reflected, "a much-indulged son who had lost a beloved mother. I find it interesting, you know, that it is an Italian family. I presume Catholic. Yes. The—er—symbolism. But I really think you needn't suspect Diaz. I never detected any violence there—any incipient aggression."

AND MENDOZA felt a little foolish about it—a little self-conscious. But he told the morgue to send Juliette up to Forest Lawn. God knew he could afford to pay for a simple funeral, but he wasn't sure why he felt obligated, and he thought vaguely as he had thought about another corpse a year or so ago, *She fell among thieves.* He wondered if Juliette had been Catholic; it was probable. He talked to Father Damian at St. Patrick's in Burbank, and the priest was sensible and practical. He held a brief graveside service. Alison attended that—"I know it's just a ceremony, but somehow I felt I ought to go"—and Mairí was there. Mairí was a very orthodox, traditional Catholic of the old school and for some reason she felt sentimental about Juliette. She said darkly, "Dying as a stranger in a strange land—and if you ask me, even if we don't know the ins and outs of it, that grandfather of hers must be a wicked old rogue."

SEVEN

ON SATURDAY, Palliser finally got around to looking up Toby Wells. The rest of the Coffey family had come in to have their prints taken and these had checked out with the other prints the lab had picked up. Wells worked at a Thrifty drugstore on Hollywood Boulevard, and he was an ordinary-looking young black fellow, round-faced, slow-spoken, and he was frank on answering questions. "You were in a little trouble a couple of years ago," said Palliser.

Wells said a little nervously, "Well, yeah, that was kind of a damn' fool thing to do—steal those clothes—but I like nice clothes, and I had a new girl then and I guess I wanted to show off to her. My grandma paid up for me and I never been in any trouble since. Oh yeah, it's an awful thing about Grandma." He shied a little when Palliser asked him about that Friday night, but answered readily, "I was out with my girl, Mae Weaver. We went to a disco down on Jefferson Boulevard. I guess it was about midnight when I got home, we both had to go to work the next day, acourse." He lived with a couple of other young fellows at an apartment on Virgil Avenue. It wasn't worth writing a further report on.

Half of them were now doing the legwork on that heister, the rest winding down the investigation at the hospital. That had been a bastard of a thing to work. They must have chased down over a hundred people, trying to identify all the visitors, looking into personal backgrounds, and all for nothing. There was no way to find out who might have done that queer killing—why or when. It was another case that would wind up in the Pending file.

On Sunday morning, the lab report came up on the Holzer car and there was nothing in it at all. The steering wheel had evidently been wiped clean and the only other prints in the car belonged to Edna Holzer and the girl, Frances. The autopsy report came in that afternoon too and she hadn't been raped, just knocked around and strangled manually. The lab hadn't picked up anything significant from her clothes.

Mendoza took the reports out to the communal office to pass on and said to Hackett, "Just damn all on everything we're working—nothing."

"Well, that's the way it goes sometimes, and then all of a sudden we'll get some breaks."

"Don't philosophize at me," said Mendoza irritably. He sat down at Higgins' desk and added abruptly, "And we're never going to hear anything from France, you know. I've got a strong hunch on that."

"I don't see that, Luis. The girl must've had friends. There's the fiancé."

"*Es cierto, sé*. But that's my hunch." He was silent for a moment and then said, "The only way we'll get anything from France is for somebody to go over there and look."

Hackett took his glasses off to stare at him. "You're not serious."

"I might be, Art. At least I've got a passport in order."

"You don't know where to start looking," said Hackett.

"But the trail starts there, damn it *¡Condenación!* Grandfather. If there was just some little lead—"

"You don't even know whether the Martin girl lived in Paris—anywhere in France—"

"The probability is Paris, I think. Such a simple, artful little setup. By God, I'll find out what was behind that if it takes a year," said Mendoza violently. "And I think we can let that hospital staff go about its business. We're never going to turn up any evidence on that damn thing." Hackett agreed thoughtfully. The autopsy on Alisio had said exactly what they expected it to say.

By now, four possible suspects on that heist had been found and questioned, but there was nothing to tie in any of them definitely. Two more heists had gone down last night with no clear descriptions. The heat wave was still with them.

Hackett said, "We get these spells sometimes. Stymied on everything. Then all of a sudden we'll start to get the breaks."

"Pollyanna," said Mendoza.

What broke on Monday afternoon was another homicide, at a junior high school down on Vernon Avenue. One of the teachers, Mrs. Vera Robertson, was found by another teacher, knifed to death in her own classroom. Mendoza and Higgins went out to have a first look and talked to a shaken and angry principal, Lee Olliphant.

"We've never had anything as bad as this," he said. "There's always the dope problem. You can't do anything with some of these damn kids, they come to school stoned on the dope, on the liquor, or both. About all we can do is try to see they don't disturb the kids who are teachable. Mrs. Robertson had complained to me of several boys in her class, the first week of school. It was her first semester with us, you know. She'd been transferred from a junior high school in Hollywood." He was a big pear-shaped man in a baggy wrinkled suit and he eyed Mendoza's fastidious dapperness with faint disapproval. The knifing had apparently happened during the lunch hour. She had been found at twelve-thirty by the other teacher, Wilma Fox.

She said, "Vera just hated it here. Heaven knows the kids anywhere are bad enough nowadays, but down here it's worse than other places, more of the kids on dope and some of the rest impossible to teach for other reasons, and I'm sorry if I sound prejudiced, but that is the plain truth. But

this— I'm going to be scared to come to work and I've got
to earn a living—''

Olliphant said heavily, "My God, I'm thankful I'm due
to retire next year. It's not unusual for the boys here to carry
knives, there's a lot of gang activity and the decent kids get
intimidated for the lunch money and so on." He sighed.
"Not an easy job. Yes, I can give you the names of the boys
she complained about—showing up high on dope, resisting
discipline—but that doesn't say it was one of them who did
it. We have a lot of difficult youngsters."

Half of the names were Latin—Ortiz, Gonzales, Lopez.
The rest of the boys were black. Classes were out by then,
the lab men busy in the classroom, but they wouldn't turn
up anything useful. They couldn't print juveniles, and with
all the kids milling around at the lunch hour nobody would
have noticed any disturbance in that classroom, and nobody would tell the fuzz if they had. Her handbag was
missing. She had kept it in a drawer in her desk. She had
been thirty-five, had a husband and two young daughters.
The husband was a bookkeeper at a savings-and-loan company in Hollywood, and he told them that she never carried more than a few dollars to school. She had had her
wallet rifled the first day she was there and there wasn't a
lock on any of her drawers. "These goddamn punk kids.
Not a white kid in that damn place. All the spicks and
dinges. And you want to arrest me for being prejudiced, go
ahead. I told her for God's sake not to turn her back on any
of them. All of those goddamn kids carrying knives or
worse. Damn it, if we hadn't needed her salary, she wouldn't
have been there—''

It was a waste of time to talk to the kids. The biggest one
of those she'd complained about was Rudy Ortiz, a hulk-
ing fourteen-year-old. He didn't like the fuzz worth a damn
but he knew they couldn't do anything to him. He said sul-
lenly what the other ones had said, as if it were the same re-

cord being played. "She just hated anybody with a Latin name—like she hated all the black kids. All the kids knew that. Nobody liked old lady Robertson, but I don't know nothing about what happened."

Her handbag turned up the next day, in a trash container behind the school cafeteria. Her wallet was in it, empty of the few dollars it had held. This was another one that would go into Pending after a couple of follow-up reports.

But on the following Thursday, the unexpected happened. The Security Pacific Bank which had issued Edna Holzer's Visa card called headquarters to report, as requested, that an attempt had been made to use that account. The routine check had showed up the hold on it. The card had been presented at the Broadway Department Store at Hollywood and Vine in the women's dress section.

Mendoza and Hackett went up there in a hurry and talked to the clerk who had checked the card. She was an amiable middle-aged woman who'd worked there for years, and she said, "It's funny how you get feelings, sort of a sixth sense, when somebody's trying to pull something, a shoplifter or something like this. I kind of had a feeling about that girl as soon as I saw her. It was funny."

"Can you describe her?" asked Mendoza.

"Oh, sure, I think I can do better than that for you. Of course, she didn't get away with the merchandise, she'd picked out a couple of dresses and a blouse, and these credit cards get stopped for a lot of reasons— I couldn't know she'd stolen it, I just let her walk out. But I'd seen her before, you know, and when the department head said the police were interested, I did some thinking on it, and I can tell you where to find her."

"By God, Art, you're a prophet," said Mendoza. "Don't tell me we're going to get a break. Where and who?"

"She's a waitress at this coffee shop just up the block. Faye's Café. I drop in there for lunch sometimes. She's about twenty-five, size twelve, she's got red hair. Yes, I'm sure it's her. I'd swear to it."

They picked her up at the café. Her name was Sally Pitman and at first she wouldn't tell them anything, just kept denying she'd done it. But Higgins came and loomed at her and she didn't like him at all, or the big businesslike detective office. Finally she said weakly, "I didn't really do anything, did I? I just thought if I could use that card to get some things—well, it'd be easy. I didn't know there was anything wrong with it. Somebody just lost it."

"Where did you get it?" asked Higgins for the third time.

"I found it. I told you. I just found it on the sidewalk." They went on pounding at her about that and finally in exasperation they left her alone for five minutes and turned Wanda Larsen on to her.

"You know, Lieutenant," said Wanda sweetly, "there's an old saying that you catch more flies with honey. Why did you try to scare the poor kid? All she needed were a few sympathetic words. I think she'll talk to you now."

"Thank you so much," said Mendoza.

Sally Pitman was still sullen but ready to talk straighter. "Oh, for God's sake," she said wearily. "I found the damn card in my boyfriend's pocket. We were just sitting around the other night and I was out of cigarettes and I looked to see if he had any in his jacket."

"Boyfriend's name?" asked Hackett briskly.

"Ray Siemens. He doesn't know anything about it either."

"Did you ask him about it?"

"He found it. He just found it in the street. He said he forgot he'd picked it up and I better throw it away, it was no good. But I just thought—but he doesn't know anything about all this. He told me to throw it away."

Ray Siemens worked at a gas station on Western. They brought him in to talk to and he laughed at them. He was a big husky dark-haired fellow about twenty-five, and he didn't appreciate being grilled by the fuzz, but they couldn't shake his story. He'd found the card on the sidewalk right outside the station. Didn't know why he bothered to pick it up. He'd forgotten he had. He told Sally to throw it away, it was no good to anybody. He went on saying that over again and of course there was no evidence on him at all. He could have found it where the X on Edna Holzer had dropped it. The car had been clean. He had a little pedigree with them—one count of assault with intent. He had served a year in the men's colony at San Luis Obispo. Both Mendoza and Hackett liked that, but without any definite evidence they'd never tie him in.

Siemens lived alone in a little apartment over the garage at the rear of a single house on Berendo Avenue, and the owners lived in the front house, a Mr. and Mrs. Dearborn. They said he was a quiet tenant, out a lot, always paid the rent on time. Mendoza got a search warrant for the place and they looked at it, Higgins trailing along. It was a shabby bare little apartment, not much furniture, but he had a nice wardrobe of clothes. In one corner of the living room stood one of the newly popular reproductions of an old Franklin stove—economical heating. Mendoza opened the door and looked in and said, "Why has he had a fire in this, *compadres?* In ninety-degree weather?" The stove was half full of ashes, partly burned lumps of unidentifiable burned matter.

"So that's what he did with the handbag," said Higgins, a hand to his jaw.

"I rather think so," said Mendoza. "Let's turn the lab loose on it."

"Impossible," said Hackett. "Nobody could say what that stuff once was."

"Well, see what they make of it."

A lab crew went out next morning. They talked to Siemens again that afternoon and he was openly contemptuous. "I don't know what the hell you're trying to tie me into, but you might as well stop wasting your goddamn time, gents, I'm clean and you'll never prove I'm not." His cocky attitude just reinforced their conviction. He said he'd been with the girl that Saturday night and she backed him up, but nobody believed her. Then Hackett went to talk to the owner of the gas station again. All he had to say was that Siemens was a damn good mechanic and he'd always liked him fine. "I don't know why the cops are picking on him," he said now. "What the hell you think he's done, anyways? When's he supposed to have done something?"

"Two weeks ago Saturday night," said Hackett absently.

"Well, there you are," said the owner. "Cops picking on him. I don't know any of his pals or what he does at night, but I just happen to remember that one. He told me his sister just had a baby and he was going to see her in the hospital."

"The French Hospital downtown?" asked Hackett mildly.

"How do I know what hospital?"

The sister's name was Marcia Field and she had been in the French Hospital.

"He's our X on Holzer. He's guilty as hell," said Higgins, "and goddamn it, we'll never prove it on him. All the evidence there ever was is long gone. Connections, but nebulous." He hunched his brawny shoulders angrily. "He wasn't the only one at that hospital that night. That Visa card could have been dropped by somebody else. There's damn all to show a judge." And that kind of thing happened too, and it was always frustrating.

But on the following Tuesday morning, Scarne showed up in the Robbery-Homicide office with a manila envelope. He was looking pleased. He said to Mendoza, "I think we've got something interesting for you, Lieutenant. It was one hell of a job. We had to use the ultraviolet and infrared film, but it came up better than I thought it would." He slid an enlarged glossy photograph out of the envelope and laid it tenderly on Mendoza's desk. "All we could salvage out of all that burned material in the Franklin stove, but maybe it's enough. There was what was left of a billfold, just the corners and a spine, and what looks like the handle of a woman's handbag, which says you're right about Siemens. The plastic slots from the billfold were completely gone, of course. Any I.D. was past recall. But this thing—" He cocked his head at it. "It was about three by five originally, and we can deduce that it was in the middle of a bunch of other papers—other snapshots possibly—in an inside pocket of the billfold. It was protected enough that all of it didn't burn, and we brought up about half of it."

It had been a snapshot, probably in color. The delicate lab processing wouldn't restore that, and the picture was gray and fuzzy from the rate of enlargement. It showed the upper half of a little girl smiling at the camera. She was wearing a polka-dotted dress and a big hair bow.

"Muy lindo," said Mendoza. "You bring about the miracles these days, don't you? Thank you so much."

"It was one hell of a job. But it might," said Scarne, "be almost as good as a driver's license."

Mendoza and Hackett took the enlargement up to Hollywood, where Frances Holzer worked at the Fidelity Federal Savings and Loan, and she took one look at it and said in surprise, "Why, it's that snapshot of Monica. My niece—Mona's little girl. Mona just sent it down about three weeks ago. Yes, Mother had it in her billfold with some other snapshots of the family, and of course Mona has a print of it too. Where on earth did you get it? And what happened to it?"

"Jackpot," said Hackett in immense satisfaction.

"Mejor tarde que nunca," said Mendoza. "Better late than never. Let's go pick him up and get the warrant."

But they never got Siemens to open his mouth. Even when they spelled out the evidence to him, he stayed cocky and silent. They had to speculate on exactly what had happened to Edna Holzer. Had he been in the parking lot at the same time, grabbed her on impulse for what she had in her billfold, or intending rape, and then, finding he had put the quietus on her permanently, stashed the car with her in it to give himself time? Had he abstracted the Visa card, intending to use it, and then changed his mind? They didn't know, and Siemens wasn't talking. But there had been only two prints of that snapshot and the other one was up in Bakersfield.

Siemens had thought he'd got rid of all the evidence. What he hadn't reckoned on was the simple yen on Sally's part for a couple of free dresses, and the little miracles the lab could perform.

AND NOTHING CAME IN from the French police. "I said so," said Mendoza to Hackett on Friday. He had just got back from a session on Siemens at the D.A.'s office. He perched one hip on the corner of Hackett's desk. "It's a dead end. There and here. Why? Why the hell hasn't someone missed her by now? By all logic, somebody should have."

"You'd think so. But you had the hunch."

"By God," said Mendoza savagely. "I'm tempted to go over there and try to pick up the trail myself."

Hackett took his glasses off. "How would you know where to start looking, for God's sake?"

"There must be a record of her somewhere, damn it. There's got to be. From this distance there's not a hope in hell of locating it—of placing her. But on her home ground—" He smoked in silence for a moment and said,

"What are you brooding about, John?" Palliser at the next desk had stopped typing and was sitting staring into space.

"There's probably nothing to it. But damn it," said Palliser, "I keep thinking about that Toby Wells. On the Coffey case. His prints were there, but so were the rest of the family's. I saw his girlfriend and she confirmed that they were at that disco on Jefferson that night. I talked to his roommates, and they'd both gone to bed before he came in. It's nothing. He's got no record of violence at all. But with the lab turning that evidence for you on Siemens— Well, Duke said something to me about shoes. If we ever got a hot suspect."

"Do no harm to have a closer look at him," said Hackett.

"By God, I am thinking about it," said Mendoza. "I'd surely to God like to know who set up that little farce, and why, and how."

Palliser abandoned his report and went out. It was Galeano's day off and everybody else was out hunting heisters or hospital visitors. They had descriptions on two more heisters now. There weren't, for once, any indictments or arraignments coming up to waste time in court. There wasn't anything to be done about the Robertson homicide. Higgins had talked to somebody in Juvenile and none of those kids she had complained about had any record with them. It wouldn't say much if they had.

There had been another teenager found dead by his mother in his own bed. It was another O.D. of the 'ludes, combined with liquor.

Mendoza wandered down to his own office and Hackett was alone when Grace came in with a possible suspect on one of the heists, so he sat in on that. It was all inconclusive. The man didn't have an alibi, but there was nothing else but his description to connect him to the heist. They decided to hold him overnight and arrange for a lineup in the morning to see whether the witnesses would pick him out.

PALLISER THOUGHT this was probably a waste of time, but he applied for a search warrant for Toby Wells' apartment. It came through on Saturday morning, and he and Galeano went out to execute it. There wasn't anybody at home in the apartment, but they showed the warrant to the manager and he agreed to let them in. He said the three young dudes who lived there seemed to be nice quiet boys. They all had jobs and paid regular.

They looked around the place. It was just a place for sleeping. No sign in the kitchen that much cooking was done there. There were two bedrooms, and the largest one contained twin beds, had a walk-in closet. In the other one there was a framed photograph of Mae Weaver on the dresser, so this was Toby Wells' bedroom. It just had a wardrobe with sliding doors. On the floor of that were five pairs of shoes—a pair of brown moccasins, a newer pair of black oxfords, another pair of moccasins—black—and some sneakers. Palliser had a look at them but couldn't see anything suggestive. He stashed them all in a plastic evidence bag and they drove back downtown to drop them off at the lab. Then they went up to that Thrifty in Hollywood to talk to Wells. He wasn't as amiable as before, when Palliser asked questions over again. "What the hell you want with my shoes, anyway? I didn't know cops could go right in a person's pad and just steal stuff."

"You'll get them back," said Galeano easily. "We may want to borrow the ones you're wearing too. Are all those the only shoes you've got?"

"For Gossakes, what am I supposed to do till then? I don't know why you guys are bothering me, I never had anything to do with that—you know what I mean. I haven't done anything at all."

"So you've got nothing to worry about," said Galeano in a friendly tone. "We can't prove you did anything. We're just looking around, Wells."

"So you can go and look around somewhere else."

"You'd like us to find out who killed your grandmother, wouldn't you?" asked Palliser.

"Oh, sure, sure, I sure hope you do. But I told you where I was that night, you asked Mae and she told you, we were out at that disco all the time."

"Yes, we know you were."

"Then why are you bothering me? Go stealing my shoes! Cops! When do I get them back?"

"When we're finished with them," said Galeano. They went back to the parking lot and sat in the car and Palliser switched on the engine for the air-conditioning. "In a sort of way," said Galeano, "I see what you mean, John. Another Baby Face. A little too innocent to be true, but on the other hand—"

"Oh, I know, I know," said Palliser. "He's got no remote history of violence—only that one little count on him, and it's an honest upright family."

"What the hell is all this business about shoes?"

"I've got no idea," said Palliser. "It was Duke suggested it. He must have something in mind. Something they spotted in that apartment. But there wasn't any mention in the lab report."

"Well, I suppose they'll tell us sometime. My God, why does anybody stay in this climate?—and the way the smog's hanging on it'll likely be the middle of October before we get any relief."

"You like to start building seniority all over again, some place where it never gets over seventy degrees?"

"Is there such a place this side of heaven?" wondered Galeano.

THAT SATURDAY NIGHT turned out to be a busy one for the night watch. It was still ninety-four at eight o'clock. September was the worst month for heat in Southern California. There was a bar on Third Street held up by two men at about nine o'clock and Conway wrote the report on that. There'd be eight witnesses to come in and keep the day watch busy making statements. They got a call to a mugging before he finished the report and Schenke went out on that. The victim had managed to get to a public phone and call in, but by the time Schenke got there he was looking green and couldn't stand up, so Schenke called an ambulance. He was a man in the sixties, Clarence Anderson, and all Schenke got was that he'd been working late in his office on Wilshire, been jumped when he came back to his car in a public lot. His home address, by the I.D. on him, was West Hollywood. He passed out as the ambulance arrived, but Schenke didn't think he was too bad. Probably a mild concussion.

However, they were supposedly there to serve the citizens, so when he came back to the office to find it empty, he called Anderson's wife and broke the news to her. Piggott and Conway came back at eleven-thirty. There'd been another affluent-looking couple jumped and manhandled and robbed in the parking lot of the Shubert Theatre. "Why wasn't there a crowd if the show was just over?" asked Schenke.

"They were about the last people to come back to the lot. They'd stopped for a drink at the Sushi bar on the way. The punks got about another fifty and some more jewelry."

"Hell," said Schenke. "I wish there was just some handle to it, some way to chase them down."

"Well, there isn't," said Conway. "And they seem to be fairly rough and ready with the M.O. One of these nights they're going to tackle somebody with a weak heart and leave a corpse for us."

"And still no way to chase them down," said Piggott dryly. The phone rang and he picked it up. "Robbery-Homicide." In the next thirty seconds his mouth went tight and the usually mild-mannered, easygoing Piggott was an angry man when he put the phone down and stood up. "We'd all better ride on this one. It's a shooting and it's one of the uniformed men."

"Christ," said Conway.

"The squad man said he didn't look too good. It's the corner of Hoover and Eleventh." They went downstairs in a hurry and piled into Conway's car.

Down there, a normally busy secondary main drag, at that time of night the streets were empty of traffic and the traffic lights had stopped working. There were three squads parked in a row at the curb in front of half a block of store buildings. One of the squads had the driver's door hanging open. The uniformed men were Bill Moss and Dave Turner and they were looking grim and shaken. "It was at the appliance store," said Moss. "A break-in." There had been a dim security light left on above the door. By the streetlight at the corner they could read the sign—PURDUE'S T.V AND APPLIANCES. "All we've heard on it is, two men, and Dubois walked into it. He looked bad, Conway—a couple of slugs in the chest. The ambulance just left. A woman across the street in the apartment at the corner of Eleventh saw it and called in, and Dubois got chased over. She called again when she heard the shooting, but they were long gone when Dave and I got here."

Turner's hand was shaking as he raised the cigarette to his mouth. "We were in the same class at the Academy," he said.

"We haven't called the owner yet. The woman's in apartment Twelve-B."

"O.K." said Conway. "You get the emergency number off the door and contact the owner. We'll go talk to her."

She was waiting for them. Her name was Alice Rabinovich and she was still excited and scared but she had kept her head. She was around forty, dark with a scrawny figure in an old cotton bathrobe over a nightgown, and scuffed bedroom slippers. The apartment was at the side of the building, looking down on Hoover Street.

She said, "I couldn't sleep, it's so hot. I was tired, we had a busy day at the store, but I couldn't sleep. I went to bed, but it was no use, and I got up and sat by the window, the fan helped some. I was sitting in the dark and you can see—" she was gesturing the men into the bedroom. There was an electric fan going on a table by the open window, and a chair, and the window looked down directly to those store buildings on Hoover. The door of the appliance store would be about a hundred feet away, seen at a slightly oblique angle.

"I saw the whole thing. It's terrible about the policeman. There were two men—it was a pickup truck, they parked right in front of the store—you can see the sign from here—and one had a flashlight and the other one had a tool of some kind. There wasn't anything in the street so late—cars or people—and they broke in the door, I could see them plain, they went in and I was sure they were burglars. I was just picking up the phone to call the police, but I was still watching and they came out with a T.V. and put it in the truck and went back in, and they brought out another T.V. and went back and it was just as they came out again with another the police car came up and the policeman got out, and I could see he had his gun in his hand, and I guess he'd have told them to put their hands up or something, but he never had the chance. One of the men just shot him—bang—like that—and he fell down and I called the police back again and told them what had happened—and the men put the T.V. in the truck and drove away fast—and about five minutes later the other two police cars drove up and then the ambulance came. I hope the poor policeman isn't hurt bad—"

"So do we," said Conway. "That's fine, Mrs. Rabinovich, you've been a big help. We're lucky you were here. Could you give any description of the men?"

She said regretfully, "Oh, no, I'm afraid not. My sight is good, but they weren't that close and it was dark even with the streetlight. But it was a Ford pickup truck. It wasn't very far from the streetlight and I saw the letters plain across the front. It was light-colored—white or light blue—something like that."

"Are you sure?" asked Conway.

"Yes, I'm sure about that."

They went back across the street. By then the owner was there and he said there were three T.V.'s missing—nothing else. They told him as they'd told her to come to headquarters to make a statement in the morning. Then they went out to Cedars-Sinai to ask about Dubois.

That was about an hour and a half after the shooting, and the doctors weren't saying anything definite. He had lost a lot of blood before he was brought in.

Dubois wasn't married, but somebody had called—Turner?—and his mother was there in the waiting room down the hall in Emergency. She was a tall thin black woman with dignified regular features and she sat there quietly without crying. She looked at the Robbery-Homicide men without speaking and Conway said, "You know everybody's concerned, Mrs. Dubois. It's one of the possibilities that goes with the job."

"Do you have to tell me that?" she said in a remote voice. "I've been afraid ever since Don put on that uniform. But he always wanted to be a police officer—ever since he was a little boy. A good, honest, honorable police officer—like his father." She raised her eyes from the floor. "His father was on the force in Chicago. He got shot by a drunk when Don was five. We came out here to live with my sister and her family then.''

"Mrs. Dubois, we're sorry,'' said Schenke. There wasn't anything else to say to her.

"We'll all be praying for him,'' said Piggott.

"I did quite a lot of praying for Don's father—twenty-one years ago,'' she said quietly.

THAT WAS THE MOST IMPORTANT item on the agenda waiting for the day watch on Sunday morning. Hackett called Mendoza at home to tell him about it and Mendoza said, *"María, y José!* I hope he makes it. But we might get some leads from the pickup truck.''

"George is talking to the DMV right now.''

"I'll be in,'' said Mendoza. "I'm flying to France on Tuesday, but I'll be in *pronto.*''

"My God, you are persistent. You'll never find out a damned thing. You haven't anywhere to start looking and you know about four words of French.''

"By God, I'll have a try at it. I'll be down. Thank God they've got computers in Sacramento.''

The computers, of course, would give them some legwork—a lot of it. The computers would sort out all the Ford pickup trucks registered in L.A. County a lot more quickly than the detectives could take the individual looks at the owners, and while there wouldn't be as many pickup trucks in an urban area as in a rural one, there would be plenty. The names and addresses were still coming in by the middle of the afternoon, and they had other cases to work, and probably other calls would go down. But there was priority on this pair, who had attacked one of their own.

Dubois was still holding his own, but still unconscious.

As the names of those owners came in, the first use they made of them was to run them through the R. and I. Office. It was possible that one or both of that pair had a prior record. It was even probable, given the instant unprovoked attack on Dubois. The break-in artist seldom went armed, and whoever had fired those shots was quick and handy with a gun.

There were more pickup trucks in the county than anyone could have predicted. They did some overtime, but they hadn't finished looking through Records with their own computers by the middle of Sunday evening.

THEY ALL LANDED at the office together, a little early on Monday morning. Palliser had come in even if it was his day off. Mendoza called the hospital. Dubois had rallied a little. There was a full day's work ahead and maddeningly, just as they settled down to it, they had a call. The job was like women's work, never done, and they were always having to drop one thing and pick up another.

And this one would just pose a lot of paperwork, and you could blame it directly on the fact that at eight o'clock that morning, at the intersection of Grand and Sixth Street in downtown Los Angeles, the temperature had hit ninety-nine degrees and was rising.

The patrolman who brought the woman into the office said, "My God, it's like a battlefield. You never saw such a hell of a thing. There were five squads out and three ambulances. I don't know how many people got killed, but I saw three bodies myself. When we got her out of the car, she looked ready to throw a fit, and then all of a sudden she calmed down. But maybe you ought to get her to a doctor."

Her name was Laura Fenn and by her driver's license she was forty-four and lived in South Pasadena. She told them in a dead and dull voice that she was a librarian at the main library and asked someone to call the library and explain that she'd be late. Then she just sat and looked at the wall and Wanda Larsen tried to talk to her.

"My goodness, you never saw such a thing," said the patrolman. Miss Fenn, driving a nine-year-old Dodge without air-conditioning, had caught a red light at that corner on her way to work. A good many other people had caught it too—on both streets. The lights were stuck, both on red. After about four minutes, the horns started, tempers began to rise, and cars began to edge cautiously into any opening. There were also a good many pedestrians on both streets. The Dodge, second in line at the light on Grand, had gone roaring up onto the sidewalk, sideswiped the car first at the light, charged across the intersection where people on foot were crossing, and finally plowed into a city bus on Grand.

When Wanda finally got her to say anything, she just said, "It was too hot—just *too hot*. I had a headache and the library's air-conditioned—and there was such a jam on the freeway—and all of a sudden it was just too *much*."

When they came to sort it out, she had killed four people and injured eleven seriously and severely damaged three cars. The Dodge was totaled.

And Mendoza said exasperatedly, "Let the D.A. worry about what to call it. People!"

IT WAS IN THE MIDDLE of Monday afternoon, with a vague idea of clearing up a muddle before he left tomorrow, that he went up to Outpost Drive and talked to Joseph Alisio.

"We'll probably never know," he told Alisio. "With so many people there, it's been very difficult to check on who was where, when. It's all up in the air."

Alisio heaved a sigh. "I can appreciate that, Lieutenant. One lunatic among all those people. My God. Poor Carl. We knew he was on the way out, the first of us to go, and I don't suppose it makes any difference whether it was now or six months from now. But it's a terrible thing he had to go like that. We've all been shook up about it, but poor Randy— I never saw anybody so broken up. He's all to

pieces and Mary says he's been drinking some. Well, he was Carl's favorite and I guess it's been a little worry to him, he'd been managing Carl's affairs for him since the cancer got diagnosed last year and Carl was so sick. It was the obvious thing to do, Carl had left him everything anyway, but it's probably made a little extra work for him." He passed a hand over his bald head. "I appreciate your coming, Lieutenant. No, I suppose we'll never know what happened. The lunatic getting into the hospital some way."

A small cold finger inched up Mendoza's spine. The other boys laughed about his hunches. Mendoza's crystal ball. But Luis Rodolfo Vicente Mendoza had been a detective a long time and he knew enough to respect his hunches.

He stood at the curb on Outpost Drive and looked at the haze of smog over the city below him. He said to himself, *"Ridículo."* His imagination working overtime.

He got into the Ferrari and drove over to Glendale to that new high-rise office building.

Randy Nicolletti was at his desk in the big office, but he looked gray and ill. He had dropped some weight. Mendoza stopped beside his desk and Nicolletti looked up at him after a moment, his expression dull and vague.

"You did it, didn't you?" asked Mendoza. "I'd like to know why."

And Randy Nicolletti said in an expressionless tone, "How did you know?"

EIGHT

HE DIDN'T WANT TO TALK ABOUT IT, and what he said after some prodding was, "It was all my fault. I know that. Uncle Carl, I was his favorite, but he was always careful about money. The only times he ever got mad at me was about the gambling— I guess that's just in my nature. And he was dying up to a month ago—the doctor said he could go any time—and since he'd been so sick six months ago, he'd signed me onto his checking account, his savings account, so I could pay all the expenses—and it was all left to me anyway—it didn't matter. I got in pretty deep with a couple of fellows at a poker place in Gardena, it was over ten thousand and I was damned worried about it—one of them's kind of a tough customer. I thought it didn't matter, I paid up by cashing in one of the T-bills on his account. He hadn't been up to looking at the statements in months. And then I dropped a couple of thousand more and I paid that—and all of a sudden he got better—the doctor said, in remission and it might be three, four, six months." He was staring dully at the floor of the little interrogation room at the jail. "He was sitting up and taking notice of things again, and just a couple of days before he'd asked me to bring in all the bank statements—and the first thing he said—that Sunday when I got there—had I brought them, and I had to say I forgot about it, but I knew he'd keep on about it, and he was always at me about the gambling. He'd raise all hell when he found out. He'd call me a damn thief. The rest of the family, they don't like the gambling either and it would be one goddamn king-size mess, and I just didn't know what to do. I'd thought by then it'd be all over, and the will in probate." He passed a shaking hand over his face. "And that day, when I went back for my cigarettes, the last thing he said to me—don't forget to bring those statements the next time you come, boy. And I—and I—" He put his face in his hands.

Mendoza said to Higgins when they came out of the interrogation room, "And God knows I was the hottest poker player in town before the domesticities ruined my game, but the compulsive gambler I never was. More fatal than the drink, that. And in the end he's made even more of a king-size mess for himself than he had already."

"You and your hunches," said Higgins. "All the damned legwork we did on that, and all for nothing."

"He was ready to break, George. If I hadn't had the hunch, he'd have come in to confess within a matter of time."

THE DOCTORS were saying that Dubois would make it, but it would be a long convalescence for him. Most of the men at the Robbery-Homicide office were on that. They still had a long list of names of pickup-truck owners to process and nobody was taking any time off. Hackett had got deflected temporarily to arrange that lineup, but the witness couldn't definitely identify the suspect and they had to let him go.

On Tuesday morning, the computers in R. and I. turned up their first lead. The owner of a Ford pickup truck showed up in the records with a pedigree of armed robbery—Alfonso Barrios, last known address the same as the current registration, Maxson Place in El Monte. Landers and Galeano were alone in the office when the word came up and Galeano said, "If he's our boy, what the hell was he doing so far from home base? Don't say it, I know—freeways. And he won't have lived in El Monte all his life. Let's see if we can find him." The lab had told them yesterday that the slugs out of Dubois had been fired from a .45 Colt.

Barrios' wife told them that he worked at a garage on Rosemead Boulevard and they picked him up there, brought him in. Higgins was back in the office by then and they stood over him and asked him questions. He was a wiry dark small man in the thirties, and he snarled back at them. "I'm clean since I got out last time, I done nothing. Just because a guy got a little record, the fuzz come down on him alla time—"

Higgins said, "All right, where were you on Saturday night?"

"Last Saturday night? I was sittin' in a game of draw with four other guys. We went on late, they can tell you." He supplied names and addresses and they went to look, stashing him in jail meanwhile. The poker game, he said, had been in a private home in El Monte; and none of the other men had any police records. The wife of the householder said, "Do I know that Barrios? Sure he was here that night. These damn fool men and their cards, they went on till two in the morning and nobody got any sleep. That damn Barrios—he took nineteen bucks off Joe and I'll be short on grocery money all this week."

You won some, you lost some. They let Barrios go. It had just been a first cast.

PALLISER HAD BEEN OUT looking for one of the heist suspects up till noon on Tuesday. When he came back to the office after lunch, Lake said the lab had been calling him. "Well, all right, put them through." He sat down at his desk and picked up the phone when it rang.

Duke said, "I'd have called you right away but I know you've been busy."

"We still are."

"You do any good on that shooting yet?"

"Not yet. What do you want?"

"Well, I'd like you to come and look at something interesting. You can get a warrant and clean one up on it. Come and see."

Palliser, slightly intrigued, took the elevator up to the lab. There in that big busy office, the long room with long tables and glaring strip lighting, the microscopes and Bunsen burners and cameras in a string of smaller offices, Duke led him to a microscope at one end of a table and said, "This is from one of Wells' shoes. The right shoe of a pair of black oxfords."

Palliser peered into the microscope and asked, "So what is it? You're the technician." He had nearly forgotten Toby Wells.

Duke said, grinning, "I didn't suppose you'd be an expert on house plants, but it's another kind of offbeat little thing like that damn snapshot. Sometimes we do turn them up. It's *Beloperone guttata*."

"Come again?" said Palliser.

"To you, the common shrimp plant. We spotted it when we were taking photographs in the Coffey apartment. There was a big potted plant knocked over and in the little fight the old lady put up, somebody trampled all over it on the floor. You could see where branches and leaves had been stepped on. I thought there was an outside chance that there'd be some trace on the soles of somebody's shoes, those leaves are pretty tough and springy—and I was right. There was one whole squashed leaf stuck on the arch of the shoe where the wet earth from the pot acted like glue. It's not that common a plant, Palliser. And if you can show that your boy hasn't been near another one since the murder—"

"By God," said Palliser. "Those will be his best shoes. He had them on for the date with the girl and he probably hasn't had them on since. By God, what a damned queer little thing."

"It's the little things that trip them up," said Duke. "Little things most people don't notice."

Palliser and Galeano went to bring Toby Wells in, and they had to spell it out for him, how they knew, what the definite scientific evidence was. He didn't take it in at first, said, "How'd anybody know one little leaf from another?"

"The men at the laboratory can tell," said Galeano. "They've got ways. You were there when that plant got knocked over, you stepped on it and that tells us you were there when your grandmother was killed." Wells thought that one over for awhile.

"Why?" asked Palliser. "Why did you go there that night?" Wells just looked at the floor.

"Your own grandmother," said Galeano. "She'd been good to you. Gave you a birthday party just the week before, hadn't she, and got you out of that little trouble a couple of years ago. Why?"

Wells said, "Oh, for Gossakes. I was out of money." He didn't look up at them. "It all goes so quick—and she had money put away. She made good money out of that business. She never spent nothing on herself. She had that couple hundred bucks to hand right over—time I took those clothes and got caught. And she gives me a lousy ten bucks for my birthday. A lousy ten bucks! I was cleaned out, time I paid the bill at that disco that night. I went to see her, ask her to loan me some bread, and she let me in and then when I asked she started to talk real sharp, how I was young and foolish and ought to be careful, save some out of my salary—and I got mad. Old people just don't know how it is for young people these days—and I hit her and she fell against that plant and I started to look around for any money. I knew she had some hid away somewheres—but she came after me into the kitchen. She was yelling and calling

me names and that hammer was laying on the counter and
I—''

"And did you find any money?" asked Galeano.

"There was only ninety bucks in her purse in the closet, I
thought there'd be a lot more. I'm sorry. I never meant to
do it. Never meant to hurt her so bad. I just needed some
money to take Mae to that show she wanted to see."

Palliser picked up the phone to ask for the warrant on
him.

THE JET DECANTED MENDOZA at Orly Airport into a chilly
gray early morning. With the time difference, it was early
morning here and already autumn in northern Europe. He
was feeling tired and stale, though he'd slept on the plane.
The travel agent had got a reservation for him at the Hotel
Crillon and he picked up a cab at the airport entrance. It was
a big hotel in the middle of the city. What he could see of
Paris in the cold morning light was just another old, dirty
city. Older than his town and parts of it dirtier, with the occasional streets of new, shining office buildings, apartments. Everybody at the hotel seemed to speak English and
he was shepherded to a good-sized room with a private bath
on the top floor. He undressed, went to bed and slept for
four hours, and woke feeling more alert. He took a shower
and shaved, got dressed again, and went downstairs for a
cup of coffee at the hotel restaurant. The elegantly uniformed attendant at the main entrance called him a cab.

He had taken an unreasonable prejudice against the Sûreté and said to the cab driver, "The Préfecture de Police,"
as distinctly as possible."

The cab driver raised a thumb. "O.K., bud," he said and
let in the clutch with a jerk.

Mendoza had got traveler's checks cashed at the hotel and
let the driver pick what he wanted of the sleazy thin paper.
The building was a square grim old pile looking like an old-

fashioned military barracks, and he found out later that that
was how it had begun life. He started out talking to a uniformed man at the desk in the lobby, who spoke some
heavily accented English and presently summoned another
man in civilian clothes who spoke more fluently, introduced himself as Delahaye, prefaced with a title Mendoza
didn't catch. "I think,"said Delahaye after deliberation,
"M. L'Inspecteur Rambeau will like to speak with you,"
and he used the phone on the desk, spoke rapid French. He
took Mendoza up in a creaking elevator to the second floor,
down a long gloomy hall. At the end of it he opened a door
and bowed Mendoza in. "The American police officer, Inspecteur."

The man at the desk in the large plain office stood up.
There was a little wooden plaque upright on the front of the
desk with lettering: INSPECTEUR LAURENT RAMBEAU.
"Ah," he said. "A pleasure to meet a colleague." He offered a firm hand. "Once I have visited your country, but
not so far as California." His English was very good. He
was about Mendoza's age and size and he had a thick crop
of wiry curly black hair and a flourishing black Gallic mustache, inquisitive bright brown eyes. "Sit down and tell me
how we can help you."

Feeling warmed and welcomed, Mendoza took the chair
beside the desk and began to tell the story. Rambeau listened absorbedly, chin planted on hands and elbows on
desk, and at the end he sat up, reached to the package of
cigarettes on the desk, offered it politely, and said, "So, do
we not all know how it goes. Day by day there is nothing but
the little stupid violences, and then all of a sudden, once in
ten years, arrives something complicated and strange. This
is very interesting. I like it. I like it as a mystery. But the poor
little Juliette." Mendoza had handed over the envelope of
photographs and he shook his head over them. "A beautiful girl. One feels for the poor fiancé."

"The Sûreté gave us nothing at all. They don't know her fingerprints and I can't give you any more information on her."

"Ah," said Rambeau. "The Sûreté. These big important men of affairs, sometimes they can be a trifle arrogant."

"Yes, we have the same trouble with the FBI at times."

Rambeau laughed. "You and I, we are the same kind of policemen, I feel. I can see things to do here. We both understand the value of the spadework. There is the telephone directory, first of all. It is a pity it is such a common name—Martin—there will be thousands in greater Paris. Ours is a bigger city than yours, Mendoza. In Paris and its environs there are more than nine million people. But," he went on briskly, "there are things to do about this. We are always busy, but I feel as you do about the little Juliette, I want to know why she is dead. Now, the telephone. We will set four or five men to check all the Martins and that will be a long job. The fiancé's surname we do not know, and Paul is a common name, too. But there is this M. Trechard—Trouchard, some such name."

"Neither my wife nor I can remember exactly."

"Yes, you were tired. Why should you pay attention? But that is not so common a name, and we will look for him also. Her employer—and she said he was not so easy to work for as his uncle. The impression you had, Juliette was a superior type— An office, she said? Not perhaps only a typist?"

"I don't know your types," said Mendoza. "She was an educated, intelligent girl."

"Yes, and the telephone directory," said Rambeau, "it is not infallible. The current ones are nearly a year old, but we will try. If the Sûreté have not got her fingerprints, then neither do we. That is no good. But you know that her passport was issued in Paris and that means that she lived

here. In one of a million places. But," he lit another cigarette and beamed at Mendoza, "but, my friend, I believe we
will find out about the little Juliette, and I will tell you why.
You yourself said it. If you had not been the one to go to
look at that corpse, no one would have suspected it was not
the so nonexistent Ruth Hoffman. It is a very pretty little
comedy, this. Here there is a Hoffman—with all the plausible identification. An end and no beginning. And there we
have Juliette—a beginning and no end. If the beginning is
hidden from us. But it was not by chance that you should see
the corpse. There are many men under you in your office?"

Mendoza said wryly, "Never enough."

Rambeau laughed. "Here too. But I believe the universe
is ordered and men are not governed by chance. Me, I am a
good Catholic, which also you should be by your name—"

"Sporadically," said Mendoza with a grin.

Rambeau shook his head in smiling disapproval. "No, it
was not by chance it was you. If the devil is always active on
one side, there is the good God to combat him, and God is
the stronger. Perhaps one of the good saints intercedes here
for the little Juliette, to see she is avenged." He looked at his
watch. "Courage—we begin the spadework. I will set men
at the telephone directory, and you and I will go to luncheon at a small place where they know how to prepare the
omelette, and then you amuse yourself and go to look at
Paris while we try to solve your mystery." He stood up and
gave Mendoza a joyous smile. "And then we will find who
is this mysterious Grandpére, and why Juliette must be
murdered. My men are the good trained bloodhounds. We
will find out."

ON WEDNESDAY, Records matched up another of the
pickup owners with a pedigree, César Montano. The pedigree said armed robbery, assault with intent, burglary. He'd

been arrested and charged the last time four years ago. Hackett called Welfare and Rehab to find out if he was loose, and Montano had been on parole for six months. The address on the registration was Harris Street in City Terrace. Hackett and Glasser went to see if he was at home or at work; his P.A. officer had got him a job with a janitorial service. They found him watching television in the dirty, untidy living room of a cheap apartment, and brought him downtown. They couldn't get the time of day out of him. He just called them a string of dirty names and after that shut up. He was a big hulk of a man about thirty with a pockmarked face and quick-shifting eyes. Dealing with the stupid louts was tedious and only from long experience did they keep their tempers and use patience. They tried for an hour to get something out of him and then they left him in jail and Higgins sent out for a search warrant.

They had another heist to work now and there were indictments scheduled for next week, Myra Arvin, Toby Wells, Randy Nicolletti. Somebody would have to be in court to cover those.

When the search warrant came in, Higgins was out looking for the owner of a Ford pickup who had a record of assault, so Hackett and Glasser went to look at Montano's apartment. It should have been Hackett's day off but they were anxious to get this one cleared up if they could.

The apartment was scantily furnished, a cheap, shabby place. There was a little stock of food in the kitchen, a wardrobe full of nondescript old clothes, nothing but underwear and socks in the dresser drawers.

"Of course whoever did the shooting," said Glasser, "may have got shut of that gun, if he's halfway smart."

"But they so seldom are, Henry," said Hackett. He went back to the bedroom, leaving Glasser staring around the squalid living room, and was busy looking through the pockets of the clothes in the wardrobe when Glasser burst out laughing. "My God in heaven! Come and look at this, Art." Hackett went back to the living room. "I just happened to see it reflected in the windowpane."

The T.V. in one corner of the living room still had a tag on it, suspended from the back of the set: the manufacturer's tag, but neatly stuck across it was a little strip of gummed paper with printing on it. PURDUE'S T.V. AND APPLIANCES. Hackett burst out laughing too. "They are so seldom smart enough to add two plus two. My God, what a stupid damn thing."

They took the T.V. in as evidence, and went to talk to Montano again. He was hardly the biggest brain in the world, but even he saw that the T.V. tied him to that job and he started to talk fast. "For Jesus' sake, you're not goin' to pin that on me, shooting that damn cop— I like to had a fit when Joe shot the cop— I didn't know he had a gun on him, even. You don't pin that on me, it was Joe, I don't take no rap for him. I don't even know him so good, I just saw him around, and he needed some eating money, he says, how about we hit that place and I—it was Joe shot that cop. I tell you where to drop on him, it's Joe Vasquez, he got a pad on Fourteenth. No, for God's sake, acourse he ain't got a job, why the hell you think we was knocking off that place?"

With a feeling of warm satisfaction, Higgins and Hackett went out to collect Vasquez, and he wasn't at home, but a helpful neighbor said he spent a lot of time hanging around the pool hall a couple of blocks up and they found him there. He didn't have the gun on him but they got a search warrant and in going through his apartment found a .45 Colt, a nearly new gun, in a box on the closet shelf. They handed it over to the lab. The lab would, of course, tell them that it was the gun that had fired the slugs into Dubois. And Dubois was conscious and sitting up. Somebody would go to see him and tell him about Montano and Vasquez.

They didn't bother to talk to Vasquez right away. Wait for the ballistics report. When he heard about that and about Montano snitching on him, he might be mad enough to come out with a confession. But it wouldn't matter much. There was the nice obvious evidence on him.

HIGGINS GOT HOME EARLY. With that case broken, just the heist to work, and with all the overtime they'd been doing, they could go slack for a day or two. When he went in the back door, Mary was just taking a cake out of the oven, the kids just home from school, Laura and Steve Dwyer, Steve looking more like Bert every day. But the memory was a little faded now, in Higgins' mind, of Bert Dwyer dead on the marble floor of the bank with the bank robber's bullets in him. They were surprised to see him and Higgins said, yawning, "We cleared up that shooting, so we can all relax some."

"How did you get them?" asked Steve, interested. Higgins told him. "Well, that was a pretty stupid thing for that guy to do."

"They're never very smart, or they wouldn't be what they are. It didn't take any brains to drop on them, just the usual routine."

"Yeah, the lab's the most interesting part of the job. Say, George. The counselor let me switch from Biology One to general science. I figured that'll be more useful to me later on."

"Fine," said Higgins. Someday, about ten years from now, unless he changed his mind, Steve Dwyer was going to be up in the police lab with the other miracle-working technicians.

OF COURSE the night watch had heard about Vasquez and Montano and were pleased about it. "But you know what he'll likely get," said Piggott. "A one-to-three and parole in a year. The courts have thrown out the rule, a third-time felony draws life.''

"You never know," said Schenke. "He might get a realistic judge." But they wouldn't bet on it.

There was a call at nine-fifteen—a dead body. It had been spotted by a squad, passing in front of an empty building scheduled for demolition on Second Street. It was just a body of a man in the twenties—no I.D. or money on him. He'd been stabbed. He smelled strongly of liquor and there was a broken bottle which had held bourbon alongside the body.

"Somebody rolling the drunk," said Schenke. All they could do was send him down to the morgue. Maybe his prints would say who he'd been—maybe not.

The end of the week was usually quiet, but they had the weekend coming up. There was always the paperwork and a report had to be typed on the body. Piggott had finished that and they were sitting around talking desultorily when the desk called at ten to eleven. Conway took it and after thirty seconds said, "Jesus, all right. What's the address?" He put the phone down. "We've got a triple homicide. All we needed."

They all rode on it. It was on Thirtieth Place and Bill Moss was waiting for them at the curb in front of the squad. He said, "My God, the rate always goes up in summer, but this is the worst I've seen in a while. I mean, the baby—it just happened about half an hour or twenty minutes ago, it took me a few minutes to get here, I was back uptown on Beverly. The woman who called in lives in the front house, a Mrs. Ballard. The people in the rear house just moved in there a few days ago. She heard screams and saw a man running away. It's one goddamned mess, boys.''

Before they went to look at it they talked to Mrs. Ballard. She was an elderly fat black woman and she was shocked and scared, but she told a straight enough story.

"They were real nice young people, Rawson's their name, they just moved to California because she had the asthma and the doctors thought she'd be better here. It was her brother rented it for them, he just lives down the street a ways. They moved in on Monday. Yes, sir, I was just getting ready to go to bed when I heard the screaming, oh, Lordy God, it was awful—coming from the back house— and I looked out the window and I saw a man come running out of there. He was a tall, skinny man. No, sir, I don't know if he was black or white. He run across the yard and up the drive into the street. And I didn't hear no more screams, but I called the police, and that policeman out there he says—he says—they're all cut up and dead—''

The little frame house in the rear had been neat and clean before carnage struck. There were no dirty dishes in the kitchen. The shabby but comfortable furniture was dusted. Clothes hung tidily in the one closet. It was a small place with two meager bedrooms, a tiny living room, kitchen, bathroom and that was all. Now there was blood all over. The man, a stocky, very black man in pajamas, was on the floor of the larger bedroom, blank empty eyes fixed on the ceiling. He had been stabbed and slashed repeatedly, but by his position it didn't look as if he'd put up a fight. Possibly he'd been attacked in his sleep. The woman had tried to get away—probably while producing the screams. She was a thin young black woman in what had been a blue nylon nightgown, and she had got as far as just inside the front door when she died. They could read it. While the killer was busy with the man, she'd wakened up, screamed, tried to run, and been caught. There was more blood in the little hall, in the living room. She'd been stabbed and slashed viciously. The baby, looking to be about a year old, was still in the crib beside the double bed, and its throat had been cut.

"God," said Conway. "What have we got here, a lunatic?"

They called the lab and a mobile van came out. All the night watch could do was write the initial report. Let the day men take it from there.

"IT MUST'VE BEEN A CRAZY PERSON, that's all," said Alexander Freeman to Landers and Palliser. "That's all anybody could say. Nobody had any reason to do such a thing to Jim and Paula. It's just crazy."

They were talking to the Freemans in one side of the duplex, half a block down on Thirtieth Place from Mrs. Ballard's house, on Friday morning. The living room here was clean and neat, if shabby. The Freemans, both medium black, looked like solid citizens. Louise Freeman had been crying; now she sat listlessly on the couch, staring at her clasped hands.

"I didn't go to work," Freeman said. "I knew the police would be here and I didn't like to leave Louise. There's just no sense to it."

"You said Mr. and Mrs. Rawson had just moved to California?" asked Landers.

"That's right. They lived back in Wisconsin, that's where Louise and Jim were raised, but the winters were awful hard on Paula and they thought they'd try it out here. I even got Jim a job, a good job, same place I work, the Parks and Recreation Department. He was working for a big nursery back there so he was experienced at that kind of job, and we were so glad to find that house for them so close. It was a good deal for them, see, because they was getting it at a lower rent than usual. Jim was going to do all the yard work for part of the rent. Mrs. Ballard's been a widow a long time and she couldn't keep up the yard. It was all in a mess, and Jim had started to work on it, just since they got here. They drove in last Sunday night and moved in there Monday."

Freeman was smoking nervously. His wife started to cry again. "There's no sense to it because Jim and Paula didn't know a soul out here and nobody knew them. Not a soul. Unless it was some drunk, a crazy person, but to kill the poor baby too—"

"They hadn't even met any of our friends," she said in a thick voice. "They'd been so busy getting settled, and Jim had to start right in on that yard. He didn't need to do it all at once, but that was Jim for you—always had to be busy. And he never could stand anything in a mess, liked everything just so. We were going to have the Pattersons and the Greens over for dinner on Sunday—"

"That's so," he said, "I told Jim to leave it, I'd help him on my day off. That place had been let go, weeds a mile high and there was even one of those old incinerators there from before the city stopped people using them. Jim said he could make a real nice barbecue out of it. And I'd have been glad to help him but I'm not off until Saturday, he hired some fella to help him cut the weeds. That's a big yard. He'd been busy at it all yesterday. A fool for work. He was starting on the P. and R. job on Monday, see."

"They didn't have any family or friends here, except you?" said Palliser.

"That's right. Look, even if there could have been any reason—only there couldn't be a reason for *that*—but you know what I mean, any reason for anybody to have a grudge on them—and Jim and Paula were both easygoing people, didn't get across anybody anytime—where was the time for it to happen? They just got here! They hadn't hardly been out of the house since Monday. Louise and Paula went to the market on Monday—"

"And the laundromat," she said. "That was all. We didn't talk to anybody."

"And Jim was getting things put away in the house and then working in the yard. I don't suppose they'd talked to anybody since they got here, except us and Mrs. Ballard and, oh, that guy he hired to help in the yard."

"Rawson hired him? It's not his yard," said Palliser.

"No, but it was in a mess. Jim said one good cleanup and it'd be easier for him to keep up without so much work."

"Where did he hire the man?"

"Drugstore down at the corner. There's a bulletin board, people put up ads. But it was a crazy man, or a drunk. I haven't taken it in yet—all of them gone—like that. Jim and Paula—they were the best—and such a cute baby. He was named for Jim." Freeman was shaking his head blindly. "Just no sense. Nobody here even knew them, to want to do such a thing—"

Landers looked at Palliser. Often there wasn't much sense in the violent crimes, but there seemed to be less in this one than most. They walked up the street and talked to Mrs. Ballard, but she knew even less to tell them, except to repeat that she'd seen the man running away. A tall, skinny man. She didn't know what color.

"There's nowhere to start looking," said Landers. "The house wasn't robbed. There was forty dollars in his wallet and thirty in her handbag."

"The lunatic or the drunk," said Palliser, rubbing his nose. "There may be prints."

"And even if there are, they might not be in Records."

"Well, time will tell. I don't see that there's much we can do on it until we see the lab report, and the autopsies should tell us something about the knife."

"For whatever it's worth," said Landers pessimistically.

HACKETT WAS JUST starting out to lunch with Higgins on Saturday when a man came into the office past Rory Farrell at the switchboard. "The desk man downstairs said to come up here." He was a pudgy middle-aged man with thinning red hair and a bulldog jaw. "With this. You're welcome to it.'' He held out a small imitation leather case, the kind made to hold a man's shaving tackle.

"What's this?"

"Well, I wouldn't know," said the man. "But I thought the cops had better see it. Sure as hell I thought so. My name's O'Hara, and I drive a cab for Yellow."

"Yes, Mr. O'Hara. Come in and sit down. What's this all about?"

In the communal office, O'Hara put the case down gingerly on Hackett's desk. "I don't want one damn thing to do with it. So I tell you. I carried five fares since I come on duty at eight. This is the hell of a town for cabs. Everybody and his brother got cars, see. And when I dropped the latest fare it was an old lady and I got out to help her up on the curb and I see that thing. Somebody's left it in the back seat, and she says it's not hers. So I don't know who it belongs to. One of the other fares."

"Yes." Hackett offered him a cigarette.

"So naturally I looked to see if it's unlocked, if there's maybe some I.D. in it to say who left it, see, and it was. And, Jesus, then I didn't want to know who owns it. You open it and look, just look."

Hackett pulled the case in front of him. It was the kind that had a zipper all around three sides and he ran it around and the case gaped open.

There were two things in it. The first was a bunched-up bath towel. It had originally been white, but it was now liberally stained with great rusty smears of long-dried blood. Something showed at the loose end of the bunch. Hackett lifted out the towel and from its folds a knife fell with a little clatter onto the desk. It was an ordinary kitchen knife with a blade about nine inches long and an inch wide, and it was deeply stained with the same rusty brown dried blood, both blade and handle.

"For God's sake," said Higgins, looking over his shoulder.

The other thing in the case was a worn imitation leather billfold. Any experienced detective was trained to be careful about disturbing possible latent fingerprints, but there were times when you had to take the risk. Hackett upended the case, the billfold fell out and he eased it open to lie flat with his pen. The first little plastic slot held a driver's license and it had been issued to Mabel Carter, forty-six, brown hair and blue eyes, five two, one hundred and ten pounds. The address was Portland Street.

"Now I will be good and goddamned," said Hackett in naked astonishment. He sat back and stared up at Higgins. "That hooker who got cut up by a john. There was nothing on it. I shoved it in Pending myself."

"That's damn funny all right. Do you have any idea which of those fares might have left this?" Higgins asked O'Hara.

"Well, I have. And if he did I don't want to lay eyes on him again. I got to thinking after I saw that damn thing. Two of the other fares were female and I got a sort of idea it's got to have been the one with the luggage. I think he had a little case like that in his hand when he got in the cab. That was the fare about ten o'clock. I picked him up at the Biltmore and took him to the Holiday Inn on Figueroa."

"I will be goddamned," said Hackett again. "That was dead. Well, thanks very much, O'Hara."

"You know who it is? He's done a murder by all that. Well, you're welcome to it," said O'Hara. "Me, I never could stand the sight of blood."

There wasn't that much urgency about it, surprising and interesting as it might be. They went out and had lunch. They got to the Holiday Inn at about one-thirty and Hackett told the desk clerk they were looking for a man who had checked in about ten this morning. The clerk shied nervously at the badge.

"I hope there won't be any trouble, we run a quiet place here." He looked at the registration book. "We've only had one guest register this morning. Dr. Walter Thomas, from Indianapolis. He's in room eighteen."

"Thanks very much," said Hackett. They rode up in the elevator, walked down the carpeted hall. "What the hell can this be, anyway?" He had the dressing case in one hand.

The door of room 18 opened promptly to a knock and they faced a large round man in an elegant silk dressing gown. He looked about fifty. He had a dough-colored face with a small prissy mouth.

"Dr. Thomas?" said Hackett. "By any chance does this belong to you?" Pending a look at this funny thing, they had restored the contents to the case.

The man seized the case, unzipped it, looked inside and said, "Dear me, yes I am most obliged to you for returning it. Most obliged." He gave them an open, friendly smile. "You see I always like to keep the souvenirs of the bad ones. You may call it a little foible of mine. I only bother to kill the bad ones. The others are not so important. I'm very glad to have this returned to me, gentlemen."

MENDOZA WAS NOT a sightseer by nature, and he was not particularly interested in Paris. As far as he could see it was just another city, as sprawled out into suburbs as his own city. He had dutifully, if uninterestedly, been to the Eiffel Tower.

This morning he had gone to Rambeau's office, but Rambeau was out, the man at the switchboard told him in rudimentary English, on a new homicide. What Rambeau called the spadework was still going on, he supposed. He wandered up the streets from the big Prefecture of Police building and presently came to a large public park. An el-

derly woman at a tobacconist shop had pressed a guide-
book on him yesterday and he consulted it now to find that
he was in the Jardin des Tuileries, and the imposing building beyond the lawns and flowers and the octagonal pool
would be the Louvre. He sat down on a bench by the pool.
Two excited little boys in knee pants were sailing miniature
boats on the pool. He hadn't any urge to go into the Louvre,
look at paintings and objects of art.

There was a little girl sitting on the grass, watched over by
a woman on the bench opposite his. She was a pretty little
girl with dark hair, about six. She reminded Mendoza of
Terry. He smiled at her and she smiled back shyly. He supposed he ought to go and have some lunch.

NINE

BOTH HACKETT AND HIGGINS had had a number of varied experiences in their combined years on the L.A.P.D., but Dr. Thomas was something new to them. He agreed quite amiably to accompany them to meet a friend and they waited while he dressed in a new gray suit, clean white shirt and tie. They took him straight out to the psychiatric ward at Cedars-Sinai and left him there, and went back to look at the hotel room. There was a suitcase full of nearly new clothes and in one of the side pockets was nearly seventy thousand dollars in cash. They also found a few of his other souvenirs, bloodstained knives and four other wallets with female I.D.'s in them, all the addresses in New Jersey.

"This is the damndest thing I ever remember," said Hackett. Somebody in the lab went out and took his prints and he wasn't in their records, so they wired them to the Feds and NCIC. Just before six o'clock they got a teletype back from NCIC. The prints belonged to Richard Conroy who was an escapee from a state mental asylum in New Jersey. He had been committed, further information added later, for twenty-five years and was known to be homicidal. Prior to the commitment, he had raped eleven women and murdered five. He had escaped five months ago and New Jersey was looking for him hard. There was evidence that since he had got out, he had raped three more women and was thought to be responsible for the murder of a prostitute in Newark. One of the rape victims had had nearly ninety thousand dollars in cash hidden in the house and he had walked away with it.

Palliser said, "Good God. The things we see."

Hackett fired off a teletype to the New Jersey State Police. On Saturday morning, a Captain Runyon called him. "Thank God you picked up that nut. We've had visions of him leaving a trail of bodies all over the state. I wonder how in hell he ended up in California, he's never been out of the East as far as we know. But of course he had all that cash. I swear to God, I sometimes wonder who is sane and who isn't. The idea of keeping that much cash loose in a box on a closet shelf—my God in heaven."

Hackett said, "People will do it. Well, he's tucked away safe. I suppose you want him back?"

Runyon said, "It's a goddamn nuisance. But, yes, we'll have to send somebody out to fetch him. How did you drop on him, by the way?" When he heard, he laughed. "We do sometimes get the breaks, don't we? Well, a lot of females can sleep easier tonight. There's been a little wave of terror around the southern part of the state where the asylum is. I'll get back to you and let you know who'll be out to get him."

"Any time," said Hackett.

It was still hot but not as bad as the last few weeks and by the middle of October it would probably slack off. The night watch had left them another heist and everybody seemed to be out on something except Palliser who was on the phone. After a minute he put it down and said, "Just trying to prod the lab on this Rawson thing. They didn't pick up any good latents in that place except the victim's. That's got to be something else insane. Like your fruitcake. The drunk running amuck, something like that."

"It sounds that way. And another one without a handle, if there's no lab evidence. God, I'll be glad when we get into fall and it cools off. This has been a rough summer. I wonder how Luis is doing in Paris. Damn it, there must be some record of that girl there. But just how to find it—"

Palliser said, "I just hope he's not getting high blood pressure arguing with the Sûreté." Landers came in with another heist suspect and he went to sit in on the questioning.

Higgins and Galeano had prodded at Vasquez some more yesterday but he wasn't about to give them a confession and it didn't matter.

There were no five possible heist suspects they were looking for. The tedious legwork was always there to be done. When Hackett came back from lunch, Lake greeted him with some relief. "I was afraid I wouldn't see any of you the rest of the day. Something new's gone down, half an hour ago. A couple of bodies on Allesandro Street."

"Oh, hell," said Hackett. "More paperwork." Galeano came in just then so they went to look at it together. It was a small apartment in an old building on that narrow street and there were two bodies—a rather pretty young blond woman in the mid-twenties and a little girl about four. Patrolman Zimmerman said, "Where the hell have you been? I called in forty minutes ago when I got sent up here. I didn't know what to do with the woman. She's sitting in the squad still crying. Well, the girl was her daughter. She found them about an hour ago." Even Zimmerman, taking a casual look at the scene, had read it as faked. "I had to turn the gas off. There wasn't much built up in here, but I figured it was safer. These old windows are so loose, there wasn't much gas in here at all, just enough smell so you'd notice it. It was the oven turned on and the pilot light off, but it could be there was a clogged line."

Galeano said, "Hell, you touched the knob."

"Well, I tried to be careful, sir. I'm sorry about any prints, but I thought it'd be safer."

The girl was on the living-room floor, on her side in front of the couch. She was wearing a white sundress and thong sandals. Hackett squatted down and looked at her. There was a dark bruise on one side of her jaw. She'd been alive when she got that or it wouldn't have showed. He felt carefully through the disheveled blond hair and said to Galeano, "She's had the hell of a crack on the skull here—just back of the temple. Feels as if the bone's caved in."

Galeano said, "Anyway, neither of them died of the gas." The bodies were the wrong color for that. Victims of gas poisoning showed bright pink skin. The little girl was in a chair in the living room, lying across one arm of the chair, her head twisted at an odd angle to her shoulders. She had on a skimpy playsuit and thong sandals.

"I'd have an educated guess her neck is broken," said Galeano.

"Yes," said Hackett. "Somebody trying to set up the fake suicide, Nick, and a damned crude one. You'd think any fool would know the autopsies would show it up. We'd better talk to this woman, find out who they were."

She was sitting in the back of the squad and she had stopped crying now. Galeano got into the backseat with her and Hackett into the front. She was a woman probably in the forties, plain-faced with greying brown hair. Her name was Ena Schwartz. She said the bodies were her daughter Gloria and Gloria's little girl, Joan. Gloria Pratt. She said, "Gloria'd never kill herself. That's just impossible. And besides, there wasn't hardly any gas— I'd never believe that, and she'd sure never want to kill Joan. They'd just moved in here, got settled, and had everything arranged and it was going to work out good— I was so glad when she left that man, he's a no-good drunken bum. I tried to tell her when she married him, but she was only eighteen and you can't talk to a girl in love. She found out—she put up with him too long, but she finally had the sense to leave him, and the divorce just got final. She was going to get alimony and support for Joan—not much, but with the job she could make it all right. She'd just got the job, going to start Monday, at a drugstore up on Vermont, and this place was handy to me. I'm just over on Rowena. She was going to drive Joan over to me every morning—"

"What's her husband's name?" asked Galeano.

"Neil Pratt. He's a no-good bum. He never supported her and he was mad when she had the baby."

"Do you know where he lives?" asked Hackett.

"They had an apartment on Fountain, I don't know if he still lives there. Why? Please, can I go home now? This has been an awful shock to me, I want to call my sister. Oh, I'm thankful my husband's dead, and that's a terrible thing to say, but this would have broke his heart, he loved Gloria so much. We tried to stop her marrying that guy—but Gloria'd never kill herself and the baby, she'd got over that man. She was going to have a better life. Everything was all arranged—"

"Are you all right to drive yourself home, Mrs. Schwartz?" asked Galeano.

"Yes, I'm all right. Thank you." She got out of the squad and walked down to an old Chevy at the curb.

Hackett said, "Let's hope there'll be some lab evidence. But it looks open and shut, Nick. Unless people have got more complicated since the last time I noticed."

"We can poke around here a little," said Galeano. "See who's home."

The apartment was on the second floor and there was a manager on the premises, in a downstairs front apartment. There were four apartments down and four up. And on a hot Sunday, only five people were at home. Four of them said they'd been watching T.V. or reading, didn't know if anybody had come visiting other tenants. But the manager, a sharp-eyed elderly woman named Potts, said, "Why, yes. I noticed a man come in about nine this morning, I'd just stepped out to get the paper—the boy comes by about then. What's this about that girl killing herself? I never had any police here before, any trouble like this. No, he was a stranger to me.''

"Could you describe him, Mrs. Potts?" asked Galeano.

She considered. ''I guess he was about thirty, dark hair, I didn't take much notice. Well, I might know him again.''

They'd let Zimmerman go back on tour. Hackett had called the lab and a man was busy in the apartment. ''You want to bet?'' asked Galeano sleepily.

''No bets,'' said Hackett. Mrs. Schwartz had given them the address on Fountain. They drove up there and found Neil Pratt blearily watching T.V. and drinking straight Scotch. He was more than half drunk and they couldn't question him like that, so they took him down to the jail and left him there. They could hold him twenty-four hours without a warrant.

RAMBEAU CALLED MENDOZA at the hotel just as he was finishing breakfast. ''It marches, my friend. On Juliette, no—the number of Martins in the Paris directory is formidable. But we have found the employer. His name is Trennard, M. Pierre Trennard. And you and I are now going to talk to him. I will call for you in fifteen minutes.''

''My God, I'd begun to think you'd never come up with anything. I'll be waiting.''

''Some of my men have the little imagination. They looked for similar names and M. Trennard was turned up ten minutes ago. It is an address on the Boul' St. Germain.''

Mendoza collected his hat and was waiting in front of the hotel when Rambeau drove up in a middle-aged Renault. ''Do you know what the business is?''

''We will discover.'' When Rambeau located the address he said, ''There,'' and pointed. It was an old four-story building with a modest sign over the entrance, BEAUMONT FOURNIER ET CIE. ''This is a district for publishers. This will be one of them if I guess right." He parked the car in a public lot across the street and in the small lobby of the building, a blond receptionist answered his questions, regarding them incuriously. There was an elevator and Rambeau pressed the button for the top floor. There, in a carpeted hallway, three doors faced them. The one opposite the elevator bore the lettered name PIERRE TRENNARD and Rambeau opened it on a square little office with windows facing the street, a desk, a covered typewriter on a lower typing desk, a desk chair, another upholstered chair. A man came out of an inner office and asked questions in staccato French, and Rambeau answered him. The man looked at Mendoza with faint interest. He was a tall dark man foppishly dressed in a dark business suit, white shirt, and rather flamboyant tie. He said in English, "Yes, I speak the English very well. You are police? The man who telephoned to ask if I know Juliette Martin?"

"This is an American police officer, monsieur, Mr. Mendoza, and he has no French so I ask you to speak in English. Juliette Martin, she is in your employ? I will ask you to look at these photographs."

Trennard looked and said, "This is Juliette, my secretary, yes. But these, they do not look— Why do you ask?"

"She is dead, M. Trennard. Murdered."

He was startled. "But this is a tragedy you tell me! She is only a young woman. In America? She was going to America—it was most inconvenient to me. No doubt she was due to take a holiday, but it was impossible to find a temporary replacement meanwhile. She was to return on the first of the month. This is very sad news, gentlemen. You had better come into my office." It was an expensively furnished office with upholstered chairs, a large mahogany desk. He sat at the desk and indicated chairs. He said formally, "I am very desolated to hear this. Mlle. Martin had been with us for five years and was a most excellent secretary. She was

useful to me, you understand, because she spoke English
and German and we have branch offices in both countries.
But I can tell you very little about her personally. You see, I
have been in the Paris office only eight months. My uncle,
M. Fournier, was the head of the firm until then and Miss
Martin was his secretary. It put everything wrong when he
died suddenly last February,'' and he gestured. ''There are
no other partners. All the staff here is experienced and capable, the business runs itself in a way, but since I am now
in sole charge— I was in our London office— I mean to
strike out on new lines. My uncle was an old man and had
not changed his business methods in many years. You understand me, I do not criticize—'' he gave a vast, Gallic
shrug ''—We have a very profitable business, we publish the
textbooks, art works, reprints of the classics, all very well no
doubt—the learned, scientific works on the archaeology,
history, travel—but one must modernize any business, and
I intend to try a line of fiction.''

Rambeau said, ''Come back to Miss Martin, monsieur.''

''But I am telling you I know nothing about the girl personally! Very likely my uncle did, I believe he had known
her family, had taken her on here for some such reason.
That is only an impression, I really do not know. He was a
bachelor, there is no family left. Miss Martin was merely my
secretary, I do not know her friends or her interests outside
the office. I am very sorry to hear that she is dead, but—''
He flung out his hands.

''You can supply us with her home address?''

''That, yes. It will be in our records.'' He picked up a
phone and issued a rapid order. ''There are, I think, some
thirty employees in this office, but I do not think any of
them would have known Miss Martin, except casually. The
readers, the editors, their secretaries, the stenographers, they
are all on the floors below and she would have no occasion
to go there. But her address we can supply.'' A moment later

a slim dark girl came in and gave him a slip of paper which he presented formally to Rambeau.

Rambeau glanced at it. "Ah, yes. This *arrondissement*—convenient to the office. I thank you." They exchanged bows.

Mendoza stood by impatiently while Rambeau talked to the employees on the next floors down in a succession of offices large and small, occasionally translating the answers briefly. When he led Mendoza back to the Renault, he lit both their cigarettes and said, "It is unsatisfactory, but I can see how it comes about. None of these people knew her personally. She is simply the secretary to the head of the firm. These women who read the manuscripts, they are all older women, and Juliette would have no contact with that office, with the editors, except now and then. The editors keep a different lunch hour, she did not go out until one o'clock. Even if they all frequented the same café, you see— they all knew her and liked her, but none of them know where she lived or that she was affianced. Or, of course, what the fiancé's name is. But her apartment will tell us more." He started the engine with a flourish. "If there is a *concierge* in the building—"

But it proved to be one of the new high-rise apartment buildings with no manager living there. Rambeau swore in French at length. "It is more delay. But we will still proceed." He took Mendoza back to his office. Mendoza had been interested to see that that office was laid out on the general lines of his own, a much larger one beyond, housing a number of desks where men typed reports, questioned witnesses. Rambeau issued peremptory orders to the man nearest the door. "It will not take long to find out," he said to Mendoza, and within twenty minutes was looking at a sheet of paper with a name and address on it. "So. The building is maintained by what you would call a management corporation. They oversee many such buildings, apartments and offices, for the owners. They will know some answers.''

Suddenly he erupted into a whirlwind of energy. He bundled Mendoza back to the car, to another tall building down anonymous streets, finally into the office of a small man in a sharply tailored suit. They went on talking with many gestures for some time and the small man brought manila-covered files from a row of file cases in a larger office. At last he went away and was gone for some minutes.

Rambeau said, "So we progress. He has gone to get us the key. And it was something I should have foreseen. Rents in Paris are very high now, and often girls like Juliette, they share an apartment with another, two other girls. That has happened here. Only the one girl officially leases the apartment, you see. Up to four months ago, that apartment was leased under the name of Claire Ducasse. Since then, the checks for the rent are signed by Juliette. The lease is to end in December. Who knows what happened?—perhaps this Ducasse has lost her job or gets married or has a little argument with Juliette. But of course the address and phone number will be in her name in the directory. Never mind. We have got there in the end.''

The small man came back and handed him a key and they exchanged formal bows. Rambeau drove rapidly back to the apartment building. Juliette Martin's apartment was on the fourth floor, and the door opened into a pleasant living room with upholstered couch and chairs, a lady's writing desk with a fold-down lid, a small T.V. in one corner, all very neat and clean. There was one bedroom with twin beds, a bureau, a chest of drawers, a lamp table between the beds. Clothes hung in the closet. A metal stand held shoes on the floor. Rambeau went back to the living room and made straight for the desk while Mendoza began to search drawers in the bedroom.

Fifteen minutes later, Rambeau said, "There is something stranger than we had thought here, my friend. There is no correspondence at all in the desk. No address book. No list of phone numbers beside the telephone, and it is across the room from the desk, it would only be natural— Me, I am a bachelor, but that is not to say I know nothing about women. Always they keep the love letters, even the little notes, the letters from friends. They keep so much!—but aside from this there should be her bankbook, the canceled checks—she is a businesslike young woman, she would keep perhaps a book of accounts—and there should be receipts for the rent."

Mendoza stood in the middle of the living room, rocking a little heel to toe, his eyes vacant. He said, "There's nothing in the bedroom *¡Media vuelta!* But, *pues sí*. They had to have her keys. That made the delay. That and maybe something else. Saturday to Tuesday."

"What are you saying?"

"They had to get her keys to get in here. I don't know if she'd have packed her address book, planning to be gone only three weeks or a month—the people she might send postcards to, she'd have known their addresses. The fiancé, friends. Our anonymous X's would have known her address from the letters to Grandfather, but they needed the keys. They got those as soon as she arrived. That autopsy report—yes, it's on the cards she was kept on enough sedatives to be docile all that while—Saturday to Tuesday—and somebody came over here to clear out the apartment. The address book, if it was here, everything personal. I think she'd have kept Grandfather's letters, you know. So that even if the police ever got this far, there'd be no definite connection." He focused on Rambeau. "Does it strike you that this place is a little too clean? It hasn't been occupied for nearly a month. There ought to be more dust."

"In the name of seven devils!" said Rambeau. "To remove all the fingerprints? That is not so easy to do."

"No," said Mendoza. "Maybe that was just somebody trying to be extra thorough. And Trennard identified the photographs, but that isn't quite the same as identifying the body. And such a businesslike, ambitious fellow, apparently he hadn't got an eye for a pretty girl, it could be argued that he couldn't be sure. Do you know what it adds up to, Rambeau? I don't think they ever expected anybody to get this far. But just in case, they made a clean sweep."

"Sacrée Mère," said Rambeau. He brought out a cigarette and then put it away again. He said, "If there is anything for the scientists to find—but now I will say something also. *Grandpère.* He becomes an obsession with me as with you. But if you are right, something else emerges, and that is—money. All of this—what we deduce—has cost someone a respectable amount of money. The bribing of the witnesses to the Hoffman business, and now a flight to Paris—"

"Yes, and it's another dead end," said Mendoza. "Where do we go from here?"

Rambeau said violently, "By the good God in heaven, we will go on from here! This animal, he insults me with his little cleverness. We will scour France for this Claire Ducasse— I will bring the technicians here, and somewhere there will be Juliette's fingerprints. We will inquire at all the shops and businesses within half a mile of here and that office—she must have purchased food, clothing, necessities at local places, and she will have gone to shops with her friends—somewhere she will be known and perhaps the friends remembered. There are the banks—we will find where she kept an account, examine the records. My friend, there must be something to lead us on."

"I wonder," said Mendoza.

PALLISER AND LANDERS walked down Jefferson Boulevard toward Thirtieth Street. The nearest parking slot had been a block away. Landers said, "This is a damned waste of time."

"Probably," agreed Palliser. They went into the drugstore on the corner. It was a dingy old place with miscellaneous merchandise on two long counters. No customers were in at the moment, and there was a man sitting on a high stool behind the pharmacy counter at the rear of the store, bent over a ledger. Palliser said, "There it is." Just inside the front door on the wall was a cork bulletin board and there were several little handwritten signs thumbtacked to it. FREE KITTENS, and a phone number. GOOD TRANSPORTATION CAR $ 300. SEWING MACHINE FOR SALE—BABYSITTING— "Freeman remembered the fellow's name was Len. I just thought we could have a look at him."

At the bottom of the board, there was a little card attached with one thumbtack to the cork. In neat ballpoint print it said, *Len, any hand work,* with a phone number. Palliser looked at it, took it down, and walked down the length of the store. The man on the stool looked up inquiringly. He was a middle-aged black man in a pharmacist's white smock. "Do you know anything about this fellow?" asked Palliser, showing the card.

"Oh, sure. I wrote that for him, I don't think he can read and write, he's kind of simple. He comes in here on errands for his mother sometimes and she always sends a note, says what she wants. I guess he could do any kind of work like cleaning or yard work—he's big enough."

"Do you know what his last name is—where he lives?"

"Sure. She writes me checks sometimes. Up on Twenty-ninth, their name is Williams. She's Martha Williams. The apartment on the corner."

They left the car where it was and walked the block up there. It was another ancient apartment building. The

mailbox said that the Williamses lived in 4-A at the rear
There wasn't any bell. Landers knocked on the door. After
a dragging minute it was opened by a tall thin black man
with a vacant face and dull eyes. Palliser asked, ''Did you
do some work for a fellow named Rawson last Friday, on
Thirtieth Street?''

Before he answered, they realized that he was drunk.

Beyond him they could see a bare, untidy living room. A
T.V. was on with the volume turned down and there were a
couple of empty bottles on the floor in front of it. He was
nearly falling-down drunk and he certainly didn't look too
bright. He said, ''Huh?'' And Palliser hesitated. There
wasn't anything to be got out of him. And then Williams
said in a thick, slurred voice. ''Tha' fella—yeah—yeah—
guess I show him! Tha' damn cheapskate dude.'' He hic-
cuped and clutched the door for support. ''Him inshult a
guy, give me ten lousy dirty bucks for all tha' damn work—
I cut 'em up good, I did!'' He staggered against the door
and slid down to the floor and passed out.

Landers said to Palliser, ''For God's sake, are you starting to have hunches like the boss? My God. And of course
it's not an admissible confession, but—''

''Three people dead, like that,'' said Palliser. ''It never
crossed my mind, Tom. I just wanted to ask if Rawson had
talked to anybody else that day.'' They looked at the long
limp body on the dirty floor and they felt a little tired. This
gave them that much more to do. ''Get the lab out here
looking for the knife. Get a warrant. Talk to him when he's
sobered up. Talk to the mother.'' And he'd probably be
certified as unsuitable for trial and wind up in the asylum at
Atascadero. They were always glad to clear one away, but
they couldn't claim any credit for this one. And whatever
happened to Len Williams, it wasn't going to bring three
people back to life.

HACKETT WAS TYPING the initial report on Gloria Pratt when his phone rang and he picked it up. "Robbery-Homicide, Sergeant Hackett."

"Oh, Art," said Alison's voice at the other end. "You aren't hypnotizing people now, are you?"

Hackett had never hypnotized anybody in his life, in any sense of the word, but he answered the sense of the question equally. "Not since the court threw it out as admissible evidence. Why? We never used it here as far as I remember. It can be useful in getting people to recall plate numbers and so on, but I suppose the court figured it's a little too close to black magic."

"Well, I thought maybe somebody down there could put me in touch with a good hypnotist—one the police had used. Luis called last night and he's hit another dead end. This French detective who's been helping him still thinks they can find something, but Luis doesn't—and I know that girl said something else, and I just can't remember, and I thought maybe a hypnotist might get it out of me."

Hackett massaged his jaw. "Well, somebody at the lab will probably know. I can find out for you."

"Find out now, Art, will you? If there's anything buried in my subconscious mind I'd like to get it for Luis."

"I'll call around and get back to you," said Hackett.

MAIRÍ MAC TAGGART said in a cross voice, "I'm not liking this at all, my girl. It's a verra dangerous thing to do, letting a doctor or anybody at all go poking around at your brain."

"Don't be silly," said Alison. "Thousands of people are hypnotized every day. I just hope I'm a good subject."

"And suppose you come home all changed around like in your brain, what would I say to the man?—him finding maybe you've forgot who you are at all."

Alison said briskly, "Don't fuss, Mairí. Nothing like that's going to happen. But I don't know how long it might take, and this Dr. Cargill's way out in Westwood. I'll be home as soon as I can."

Mairí said gloomily, "And I only hope it'll be with your brain in one piece, *achara*."

HACKETT GOT HOME late. It was starting to cool off the last couple of days, had only gone to eighty today, and please God they had seen nearly the last of this summer. The ridiculous huge mongrel Laddie was chasing around the backyard with Mark and Sheila. They all came running to greet him and Laddie nearly knocked him over. He went into the kitchen and kissed Angel. "I suppose the freeway was murder," she said.

"I stayed overtime to finish a report. Alison went to be hypnotized this afternoon, did she tell you about it?"

"For heaven's sake, what for?"

"Try to trigger her memory about that girl." Hackett yawned. "I am bushed. I think I'll have a drink. But at least we've cleaned up those two homicides."

HE AND GALEANO had gone over to the jail to talk to Neil Pratt when it could be presumed that he was sobered up. Unless they got anything definite out of him they couldn't hold him any longer.

But Pratt was another stupid lout, which they could have deduced from that clumsily faked suicide. He was surprised and aggrieved that they'd seen through it. When they explained how they knew, it passed straight over his head. "I thought everybody'd think she did it herself," he said naïvely. "It was the way I set it up to look." After he had been seen by that sharp-eyed manager, who would probably recognize him, and batted them on the head with some weapon before turning on the gas—and leaving the bedroom window wide open.

"Why did you want to set it up?" asked Galeano.

"Goddamn it," said Pratt, still annoyed. "Everybody should've thought she'd done it herself. Well, goddamn it, I couldn't afford to give her all that money! That goddamn judge said a hundred and fifty a month and I couldn't afford it no ways. I don't know why she had to have that damn kid in the first place. I need all the money I make to live on. Goddamn it, I still don't see how anybody knew she didn't do it herself!"

MENDOZA WAS IN THE MIDST of a graphic dream. He dreamed that Laurent Rambeau had found Grandfather for him and they were questioning him in the first interrogation room down the hall at the Robbery-Homicide office at Parker Center, which seemed quite logical to the dreaming mind. Grandfather looked exactly like the picture of Fagin in the illustrated Dickens Mendoza had read in high school. He was small and hunched, with a scraggly white beard and beady little crafty eyes. Rambeau was thundering at him, "You villain, what have you done to the little Juliette?" And Grandfather leered at them and said solemnly, "You will never prove it. We have buried her in a filing case at the main library." This struck Mendoza as the most fiendish method of homicide he had ever heard of and he was recoiling from Grandfather in loathing and disgust when he became aware that there was some intrusive extraneous sound.

He swam up from the depths of sleep and heard the telephone ringing. After a moment he was enough awake to sit up and grope for the switch on the bedside lamp. The phone went on ringing. He picked it up and answered it.

"Oh, Luis, thank goodness you're there, I thought you were out, they've been ringing you for ages—"

"*Qué es esto?* What's wrong?—the twins, the baby—"

"Nothing's wrong, why should there be? I knew you'd want to hear—"

"It's the middle of the night here, *cariña,* and I was sound asleep."

Alison laughed. "Good Lord, I am sorry, Luis, the time difference went right out of my mind—and I suppose Mairí would say it's all the poking around. But listen, I saw this Dr. Cargill, and he hypnotized me, he says I'm a pretty good subject, I went under right away. And he had a tape going and he got it out of me—what the Martin girl said that I couldn't remember. It was there in my subconscious mind."

"*Maravilloso.* And what was it?" He groped for cigarettes on the table.

"Well, it was just after I'd asked her if she lived in Paris that I went to sleep. But my mind took in what she said. She said she had lived in Paris for five years since she worked for Mr. Fournier. But before that, they had always lived at Evreux because her father was attached to the museum there. That was all I came out with. But, Luis, it could help, couldn't it? If you can trace her parents, there'll be other people—"

"It could help one hell of a lot, *mi vida,*" said Mendoza. "It was a brainstorm. *Muchas gracias.* Everything all right there?"

"The twins have discovered that first grade isn't as much fun as they'd expected. That old Sister Grace is awful strict. And El Señor caught a toad and was sick. Everything else is fine."

"*Muy Bien.* Keep your fingers crossed, *querida.* This might mean a big break."

"EVREUX!" said Rambeau. "The museum!" He smote himself on the forehead. "Le Musée de l'Archeologie et de l'Histoire Naturelle. And Maman and Papa died only six months ago. Now, indeed we will march! *Allons!*''

He drove out of Paris at a rate to frighten Mendoza, who didn't like being driven. It was not far out of the city, and Rambeau seemed to know his way. He braked outside an old stone building with several wings, bustled Mendoza in and demanded the director. Within five minutes they were talking to an alert-looking elderly man with a fringe of white hair, Professor Rigaud. ''I ask you to speak in English if it is possible, for the benefit of my colleague.''

Rigaud's English was hesitant, but adequate. Indeed he had known Dr. André Martin and his wife, Dr. Martin had been with the museum for nearly thirty years, he was a most distinguished Egyptologist. It had been a great tragedy when they were killed by the drunken motorist. Indeed he had met the daughter—a charming girl and quite brilliant. He did not mingle a great deal in social circles, and the Martins had been younger. Perhaps their closest friends had been the Boyers, Édouard and Léonie Boyer. Dr. Boyer was absent on a field trip in Egypt but he could direct them to the house.

It was a pleasant little stone house with a walled garden where a few roses still bloomed. Léonie Boyer was a pretty woman still, though she was probably in the fifties, with delicately tinted blond hair, skillful makeup, smart clothes. Rambeau was magnificent with her.

''Madame, the reason for this I will recount to you later,'' he said after introducing himself and Mendoza and ascertaining that she spoke English. ''I can only tell you that you will be of inestimable aid to Juliette Martin, to my colleague, and to myself if you will answer our questions freely.''

''Of course, Inspector.'' She looked a little bewildered, but she responded automatically to his gallantry. ''Come in and sit down. Ask whatever you please. As you hear, I speak

English very well. I used to speak it with Élise, Julie's
mother, I do miss her so very much,'' and her eyes were sad.
"We were dear friends, and I look on Julie as a niece, almost a daughter. I have no children, you see."

"I'd like to ask you something about her, too," said
Mendoza. "Had you known her since she came to France,
Mrs. Boyer?"

"Oh, yes. Since she and André were married. She became Élise then. In America, her name was Elsie, such an
ugly name. Like thud, thud. But always she had an affinity
for France and the French language."

"Then you know about her father and about Juliette's
visit to him."

"Yes, indeed. I look forward to hearing about that when
Julie is home. Élise, it did not trouble her very much that he
was so angry about her marriage. He was a cold hard man,
she always said, and her mother had died when she was fifteen. There was no real home for her there. But also he was
jealous, you comprehend—no man she wished to marry
would have pleased him, for she was his favorite and the
only daughter.''

"And then after all, and after all these years, he wishes to
be reconciled to his granddaughter," said Rambeau.

She said, "I understood why Julie felt she should write to
him. There is such a thing as the family feeling. Of course
we did not have a proper address, there had been no com-
munication for thirty years—well, twenty-five—for Élise
had written him when Julie was born but never had a reply.
All I could tell Julie," she smiled, "it was a little joke between Élise and me—her old home in America. It was all so
different for her here, the country—the people—a cosmo-
politan surrounding. But she had become very French. Ah,
that curious address in America." She pronounced it carefully. "Indian Canyon Road, Rural Route Two, San Fernando. So very American. And Julie's letter sent on, he is

not there any longer, but he wrote to her. Yes, he was very
pleased to have her letter. He wrote that he had often wanted
to get in touch with Élise, but of course did not know where
to write. He is," she sighed, "very old and feels remorse,
and he was pleased to know about Julie. He asked her to
send a snapshot, and of course she looks very much like her
mother. They had corresponded since then. He sent Julie the
money for the airplane fare."

"Ah," said Rambeau. "He has money, then."

"Oh, no, I do not think so." She was surprised. "It was
a very poor place they lived when Élise was a young girl."

"Do you know the name of Claire Ducasse?"

"Why, of course. She is Julie's closest friend. They were
at school together. They shared an apartment in Paris until
Claire was married a few months ago. Her husband has been
transferred to Bordeaux, he is in a wine merchant's office.
And Julie had missed her, but she said she would keep the
apartment alone until she and Paul are married in January."

"The fiancé, Paul—"

"Paul Goulart. He is a fine young man. A doctor like his
father, he is finishing out his term at, what is it in English,
internship at the Paris General Hospital, and then he will go
into practice with his father. He is such a handsome young
man, they are so much in love. I have been very happy for
Julie."

"What," asked Mendoza, "is Élise's father's name?"

"Oh, that is very American, too. Elias K. Dobbs—more
thud, thud," and she laughed.

"Juliette's first letter to him was sent on. To where?"
demanded Rambeau. "She agreed to visit him, he sent her
the money for the plane ticket, somewhere in or near Los
Angeles—where?"

She put her hand to her cheek. "I could not tell you. I am
sorry. Julie must have said the name, but I am not familiar

with American names and I do not remember. It was not
important. Julie has gone to see him—of the family feeling. The old man, sentimental and sorry—it is only for a
short time. Inspector, I must ask you why you are asking me
all these questions. I do not understand."

Rambeau leaned forward and patted her hand. "Now,
you will be brave, madame. We must tell you that Juliette
Martin is dead. That is right, you weep for her. I can only
say you have helped to avenge her death."

But when they came back to the Renault, parked in the
quiet street, he was looking distracted. He stopped on the
sidewalk and said, "But why does that name ring a small
bell in my head? Paul Goulart, Paul Goulart. However, we
now have the name of Grandpère."

"And like the ones I handed you—a common one. But we
have telephone directories, too," said Mendoza.

"So again, allons! You will get there, my friend. You will
find Grandpère." Rambeau reached the key to the ignition
and stopped. He sat frozen, motionless for thirty seconds.
And then he said very quietly, "Sacrée Mère. I have just remembered. Paul Goulart." He lit a cigarette and sat smoking silently, staring through the windshield of the Renault.
"He was murdered," he said softly. "The reports that pass
across my desk, other men investigating other cases than
concern me—the names cross my mind and go. But that
much I remember. This Paul Goulart has been murdered."
He switched on the engine. "We will go to the office and
look up the report on him. Your mystery—it gets to be
stranger and deeper, my friend."

THEY TALKED to Dr. Jules Goulart briefly that evening, in
the parlor of his rather shabby comfortable old house in a
suburb north in the city. "I have nothing left," he said. He
was a leonine man with an aristocratic profile. "Paul was a

fine doctor, a son to take pride in—and his life is taken for no reason. A burglar stealing what little he had—perhaps a drug addict. He was to have taken my practice. And now you tell me Juliette is dead, such a dear girl, the right wife for Paul." After a silence, "If it is possible, I would like to have the ring back. Paul gave it to her as an engagement ring. I had it made for his mother when he was born. It is unique, a diamond and sapphires."

"You know," said Mendoza in the Renault, "that ring is somewhere in the sewers of Los Angeles."

"It is always well to be thorough," said Rambeau.

It was a small jewelry shop in the Rue Lafayette. The youngish man behind the counter said, "I remember the ring, sir. M. Goulart brought it in for cleaning, to see if the stones needed tightening. My father was interested, for he designed it. He is in the rear office—you may talk to him."

M. Duprés said, "Indeed, it is a unique ring. I designed it, it would be some twenty-six years ago. The account book would give the date." He was fussy and slow, looking up the record. "I can give you a sketch of the design. My memory is excellent, despite what the young people say. It is a yellow-gold ring—eighteen-karat gold—a diamond and two sapphires, all the stones are of half a carat weight." He insisted upon drawing a neat little sketch.

Rambeau said at the hotel, "So, my friend, you go home to find the solution to your mystery. And when you do, write and tell me, for I am interested to know. I shall never forget the little Juliette."

HACKETT AND HIGGINGS had just come back from lunch when a man from Communications brought in a cable. Hackett scanned it rapidly POSITIVE PROOF IDENTITY. BRINGING DEPOSITIONS. LEAN ON DAGGETTS HARD.

Hackett said, "Well, I will be damned. He seems to have got what he went after."

Sergeant Lake looked up from the switchboard. "You've got a new one just gone down—a body."

TEN

HACKETT, HIGGINS, and Palliser confronted the Daggetts and Helen Garvey in Mendoza's office; there wasn't space for all of them in one of the interrogation rooms. The two women were silent and Daggett tried to bluster. Higgins said, "We've spelled it out for you, Daggett. Now we can prove you've all been lying. We've got legal proof of who the girl really was. That she hadn't been living in that apartment—that her name wasn't Ruth Hoffman—and now we'd like to hear what you know about it. Who primed you with that story?"

Daggett's Adam's apple was jerking wildly. He said, "I don't know anything about it. Not a thing. Just what I told you."

"Don't waste time trying to deny it," said Hackett. "How did the girl get there and when? Who told you what lies to tell?"

Daggett looked at his wife and he looked like a frightened rabbit cornered by hounds. "We never did anything to that girl. We don't know anything about that girl."

"So what do you know about?" asked Palliser.

Daggett shifted in the chair, still looking at his wife. "We never wanted to get into any trouble—"

"Well, you're in a hell of a lot of trouble now," said Higgins brutally. "You'll have to tell us about it sometime, and it had better be here and now."

The woman said evenly, "I guess we better tell them, Fred. I thought we put it over—even when that other one asked questions. But I guess we'll have to tell them the rights of it now."

He licked his lips. "Well," he said, "it was the money. I told you that building's going to be torn down and I'll be out of a job. I'm fifty-seven years old and it won't be easy to get another. I worked around a lot—construction and clerking in stores—but it won't be easy to find any kind of decent job at my age. I managed that apartment for ten years, we get the place rent free. But it's coming down. They're gonna build a big office building there. The land belongs to some big company, they couldn't care less about the likes of me, and we've been worried about it. I've been damn worried about it. It was around the first of August I got the phone call." He was hunched forward, clasped hands between his knees, head down. "And I can't tell you anything about the guy. I never laid eyes on him. It was just a voice on the phone—an ordinary voice. He asked me if the wife and me would like to earn ten thousand bucks each. We wouldn't have to do much, he said. Just tell a little story to the police. I didn't like the idea of police being in it. I never had anything to do with the police, but they can be nosy— and when he said what we'd have to do, I didn't like that so good either. But he said there couldn't be any trouble, the police would only come once and they'd believe what we said because there'd be things to back it up so the police would believe us. He said he'd let us think it over and call me back. Well, the wife and I talked it over and decided to do it—for the money. But I thought about Helen, see. She and Ethel been pretty good friends, time we'd been here, and I know things hadn't been easy for her either. And I thought it'd look better if somebody else was to back us up on that story. We talked it all over and when he called back I put it to him. I said Helen'd back us up for another ten thousand, and he said that was O.K."

Hackett said, "Not so much money for a thing like that, was it? With a dead body involved."

Mrs. Daggett looked at him almost contemptuously. She was a short fat woman with sandy blond hair and hard pale blue eyes, a small tight mouth. "Mister," she said, "I don't know how old you are or how much you make at this job, but sooner or later you'll find out like the rest of us, in this life, it's dog eat dog. You got to look out for yourself first. Sure it was a little risk to take. But we figured it was worth it for the money, and so did Helen." Helen Garvey was sitting silent, her much-made-up face gaunt in the bright sunlight pouring in the window. "The fellow told Fred just what was going to be in that apartment. There'd be things to make the story look on the level."

Daggett said, "He told me just what I had to do. All I had to do was just what he said. He didn't know exactly when it would be, but he'd let me know beforehand. He said I was to tell him the number of the apartment. Well, that was easy. People moving out the last three months—not five tenants left in the place, and Helen was the only one left on that floor, so I told him the one opposite her. He said when he called I was just to leave the key in the door and the only thing I had to do, make out rent receipts like the Hoffman girl had been living there. Leave the top ones in the apartment and have the carbons ready to show the police, and the next morning I was supposed to go up there and call the police and say how I'd found her."

"You all knew you were getting mixed up in a murder, didn't you?" asked Higgins.

"You can't say any such thing! We never—how'd we know that?"

"When the fellow told you a month in advance," said Hackett, "that there was going to be a dead body in that apartment? You're not that much of a fool, Daggett."

He looked wildly from side to side. "I didn't want to know anything about it—it wasn't anything to do with me—with us. I didn't want to think about it."

His wife said, "We'd never have taken the risk except it looked like he had it all set up so the police wouldn't think it was a lie. Well, we lost the gamble, that's all."

Palliser asked, "And what happened next?"

"We had to be sure he'd pay up. He sounded like he meant business all right, and even before I asked him he said he'd pay us half first. The money came in the mail. It was a little package came by first-class mail and it was all cash—all in twenties. Fifteen thousand dollars. I never heard from him again until just the night before. He called and said we should get ready—to do it—the next morning. I—right then, I'd have liked to back out of the whole deal. I hadn't really thought about—about the body, but we were in it then—and I said O.K." He took a deep breath. "And he said, leave the key in the door and leave your own door shut—just sit and watch the T.V."

"And that was what you did?" said Palliser.

Daggett nodded. "And next morning I went up there. It was all just like he said it'd be, and the rest of the money was there on the table—another fifteen thousand in twenties. So I just did what he said to. We all did."

Higgins said, "You know you've laid yourselves open to a charge of accessories to a murder, don't you? That's what it adds up to. Is that all you can tell us about him?"

"We don't know anything about a murder. I never laid eyes on him. That's all I can tell you. Just a voice on the phone. We never knew anything about that girl. You can't say we knew nothing about a murder. It was just a chance to make all that money. It didn't seem much to do for that much money."

Hackett said, "It's put you in one hell of a lot of trouble, Daggett. You're all going to jail and the money won't do you much good there." Mendoza had predicted something like this, but it was unsatisfactory. It left the thing still shapeless. They talked it over a little after they'd booked the

Daggetts and Garvey into jail. There had, of course, been an inquest on the supposed Ruth Hoffman, and at Mendoza's request the coroner had instructed the jury to leave it open. Now it was to be hoped that he had enough further evidence to conclude the inquest with a verdict of murder. He hadn't said when he'd be back. He might be on the way now.

ROBERT SHAFTON said to Landers and Galeano, "This neighborhood's run down in the last twenty years. It was convenient to my business. But nearly anywhere in the city these days you get all sorts of crime—the violence. We bought the house on Scott Avenue twenty-five years ago, it was handy to the store, but we'd like to get out of the area now. Only who can afford the interest rates? Any other place we'd get, we'd have to get a loan on. And nearly anywhere these days—" He spread his hands. They were talking to him at his store on Glendale Avenue. It was a stationer's and office-supply store, a fairly big place. He had this little office at the rear of the store, and there was a woman clerk in front.

"We talked to the patrolman," said Landers, "but we'd like to hear what you can tell us, Mr. Shafton."

"Certainly," said Shafton. He was a short spare man with gray hair and glasses. "I'd been home for lunch. I like to get a little exercise, and it's only six blocks to the store— I usually walk. I was on Scott Avenue—about halfway up the block from Glendale, and this woman was ahead of me— almost at the corner. There wasn't anybody else on the street. She seemed to be having trouble getting along— walking very slowly and bent over, and I was just wondering if she was ill or perhaps drunk when it happened. These two—well, I don't know whether to call them men or boys— I'd say they were around seventeen or eighteen, but both pretty husky. They came around the corner from Glendale

Avenue and saw the woman, and just—well—tackled her. One of them knocked her down and the other one grabbed her handbag and they ran back up Glendale Avenue. It happened so fast I couldn't have done a thing, I wasn't close enough. Not that I could have done much—they were both bigger than me."

"You might have got clobbered too," said Galeano.

"I went up and looked at her. I saw she was quite elderly and looked as if she was badly hurt. She'd hit her head on the sidewalk. So I went up to the corner where there's a public phone and called the police and an ambulance."

"Would you recognize either of those two? Can you give us a description?" asked Landers.

"They were just the typical young louts you see around. Long hair, jeans, sweatshirts— I think they both had dark hair, but that's really all I can say. Was that ambulance attendant right—that she was dead? The patrolman thought so."

"Yes, I'm afraid she was," said Galeano.

They had talked to the uniformed man, who had one piece of information for them. The woman's handbag had been gone, of course, but she'd been wearing an identification bracelet with a name and address stamped on it and he had noted it down. PHILLIPS, an address on Morton Avenue. They went to look there, to notify any relatives. It was a small apartment building, not new, but well maintained with a strip of lawn in front. There wasn't a manager, and they tried the first right front apartment downstairs. A woman about thirty said they'd just moved there, didn't know any of the other tenants. Nobody else was home downstairs. They climbed stairs, tried the first right-hand door there. The woman who opened it said, "Phillips?" She was stout and henna-haired. "She lives right across the hall." She was shocked to hear what had happened. "Well, I don't know about any relatives. There was some woman came to see her nearly every day, I'd meet her in the hall sometimes, I don't know who she is. Of course you want to find out. I wonder if the door's locked. She hardly ever went out, I don't think.'' She stepped across the hall and tried the door, and it was unlocked. ''There. I expect there'll be something inside to tell you about any family,'' she said brightly.

Landers shut the door on her with thanks and they looked around. It was a typical place for its age and for the area. The neutral upholstered furniture, everything orderly, the kitchen clean. The phone was on one of the end tables by the couch and taped just above the dial was a neat card with firm printing on it: GREGSON and a phone number—NURSE and another number. Landers sat down on the couch and tried the first number. On the sound ring a masculine voice answered. ''Mr. Gregson? This is the police. I believe you know a Mrs. Phillips on Morton Avenue. I'm sorry to have to tell you she's met with an accident— Yes, sir, I'm afraid she's dead. We're at the apartment, sir, yes. If you could tell us about any relatives—''

He said, ''Yes, I can tell you. I'll come as soon as I can get there.''

He came half an hour later. He was a tall elderly man, once very handsome and still good-looking, with a thick crop of gray hair and steady blue eyes. He was wearing neat sports clothes. He sat down on the couch and listened to Landers' account and said heavily, ''Oh, my God. What a terrible way for her to die. I hope it was quick for her—that she hadn't time to be frightened. I'm so very sorry.''

''You're a relative, sir?'' asked Galeano. ''There has to be an autopsy. You'll be notified when you can claim the body.''

''Yes, there'll have to be a funeral. I'll see to it. No, not a relative.'' He lit a cigarette and sat back with a little sigh. ''No, but I've known her for a long time. She was eighty-five. It had been nearly fifty years. I was—responsible for her, you could say. It's queer the way things happen. You don't know who she was. Neither of you is old enough to recognize the name. Isabel Page. She was a big star in the twenties, the thirties, up to the war. She was a beautiful woman. She made a lot of big money and she spent it. Those days the income tax wasn't so high. The house in Beverly Hills, the cars, the parties. I was her butler.'' He laughed ruefully. ''Life's a queer proposition. I'd started out to try to make it in show business too, but we found it was a hell of a lot steadier work to take the servants' jobs. I was her butler and my wife was her housekeeper. She was a good woman—a silly woman some ways—sentimental, but very generous and warmhearted. Too much so. She was married four times and all four of them took her for a bundle, but it was the last one, Phillips, who cleaned her out. That was twenty-five years ago. We'd been with her for seventeen years.'' He was smoking quietly, his eyes vacant on the past. ''Such a childlike person she was. How often she'd get in some muddle and then it'd be, But you'll fix it for me, Gregson—and I usually could—until the very last.''

''What happened?'' asked Galeano.

''You see, we could never forget her kindness to Enid. My wife. She contracted polio, and you know back then they didn't know much about it, couldn't do much. And nobody had medical insurance then. Isabel Page paid for everything. Enid was in the hospital for weeks, and there were specialists, the private nurses. You might say that it was nothing to her, she had the money. But it wasn't just a gesture—she was a very warmhearted woman—genuinely concerned. We both feel it was all the expensive attention and care that pulled Enid through—though it left her with a slight limp. And then, Miss Page let us keep our little girl at the house. A good many people wealthy enough to have live-in servants won't be bothered with children, but she didn't mind. She was always so kind to Doreen too, Christmas and birthday presents. We were with her up to the end. Phillips cleaned her out, he'd tried to manage the money she had left and lost all of it. She never had any judgement about people, of course. All there was left after he took off with some floozy was the house in Beverly Hills. I sold that for her—got a hundred and fifty thousand. God, it'd go for a million now. And I put it into some solid stock, she could live on the income in a modest way. I had another job with one of the big producers up to when I retired five years ago. But the last ten years, all this damned inflation—'' He put out his cigarette. ''Well, I'd saved and made some sound investments, rental property, and Enid and I are O.K. I couldn't afford to keep her in luxury, but I could pay the rent here. Only just lately it's been worrying, the way she was going. She'd been failing the last couple of years—up to then she could look after herself fairly well. One of these visiting nurses came in every day, saw she had a bath and a hot meal. But I was afraid she'd have to go into a nursing home, just lately she'd taken to getting out and wandering all over—the reason I got that I.D. bracelet for her. She wanted to go home, you see—to the house in Beverly Hills. She was trying to get home. Well, it's finished. A terrible way for her to go. I hope she hadn't time to be frightened.''

''You'll be notified about the body,'' said Landers. ''It was very good of you to look after her like that, Mr. Gregson.''

He had stood up. He looked at Landers with a little surprise. ''I don't see it quite like that,'' he said. ''We have to pay our debts, you know.''

MENDOZA GOT HOME on Wednesday afternoon. When the cab let him off at the door of the big Spanish house, he handed over the exorbitant fare and a tip and carried his bag into the house, into the blessed air-conditioning. It wasn't as hot as when he had left, but the-air conditioning was still welcome. He found Alison in the living room, curled up in an armchair reading, and she scrambled up in surprise, scattering cats. "Luis, we didn't know when to expect you." When she emerged from his embrace she added, "You look tired to death, *querido*."

"Jet lag," said Mendoza. "I want a shower and shave and there's time to get down to the office—"

"Time to go nowhere," said Alison. "You're going to lie down for the rest of the afternoon and get some sleep. You're not as young as you were, and you know you're exhausted. I suppose you went to the Folies Bergère every night to whistle at all the lovelies." He followed her meekly up the stairs, yawning his head off. He wasn't sorry to be overruled.

So it wasn't until Thursday morning that he sat at his desk with Higgins, Hackett, Palliser gathered around him, Hackett missing another day off, and said, "So, Paul Goulart, the fiancé, got himself murdered too. And it could have been a coincidence—the crime rate's up in Paris too—but I don't think so and neither does Rambeau. Goulart was on a late shift at the hospital and would get home at his apartment about midnight. It looked as if he'd surprised a burglar. The place was ransacked and he was stabbed. The door had apparently been jimmied opened with a chisel or something, but the lock wasn't broken. There was a good solid deadbolt. What the detective on the case thought, and what I think, was that somebody was waiting for him. Went in with him on some excuse and set up the burglary. He wasn't known to have any, in the melodramatic word, enemies. No trouble with anyone recently. But Goulart!" said Mendoza. "Of all the people who knew her, Goulart would never have rested until he located Juliette. He wouldn't have been fobbed off with any polite excuses from the French police or us. And there was no address book in that apartment, and that's an item the burglar seldom bothers with *¡Cómo no!* And he must have known Grandfather's address. He's the one who would have had it, damn it.''

"I'm following you," said Hackett cautiously. "But—"

Mendoza impatiently lit a cigarette from the stub of his old one. "Look at it. Just look at the probabilities. What would happen when Juliette didn't come home from America? The Ducasse girl is all wrapped up in a new marriage, and living in another town. I doubt that she'd have Grandfather's address. Juliette was only going to be gone for three weeks, a month. The Ducasse girl would expect to hear from her, she'd be surprised when she didn't. She'd write to the Paris address. Eventually, she might contact the Boyer woman, and she'd have been surprised and worried at not hearing too. But what would they do? How soon? By December the lease would be up on that apartment, but the rent would have been overdue before then, and sooner or later the managers would go in, find personal possessions, assume she'd decamped. Theirs not to reason why. I doubt if they'd take the trouble to look at her accumulated mail. Take Goulart's father. He liked the girl very much, but when she didn't contact him when she was supposed to be back, what would he think? Put her down as a heartless female— not worthy of Paul. But Goulart! A young, energetic man with some standing—he'd have been a tiger after her when she didn't come home. He was in love with the girl, he knew where she was going. He'd have moved heaven and earth to find out what had happened to her. Goulart was the key. If Juliette was to vanish quietly away, he had to go. However, he had to be disposed of.''

"I see it," said Higgins. "But, my God, Luis. Talk about a wholesale operation—"

"Her other friends, and she probably had a lot of them, mostly middle-class working girls like herself, they'd wonder and speculate. They wouldn't do anything. And if in

December or January or February Mrs. Boyer did contact
the French police and they contacted us, what is there to
find? She landed at International that day and—as Mr.
Shakespeare puts it, the rest is silence." Mendoza laughed
and leaned back in his desk chair. "So everybody is at a
dead end. She had a visitor's permit, good for six months.
Muy bien. Immigration isn't going to send out the troops
looking for her. But Goulart, that was a different breed of
cat, *compadres.* They had to get rid of Goulart." He
brooded over his cigarette. "He was killed on the Monday
night, after Juliette landed here on Saturday. Somebody had
been busy. They had to get her keys, possibly her address
book if she brought it with her, for Goulart's address.
Somebody started for France that Saturday night. They'd
know her address from her letters, of course. Somebody
cleared that apartment of anything personal—Grandfather's letters, other letters. And if the address book was
there—that, and any list of phone numbers. And somebody set up a little ambush for Goulart."

"And," said Palliser. "Another thing you can deduce. If
the Boyer woman or the Ducasse girl had done anything,
what would they do? Go to Goulart."

"*Exactamente.* He had to go. And that was just the way
it's been at this end—simple and yet—mmh—cunning. Rudimentary, but very damned thorough. And money and lives
no object."

"For God's sake, what could be behind it?" said Higgins.

"Elias K. Dobbs," said Hackett. "Another common
name. We can start out with the phone books and city directories."

"It would probably have worked out as smooth as
cream," said Mendoza, "if I hadn't seen the corpse. Oh,
such a nice little plan. And executed so damn smoothly
too."

"Why?" wondered Palliser.

"And we still don't know," said Mendoza.

"The phone book," said Hackett.

There were six phone books covering the county. This one had been a bastard to work all the way. Dobbs wasn't as common a name as Smith or Brown, but common enough. And there were a hundred or more in each of the books, even just looking for the initials. And of course the number might be unlisted. They started to work on it, on four books. That was at eleven o'clock, and at noon a bank job went down at a Bank of America on Beverly. Everybody else was out hunting heisters and there'd be dozen of witnesses to question. They all went out on that, and what with talking to the witnesses and taking statements, it occupied the rest of the day.

THE NIGHT WATCH had only one call, but it was a homicide. And it would likely give the day boys some more legwork to do. Conway went out to look at it. The uniformed man was waiting for him with a civilian in front of a little old single-frame house on San Marino Street. The civilian was a middle-aged man, sitting on the front steps with his head in his hands. His name was Richard Scoggins. He said to Conway numbly, "We were worried when she didn't answer the phone. My mother. She's nearly eighty and pretty frail. We usually phoned to check on her every day. We didn't like her living alone down here but of course she owned the house. My wife couldn't get her all day. I thought I'd better check. Of course I've got a key to the house—and when I saw—" He put his head in his hands again.

The old lady was lying on the floor of the bedroom. It looked as if she'd been strangled. There were a few drawers pulled out, an old jewelry box on the dressing table was empty with its lid open. Conway sent the patrolman back on tour after he'd called the lab and while he waited looked through the rest of the house. He told Scoggins that later they'd want him to look and see what was missing here, and Scoggins just nodded silently. It didn't look to Conway as if the back or front doors had been forced, or any of the windows. But that was the lab's business. Let them get on with it. He went back to the office to write the initial report.

MENDOZA SWORE over the night report. It was Galeano's day off. They were still taking statements from the witnesses on the bank job and now they had this damned homicide to work. And all the damned phone books— He got Jason Grace to get back on that with him. The first thing they had checked on had been unlisted numbers and no Elias K. Dobbs or any E. Dobbs in the county had one. There wasn't an Elias Dobbs listed in any of the six books, but there were at least a hundred and fifty E. Dobbses.

"There's an easier way to do it, you know," said Grace reasonably.

Mendoza said savagely, "Hands off the phone, Jase! Grandfather's part of this damn thing and I don't want to set off the alarm on him *¡Dios!* We'll have to take a personal look at every one of these damned Dobbses, and whoever pulled this off may be damned canny and crafty but I'll take a bet that when we find Grandfather and let him know that we've connected him with Juliette he'll be surprised enough to show it."

"Yes, I see what you mean," said Grace. They set to work to compile a list of possible Grandfathers. And adding insult to injury, they were all over the damn county. There'd be mileage piled up on all their cars, and the only consolation was that the heat wave seemed to be dying a natural death.

Then Lake buzzed him and said there were a couple of Feds to see him, and Mendoza snarled. "And what the hell do you want?" he asked the two big men who came in.

"Well, this bank job yesterday—"

"If it's any of your business," said Mendoza. Time was the bank jobs had belonged exclusively to the Feds, but these days they were left up to the locals.

"Now don't be so goddamned touchy, Mendoza. We're just offering some friendly help," said the other Fed mildly. "We got the word from a snitch up in Hollywood. Norm and I have been on a big Narco case, there's some bunch bringing the stuff in from Mexico pretty damn wholesale. We've been sniffing around on it for a couple of months, and the snitch, who's a former pusher just out on P.A., is evidently carrying a grudge. He tells us that job was pulled by Angelo Morales and Tony Montez because they needed the bread to make a payment on a new shipment."

"Por Dios," said Mendoza. "There were two men—both Latins by the witnesses."

"Well, there you are," said the Fed. "By what the pusher said, he got it on the grapevine that Morales dumped a bundle at draw somewhere, and it was the stake for the shipment."

"Es que ya me canso de las estupideces. I do get so damn tired of all these stupidities. All right. Thank you both so much. We'll look into it."

"We're just trying to be helpful," said the first one plaintively. When they had left, Mendoza went out to see who was in. Landers had just come back and Mendoza passed the information on.

"You'd better check with Records— I assume they've both got pedigrees—and see what comes of it."

"Oh, hell," said Landers. "More legwork."

After lunch Mendoza and Grace started out separately to look at Dobbses, but with all the driving, they only got to four between them that afternoon and none of them was Grandfather.

But Mendoza had spent awhile poring over the County Guide before he left the office, and on Sunday morning as he left the house on the hill he didn't turn left to hit the east on-ramp of the Golden State Freeway, the other way for the west on-camp. Nine o'clock found him on a narrow black-top road some little way north of the town of San Fernando, and heading north. Behind him was the teeming, crowded San Fernando Valley, one big city sprawl these last twenty-five years. But up here it was all empty land. Gentle bare little hills burned brown by the sun, a few scrub-oak trees. He drove slowly around the various windings of Lopez Canyon Road and nearly missed the little sign off to the right that said INDIAN CANYON ROAD. That was even narrower and led him northeast past more bare land. About half a mile up on the right was a house with a FOR SALE sign on it. A quarter mile farther on the left was another house, or, he amended to himself, what had been one. Nobody had lived in it for a long time. It had been a square frame house but the roof had fallen in and the front porch was broken. There was a post which had held a mailbox in front and the remains of the mailbox lying alongside it. The post office hadn't delivered any mail here for years. Mendoza parked the Ferrari on the shoulder, went back and looked at the mailbox. There was no lettering visible on the uppermost side, but when he turned it over with one foot, just decipherable were the remains of a few once-white-painted letters. E-D-BS.

"Allá va," he said to himself. He turned the car and went back down the hill to the other house. It had been maintained fairly well. There was a wire fence around about half an acre of land. The realtors' name on the sign was Hawley and Calkins in San Fernando.

"Oh, sure," said the salesman in that office. "It's an old lady owns it. Got too old to live alone. I don't suppose we'll sell it very easy, all the commercial growth is west and it's not out far enough for a weekend cabin. Sure I can tell you. Her name is Deeming. Harriet Deeming. It's an address in Van Nuys."

It was an attractive beige stucco house on a good residential street, and the woman who opened the door looked in surprise at the badge. "Well, I can't imagine what the police want with Mother Deeming, but she's always pleased to talk to anyone. Come in." She took him into a pleasant living room and introduced him to a little old woman in a clean cotton housedress sitting in a rocking chair knitting, a cane propped at her side. She had white hair and bright brown eyes, sharp and intelligent on him. Mendoza sat down and asked, "When you lived in that house up on Indian Canyon Road, did you ever know Elias Dobbs?"

"Now you do bring back some old times to me," she said interestedly. "Indeed we did."

"What can you tell me about him and do you know where he lives now?"

"Not exactly, no. My, how I did hate that man one time. But I've got past that now. I could tell you this and that about him." She didn't ask why he wanted to know. "He was a hard man, a regular miser. Frank and I bought that old place, well, paying on it, you know, in nineteen-thirty, we were both raised in the country and thought we could grow a lot of our own food there. Times were awful bad then and we had it pretty tough, Frank out of work and the baby coming. Dobbs lived up the road, and I always felt sorry for his family. There were three kids by the end of the war—a girl and two boys. We didn't know him so well then when we moved there, and when he offered to lend us that money, well, we didn't like to borrow but we had to—and goodness, he was around to collect the interest right on the

dot till we managed to pay it back. How that man loved
money—well, he got it. All he could use in the end, and I
wonder what good it ever did him. One thing life's taught
me, Mr. Mendoza, is that all you need is enough. You can't
eat more than one meal at a time—and life goes so quick.
Seems yesterday I was hoeing that garden and Tommy just
a toddler, and here I am coming to the end and Tommy with
grown-up kids of his own and their kids coming along, and
he's got that good hardware business. We had it rough back
there, but we made out. And when the war came along,
Frank got that good job at the assembly plant and everything was better. But we went on living there because it was
home then, and we got it paid off. I guess I was stubborn
about it, I stayed there too long after Frank went, ten years
back. Tommy and Faye at me to move in with them, but I
like to be independent. It wasn't until I had that bad fall a
few months back I saw it was only sensible. When we were
first there, there wasn't a house around for quite a ways, real
country. But then you know how the valley started to build
up after the war—the freeway coming through and houses
and businesses getting built all over. It's all just like one big
city now—and that's where Dobbs got all his money, it
seems he owned thousands of acres out there. He got left
some and I guess he bought up a lot more when it was just
wasteland at ten cents an acre or something. Right where the
freeway came through and all around."

A great flood of enlightenment hit Mendoza. "What did
he do with the money, do you know?"

"That was back in the early fifties," she said. "Thirty
years ago. He started his own big real-estate company. He
called it the Golden D. He went on living there awhile, that
tumble-down old house. His wife was dead and the girl off
somewhere, but about twenty years back he moved out. The
boys, they were helping to run the business then. Good-

ness, they'll both be in the forties now, doesn't seem possible.''

"There was a letter for him about six months ago—"

She looked at him over the top of her spectacles. "Oh, you know about that. Yes, it was funny. The mail carrier asked about the name, he'd never heard it—and I told him to send it to the business.'' So Juliette's letter, fatally, had got sent on.

"That's all very interesting," he said.

"People, they're mostly interesting," said Mrs. Deeming.

He found the nearest public phone and looked up the address, and swore. It wasn't a realty company, which would be open on Sunday. It was the Golden D Management Corporation, with an address out on Sunset in Beverly Hills.

ON MONDAY MORNING he landed there with Hackett at nine o'clock. The office occupied three floors in a new high-rise building. The top floor contained the managers' offices. It was all expensively and lavishly furnished. They talked to a svelte receptionist with lacquered blond hair and Mendoza asked for Mr. Elias Dobbs. "Oh, the old gentleman isn't in the office regularly, sir. Mr. David Dobbs won't be in until this afternoon, but Mr. Robert Dobbs should be in this morning."

"It's rather important that I see Mr. Elias Dobbs," said Mendoza. "Could you give me his address?"

She shrugged, incurious. "He's in one of our condos in Santa Monica—Carlyle Terrace.''

In the car, Hackett said, "You took a shortcut, all right."

"Just following my nose. And here," said Mendoza in satisfaction, "is the money. In spades. And I have a small hunch we've been maligning Grandfather. I think I see a glimmer at the end of the tunnel, Art."

The condominium was high up in another tall building on a quiet street, and the man who opened the door was about thirty-five, with a Scandinavian look to him, light hair and a round genial face. He said, "Oh, I'm sorry, sir. Mr. Dobbs is in the hospital, just since yesterday." He looked at the badge and gave them a curious stare.

"We'd like to ask you some questions," said Mendoza. "What's your name? Do you live here?"

"Brant. Bernard Brant." He lost a little of the punctilious manner. "Yes, I've been looking after the old gentleman for a couple of years, since he broke his hip. I've been a male nurse ten years, and I like the work fine, but this was the easiest job I ever had. He didn't really need nursing, just a little help. All there was to do was get his meals, drive him wherever he wanted, like that. He got back on his feet again after they put a pin in his hip, and he was sharp as a tack, mentally, you know. What's this all about?" He had stepped back to let them in. The living room was elegantly furnished with a big T.V. console in one corner.

"About his granddaughter," said Mendoza. "The girl from France. Did you know about her?"

"Oh, sure. Everybody did," said Brant. "Mr. Dobbs was excited about her coming. He liked getting letters from her. I really think it was the reason he just went downhill the last month, after he got the letter to say she couldn't come after all. It was a big disappointment to him. I think it sort of contributed to his having the stroke yesterday."

"Oh," said Hackett. "She wrote to say she wasn't coming?"

"Yes, and he took right against her when he got that letter. He'd been so interested in her, he had her picture beside his bed, he was always telling me how much she looked like her mother and she was just as smart, too. He was proud of her. He wanted to see her and show her off to people. And you know, I think that girl made a big mistake not coming," said Brant reflectively. "Because he said to me more than a few times that Juliette would get a surprise when he died, he was going to make a new will and leave her a lot of money—make it up to her for how he'd treated her mother. One time when he was mad at his two sons he said, by God, he'd leave her the whole kit and caboodle."

"That's interesting," said Hackett.

"But when he got that letter, he turned right against her. She said that fellow she's engaged to wouldn't let her come, didn't want her leaving France—and she didn't send back the money Mr. Dobbs had sent her to get the plane ticket. He was mad about that." Mendoza laughed. "He said, like mother, like daughter, and he tore up her letters—he used to read them over—and her picture."

"I see," said Mendoza. "Did his sons come to visit him often?"

Brant grinned. "From what I heard they had to. He was sharp as a tack like I say and he was still active in the business. He'd kept all the reins in his own hands like they say. Those two, they had to bring all the papers for him to sign. He knew everything that was going on at the office. Why in hell are the police interested in all this?"

"You may be reading about it in the *Times*," said Mendoza.

At the curb beside the Ferrari he said reverently, "But it's beautiful, Arturo. So simple and so beautiful. The old man getting sentimental in his old age, besotted about the pretty granddaughter—and his mind still sharp. The business still in his own hands. So there'd be no hope of getting him declared incompetent. There are a hell of a lot of bribable people in the world, but not many of them will be reputable psychiatrists. David and Robert Dobbs stand to inherit everything, and that business must be grossing millions. God knows what they own all over the country. And I haven't any doubt that if the old man said it to Brant he'd said it to them, leave her everything, maybe. They wouldn't remember much about the older sister who went to France. And here's this upstart of a girl going to rob them of everything they had—everything they'd sweated for. He can't have been an easy man to deal with. They'll have had to kowtow to him—yes, Father, no, Father. And the strange girl stepping in to take the whole kitty because she reminded him of her mother and wrote the friendly letters." He laughed sharply. "Just from the family feeling. Oh, by God, of course they had to do something about it. So there were two trips to Paris."

"How do you make that out?"

"The letter. The letter saying she couldn't come. Somebody had to fly over to mail the letter, for the Paris postmark. They'd have heard all about her letters. They knew about Goulart. They had that plan all ready a month before, by God. I wonder if they're both married. Some woman took out that library card. But that Social Security card—well, we'll have a look at them—see what shows."

"And just the unlucky chance tripping them up," said Hackett.

"Maybe not chance, Arturo," said Mendoza.

HE WENT TO THE HOSPITAL just to look at Grandfather, who was in a coma and by what the doctors said unlikely to come out of it. It was an old wrinkled lantern-jawed face on the pillow, with a mean narrow mouth. Not a pleasant character, Grandfather, but not such a villain as they had imagined.

HE SURVEYED the Dobbses in his office enjoyably. David Dobbs was unmarried, but Robert's wife was a flashy blonde named Gaylene, in expensive clothes and wearing too much jewelry. Both the men resembled their father strongly, the same aquiline features and long jaw. They were both impassive. The blonde looked sulky.

"It was a very pretty plan," Mendoza told them. "Of course your company had that derelict building on its books and a rudimentary look at it would have suggested Daggett as open to bribery. That was very competently accomplished. Which of you went to France?—first to mail the letter and a week or so later to murder Goulart and clear out Juliette's apartment? We'll have to look for a passport, of course. Somehow I think it was Mr. David Dobbs. I appreciate the touch about the money not being returned. That would have been the last straw, to set the old man against her. And Robert and his wife met Juliette at the airport—her pleasant new relatives—all smiles and welcome. You didn't take her home for the neighbors to see, of course. But you could have rented the nice little beach house for a week, or possibly the company owns a suitable place. And you gave her some plausible excuse why she couldn't see Grandfather right away—it only needed to satisfy her long enough for you to get her inside somewhere and get a drink down her—well-laced with a sedative. You kept her half-doped from Saturday to Tuesday, when David got back from France and told you it was all clear, Goulart was out of the way. So you called Daggett and that night you three took the girl to that apartment, left the artistic evidence scattered around, the rest of the money for the Daggetts and Garvey, and went home rejoicing. It all should have been quite safe, but Nemesis outguessed you." Mendoza laughed.

"I'm afraid I don't know what you're talking about," said Robert Dobbs woodenly.

THEY ASKED THE AIRLINES and got confirmation of David Dobbs two flights to Paris. They heard from a garrulous friend of Gaylene Dobbs' that her name had been Hoffman before she married Robert, and she'd always hated her real first name, Ruth, used her middle name. So that was where the Social Security card had originated; but Mendoza had overlooked one small point about that. The original card, unlike the replica, would have have borne the date of issue; and that card had probably been issued to Ruth Hoffman when Juliette was hardly more than a baby. But when they got the search warrant for the Robert Dobbs' million-dollar house in Bel-Air, they hit a jackpot. At the bottom of a carved wooden jewel case in the bedroom, among all the other expensive jewelry, they found Juliette Martin's engagement ring. The unique ring designed and made by M. Duprés in the Rue Lafayette twenty-six years ago.

And with the only display of emotion Mendoza was ever to see Robert Dobbs display, before that or during the trial, he rounded on his wife with a string of vicious obscenities. "I told you to throw that damn thing down the john—"

"But, Bob," she said stupidly, "it's a valuable ring, it's worth a lot of money."

MENDOZA GOT HOME late that night. It had suddenly turned much cooler and up on the hill above Burbank a strong breeze was blowing. It was nearly dark, but he could see the vague white forms of the Five Graces huddled in the pasture. At the house, the garage light was left on for him and he went in the back door, past Cedric slurping water from his bowl in the service porch.

"Well, you are late and all," said Mairí. "I kept your dinner warm in the oven—"

"Never mind, I had something downtown." He went down the hall to the living room. The twins and the baby would be in bed. Alison was reading in her armchair, surrounded by cats. "Well, *querido,* you finally remembered you have a home?"

Mendoza bent to kiss her. "Things should quiet down a little now that the heat wave's ending." Now they just had the latest homicide and two heists to work, and could hope that not too many new calls would go down. "You get on with your book, *cariña*. I want to write a letter to Rambeau."

He went back to the kitchen for a drink first, and El señor was waiting for him on the counter below the relevant cupboard.

A J.K.G. Jantarro Mystery

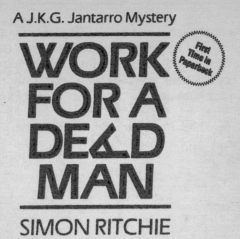

WORK FOR A DEAD MAN

First Time in Paperback

SIMON RITCHIE

**JANTARRO DIDN'T LIKE TO LOSE A CLIENT...
ESPECIALLY NOT TO A MURDERER.**

When megabuck film producer/director Alan Laki is poisoned, private investigator J.K.B. Jantarro takes special interest. He'd been hired by Laki to investigate the bizarre spending behavior of the man's gorgeous wife, Camelia. But now Laki's been murdered, his empire is in chaos and Jantarro is working for a dead man.

As for motives, Camelia Laki had millions of them... all dollar bills. Toss in a greedy business partner, a gossip columnist and her guilty secret, a hothead and a resentful brother-in-law, add three goons with homemade baseball bats, and it's lights...camera...action, as Jantarro plays the lead in a script full of scheming passion, dirty deals and death.

"Ritchie deftly blends literate writing, a light touch of humor, a likeable hero and memorable characters for a terrifically suspenseful tale."

—*Publishers Weekly*

WORLDWIDE LIBRARY

WFDM

AVAILABLE IN JANUARY

From the author of the highly acclaimed
Father Dowling novels now seen on ABC-TV

RALPH McINERNY

AN ANDREW BROOM MYSTERY

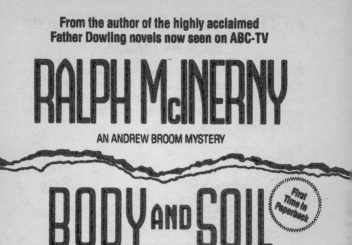

BODY AND SOIL

First Time in Paperback

TILL DEATH DO US PART...

After nearly thirty years of unhappily ever after, Wyler, Indiana's most affluent and argumentative couple decided to call it quits. At least Pauline Stanfield did. Hal Stanfield knew a divorce would unearth secrets—both the financial and extramarital kind—he preferred to keep buried.

But when Hal is found bludgeoned to death in his kitchen, attorney Andrew Broom finds himself defending a wife suspected of choosing murder over divorce. Soon he discovers that even the best-laid plans of marriage—or murder—can go dangerously awry when a twisted killer decides to play judge, jury... and executioner.

"*Body and Soil* confirms McInerny's mastery of the light mystery." —*Publishers Weekly*

WORLDWIDE LIBRARY

BAS

AVAILABLE IN JANUARY